Emma Chase, the *New York Times* and *USA Today* bestselling author who created the "hot, hilarious, and passionate" (Katy Evans) novels in the *Tangled* series, turns her award-winning talents to the erotic escapades of lawyers in love, lust, and compromising positions . . . the Legal Briefs series!

Raves for Emma Chase and her sexy bestsellers

Tied

One of PopSugar's Best Books for Women 2014

"Sublimely irreverent, massively sexy, and so frigging perfect, readers will be bursting with giddy smiles. This . . . praise Emma . . . the ending we all wante . . .

. . . tselling

. . . *l Secret*

"W . . .

po . . . disap-

. . . *Driven*

Twisted

"A great escape."

—Katy Evans, *New York Times* bestselling author of *Real* and *Ripped*

"A delicious treat . . . funny, witty, and very sexy."

—The Book Bella

"I laughed. I cried. I yelled. I wanted to stop reading, but I couldn't... Emma Chase really knows how to evoke emotion from her readers!"

—Harlequin Junkie

"Emma Chase grabbed me from page one and put me through the wringer."

—Caffeinated Book Reviewer

"A yummy read . . . interesting, intense, sexy, and challenging."

—Literary Cravings

"Is emotional whiplash considered a sickness? I am more in love with this series than I was before, my heart just took a severe beating along the way."

—The Geekery Book Review

Emma Chase was chosen as the Debut Goodreads Author in the Goodreads Choice Awards for 2013 for her sensational novel

Tangled

Also a Goodreads Best Book of 2013!

"Well-written, clever, and charming."

—Maryse's Book Blog

"Total stop, drop, and roll reading. . . . Oh, and the sex . . . completely and utterly scandalicious."

—Scandalicious Book Reviews

"Addictively entertaining. If you're looking for a witty, laugh-out-loud insight into the male psyche look no further: it's *Tangled.*"

—Miss Ivy's Book Nook

"If you're looking for a laugh-out-loud, can't-put-it-down, quick read, you won't be disappointed."

—Hardcover Therapy

"I give *Tangled* . . . Five Spectacular, Swoony, Fun, Laugh-Out-Loud Stars!"

—A Bookish Escape

"I seriously enjoyed this book; any erotic romance that you can laugh out loud while reading and then be turned on in the next paragraph is an exhilarating book to read."

—Schmexy Girl Book Blog

"A perfect romantic comedy told through the eyes of a very cocky and sexy man."

—Literati Book Reviews

"So, not only is it funny, it's deliciously hot too! The sex scenes are great. Laced with humor and Drew's honest, frank way of thinking, they're just another stroke of genius that make this book such a must-read."

—Smitten's Book Blog

ALSO BY EMMA CHASE

The Tangled Series

"It's a Wonderful Tangled Christmas Carol" in *Baby, It's Cold Outside*

Tied

Tamed

Twisted

Tangled

OVERRULED

EMMA CHASE

GALLERY BOOKS

New York London Toronto Sydney New Delhi

G

Gallery Books
An Imprint of Simon & Schuster, Inc.
1230 Avenue of the Americas
New York, NY 10020

First Gallery Books trade paperback edition April 2015

GALLERY BOOKS and colophon are registered trademarks of Simon & Schuster, Inc.

For information about special discounts for bulk purchases, please contact Simon & Schuster Special Sales at 1-866-506-1949 or business@simonandschuster.com.

The Simon & Schuster Speakers Bureau can bring authors to your live event. For more information or to book an event, contact the Simon & Schuster Speakers Bureau at 1-866-248-3049 or visit our website at www.simonspeakers.com.

Manufactured in the United States of America

10 9 8 7 6 5 4 3 2

Library of Congress Cataloging-in-Publication Data is available.

ISBN 978-1-5011-0203-5
ISBN 978-1-5011-0206-6 (ebook)

To my Mom and Dad, for showing me how this parenting thing is done.

Acknowledgments

Beginning a new series has been both thrilling and terrifying. Thrilling, because there are new characters to explore, new places to discover, new storylines to lose myself in. The possibilities of "Chapter 1" are exhilaratingly infinite. And terrifying, because . . . well . . . one word: *new*. It's something different, a change. A quieting of the characters I already know and love, who have become my sweetest, dearest friends.

Many writers regard their books as their babies—their offspring. But I didn't really understand that comparison until I began writing *Overruled*. Child #1 was my everything—easily the most magnificent thing I'd ever done. Would I feel the same way when Child #2 arrived? Was it really possible to love another as completely as I already loved Child #1?

The answer, of course, was yes. It was not only possible but a wonderful, absolute certainty.

As pages turned into chapters, I came to know the characters of the Legal Briefs series—their histories, their voices, their quirks and strengths. And now I can say, without a doubt, that I adore them every bit as much as the characters of the Tangled series. In different ways, for different reasons—but certainly no less.

I'm so grateful to so many who have helped bring this new story to bookshelves and new characters to life. Most of you know who you are, but it's an honor to acknowledge you here in black and white.

My super agent Amy Tannenbaum, and everyone at the Jane Rotrosen Agency—I'd be lost without you! Really, really lost.

My publicists, Nina Bocci and Kristin Dwyer—I'm so lucky to have you in my corner!

My editor, Micki Nuding—it's such a privilege to work with you. Thank you for understanding exactly where I want to take my characters and for knowing just what to say to help me get them there.

My assistant, Juliet Fowler—your innovation and organization are invaluable! Thank you for staying on top of everything so I can stay buried in the writing cave.

Kim Jones, author of *Saving Dallas*—thank you for taking the time to talk and text with me about all things Mississippi! Stanton is a better man—a better Southern man—because of you.

My publishers at Gallery Books, Jennifer Bergstrom and Louis Burke—I still pinch myself to make sure working with you isn't just a dream! Thank you for believing in me and for your continued support.

To all of my talented, warm, and hilarious author friends—you are my idols and a fantastic source of encouragement.

To all my blogger friends—thank you for your tireless work, your humbling support, and for doing all that you do so very well.

My dearest husband and two children—I'd never be able to write about the joys in my characters' lives if you were not the joys in mine.

Finally, to my amazing readers—I think of you all while I write, always with the hope of entertaining you, making you laugh, gasp, swoon, and smile. Thank you for taking this journey with me and I hope you fall for these new characters as completely as I have.

OVERRULED

1

Senior year high school, October
Sunshine, Mississippi

Most stories start at the beginning. But not this one. This one starts at the end. Or, at least, what I thought was the end—of my life, my dreams, my future. I thought it was all over because of two words.

"It's positive."

Two words. Two little blue lines.

My stomach free falls and my knees lose their will. My green Sunshine High School football jersey clings to my torso, stained with dark sweat spots under the pits—and it's got nothing to do with the Mississippi sun. I take the stick from Jenny's hand and shake it, hoping one blue line will disappear.

It doesn't.

"Sonofabitch."

But even at seventeen, my debate skills are sharp. I offer a counterargument—an explanation. Reasonable doubt.

"Maybe you did it wrong? Or maybe it's defective? We should get another one."

Jenny sniffs as tears gather in her baby blues. "I've been gettin' sick every mornin' for the last week, Stanton. I haven't had my period in two months. It's positive." She wipes at her cheeks and raises her chin.

"I'm not stealin' another test from Mr. Hawkin's store to tell us what we already know."

When you live in a small town—particularly a small southern town—everybody knows everybody. They know your granddaddy, your momma, your wild big brother and sweet baby sister; they know all about your uncle who got locked up in the federal penitentiary and the cousin who was never quite right after that unfortunate tractor incident. Small towns make it too awkward to get condoms, too hard to go on birth control pills, and impossible to buy a pregnancy test.

Unless you *want* your parents to hear all about it before your girl even has time to piss on the stick.

Jenny wraps her arms around her waist with trembling hands. As scared shitless as I am, I know it's nothing compared to what she's feeling. And that's on me. I did this—my eagerness, my horniness. Fucking stupidity.

People can say what they want about feminism and equality and that's all fine and good. But I was raised on the idea that men are protectors. Where the buck stops. The ones who go down with the ship. So the fact that my girl is "in trouble" is no one's fault but mine.

"Hey, c'mere." I pull her small body against my chest, holding her tight. "It's gonna be okay. Everything's gonna be all right."

Her shoulders shake as she weeps. "I'm so sorry, Stanton."

I met Jenny Monroe in the first grade. I put a toad in her backpack because my brother dared me to. For two months she shot spitballs at the back of my head in retribution. In third grade I thought I was in love with her—by sixth grade I was sure of it. She was beautiful, funny, and she could throw a football better than any girl—and half the boys—I knew. We broke up in eighth grade when Tara-Mae Forrester offered to let me touch her boobs.

And I did.

We got back together that next summer, when I won her a bear at the county fair.

She's more than just my first kiss—my first everything. Jenny's my best friend. And I'm hers.

I rear back so I can look into her eyes. I touch her face and stroke her silky blond hair. "You've got nothing to be sorry for. You didn't do this by yourself." I wiggle my eyebrows and grin. "I was there too, remember?"

That makes her laugh. She swipes a finger under both eyes. "Yeah, it was a good night."

I cup her cheek. "Sure was."

It wasn't our first time—or our tenth—but it was one of the best. The kind of night you never forget—a full moon and a flannel blanket. Just a few feet from where we are right now—next to the river with a six-pack of beer kicked and music floating out of the open windows of my pickup. It was all soft kisses, hot whispers, sweaty bodies, and grasping hands. Joined so deep I couldn't tell where I ended and she began. Pleasure so intense I wanted it to last forever—and prayed out loud that it would.

We would've thought about it—tried to relive it—years from now, even if we weren't having a baby to commemorate it.

A baby.

Fuck me. As the reality truly starts to set in, my stomach drops all the way to China.

Like a mind reader, Jenny asks, "What are we gonna do?"

My father always told me being scared was nothing to be ashamed of. It was how you reacted to that fear that mattered. Cowards run. Men step up.

And I'm no coward.

I swallow roughly, and all my aspirations, hopes, and plans for leaving this town get swallowed too. I look out over the river, watching the sun sparkle off the water, and make the only choice I can.

"We're gettin' married. We'll stay with my parents at first. I'll work on the farm, go to night school—we'll save up. You'll have to put off nursin' school for a little while. Eventually we'll get our own place. I'll take care of you." I put my hand on her still-flat stomach. "Both of you."

Her reaction isn't what I imagine.

Jenny steps back out of my arms, eyes wide and head shaking. "What? No! No, you're supposed to leave for New York right after graduation."

"I know."

"You gave up your Ole Miss football scholarship to go to Columbia. It's Ivy League."

I shake my head. And lie.

"Jenn, none of that matters now."

There's not a single guy in this town who wouldn't give his eye teeth to play ball at Ole Miss . . . but not me. I've always wanted different—bigger, brighter, farther.

Jenny's flip-flopped feet kick up sand as she paces on the riverbank. Her white sundress flares as she turns a final time to me, finger pointing. "You're goin' and that's all there is to it. Just like we planned. Nothin's changed."

My voice rails with resentment she doesn't deserve. "What are you talkin' about—*everything's* changed! You can't come visit me once a month with a baby! We can't bring a baby to a dorm room."

Resigned, she whispers, "I know."

I take my own step back. "You expect me to leave you here? That was gonna be hard enough before, but now . . . I'm not gonna fucking walk away when you're pregnant. What kinda man do you think I am?"

She grasps my hands and gives me a speech that rivals "win one for the Gipper." "You're the kind of man who's gonna go to Columbia University and graduate with honors. A man who's gonna be able to name his salary when he does. You're not walkin' away, you're doin' what's best for us. For our family, our future."

"I'm not goin' anywhere."

"Oh yes you are."

"And what about your future?"

"I'll stay with my parents—they'll help me with the baby. They're practically raising the twins anyway."

Jenny's older sister, Ruby, is the proud mother of twins, with baby number three on the way. She attracts losers like cow shit attracts flies. The unemployed, the alcoholic, the lazy—she can't get enough of them.

"Between them and your parents, I'll still be able to go to nursin' school." Jenny wraps her slender arms around my neck.

And, God, she's pretty.

"I don't want to leave you," I murmur.

But my girl's mind is made up. "You'll go and come home when you can. And when you can, it'll get us through until the next time."

I kiss her lips—they're soft and full and taste like cherry. "I love you. I'll never love anyone the way I love you."

She smiles. "And I love you, Stanton Shaw—there's only ever gonna be you."

Young love is strong. First love is powerful. But what you don't know when you're young—what you can't know—is how long life actually is. And the only dependable thing about it, besides death and taxes, is change.

Jenny and I had a whole lot of change headed our way.

She takes my hand and we walk to my truck. I open the door for her and she asks, "Who are we gonna tell first? Yours or mine?"

I blow out a breath. "Yours. Get the crazy side over with first."

She's not offended. "Let's just hope Nana never finds the shells to that shotgun."

• • •

Seven months later

"Ahhhhhhhhh!"

This can't be normal. Dr. Higgens keeps saying it is, but there's no way.

"Gaaaaaaaaaaaa!"

I grew up on a farm. I've seen all types of births—cows, horses, sheep. None of them sounded like this.

"Uhhhhhhhhhh!"

This? This is like a horror movie. Like *Saw* . . . a massacre.

"Rrrrrrrrrrrrrrrrr!"

If this is what women go through to have a baby, why would they ever risk having sex at all?

"Owwwwwww!"

I'm not sure *I* want to risk having sex again. Jerking off looks a lot better now than it did yesterday.

Jenny screams so loud my ears ring. And I groan as her grip tightens on my already tender hand. The air is thick with sweat—and panic. But Dr. Higgens just sits there on a stool adjusting his glasses. Then he braces his hands on his knees and peers between Jenny's spread, stir-rupped legs—the way my mother squints into the oven on Thanksgiving, trying to decide if the turkey's done.

Gasping, Jenny collapses back against the pillows and moans, "I'm dyin', Stanton! Promise me you'll take care of the baby when I'm gone. Don't let it grow up to be an idiot like your brother, or a slut like my sister."

Her blond bangs are dark with sweat. I push them back from her forehead. "Oh, I don't know. Idiots are funny and sluts have their good points."

"Don't patronize me, dammit! I'm dyin'!"

Fear and exhaustion put an extra snap in my voice. "Listen up—

there is no way in hell you're leavin' me to do this on my own. You're not dying."

Then I turn to Dr. Higgens. "Isn't there somethin' you can do? Drugs you can give her?"

And me?

I'm not usually much of a stoner, but at this moment I'd sell my soul for a hit of pot.

Higgens shakes his head. "Won't do any good. Contractions are comin' too fast—you got an impatient one here."

Fast? *Fast?* If five hours is fast, I don't want to know what slow looks like.

What the hell are we doing?

This isn't how our lives were supposed to go. I'm the quarterback. I'm the fucking *valedictorian*—the smart one. Jenny's the homecoming queen and head cheerleader.

Or at least she was—until the baby bump got too big for her uniform.

We're supposed to go to prom next month. We should be thinking about graduation parties and bonfires, screwing in the backseat of my truck and having as many good times with our friends as we can before college. Instead we're having a baby.

A real one—not the hard-boiled-egg kind they make you carry around for a week in school. I cracked mine, by the way.

"I'm gonna throw up."

"No!" Jenny screeches like a mad cow. "You're not allowed to throw up while I'm bein' ripped in half! You just suck it up! And if I survive and you touch me again, I'm gonna cut your pecker off and feed it into the wood chipper! Do you hear me?"

That's something a man only needs to hear once.

"Alright."

I learned a few hours ago it's best to agree with anything she says. *Alright, alright, alright.*

Lynn, the perky nurse, wipes Jenny's brow. "Now, now, there'll be no cutting off of things. You'll forget all about this nasty business when your baby is here. Everyone *loooves* babies—they're blessin's from Jesus."

Lynn's way too happy to be real. I bet *she* took all the drugs—now there's none left for the rest of us.

Another contraction hits. Jenny's teeth grind as she pushes and grunts through it.

"Baby's crownin'," Higgens announces. He pats her knee. "A nice big push on the next one should do it."

I stand up and glance over Jenny's leg, and I see the top of the head, pushing against my favorite place in the whole world. It's bizarre and disgusting, but . . . but kind of incredible too.

Jenny falls back, pale and drained. Her sobs make my throat want to close. "I can't. I thought I could do it, but I can't. Please, no more. I'm so tired."

Her momma wanted to be here in the delivery room—they argued about it. Because Jenny said she only wanted it to be us. Her and me—together.

Gently, I lift Jenn's shoulders and slide behind her onto the bed, bracing my legs on either side of her. My arms encircle her stomach, my chest supports her back, and her head rests against my collarbone. I brush my lips against her temple, her cheek, murmuring soft nonsensical words, the same way I'd whisper to a skittish horse.

"Shh, don't cry, darlin'. You're doin' so good. We're almost there. Just one more push. I know you're tired, and I'm sorry it hurts. One more and you can rest. I'm right here with you—we'll do it together."

Her head turns to me wearily. "One more?"

I give her a smile. "You're the toughest girl I know. You always have been." I wink. "You got this."

She takes a few deep breaths, psyching herself up. "Okay." She breathes. "Okay." She sits up straighter, bending toward her raised knees. Her fingers clamp down on my hands when the next contraction comes. The room fills with long, guttural groans for a dozen seconds and then . . . a sharp cry pierces the air. A baby's cry.

Our baby.

Jenny pants and gasps with sudden relief. And Dr. Higgens holds up our squirming, cheesy child and pronounces, "It's a girl."

My vision blurs and Jenny laughs. With her own tears streaming down her face she turns to me. "We have a baby girl, Stanton."

"Ho-ly shit."

And we laugh and cry and hold on to each other all at the same time. A few minutes later, Happy Nurse Lynn carries the pink bundle over and places her in Jenny's arms.

"Oh my God, she's perfect," Jenny sighs. My awed silence must worry her, because she asks, "You're not disappointed she's not a boy, are you?"

"Nah . . . boys are useless . . . nothin' but trouble. She's . . . she's everything I wanted."

I wasn't prepared. I didn't know it would feel like this. A tiny nose, two perfect lips, long lashes, a wisp of blond hair, and hands that I can already tell are miniature versions of my own. In an instant, my world shifts and I'm at her mercy. From this moment on, there is nothing I wouldn't do for this beautiful little creature.

I brush my fingertip against her soft cheek, and even though men aren't supposed to coo, I do. "Hey, baby girl."

"Y'all got a name for her?" Nurse Lynn asks.

Jenny's smiling eyes meet mine before turning back to Nurse Lynn. "Presley. Presley Evelynn Shaw."

Evelynn is after Jenny's nana. We figured it might go a long way if she ever finds those shotgun shells. She's been searching particularly hard since Jenny and I announced we weren't getting married—yet.

Too soon Nurse Lynn takes the baby back so she can get printed and poked. I climb off the bed while Dr. Higgens busies himself between

Jenn's legs. Then he suggests, "Why don't you go outside and give your family the good news, son? They've been out there waitin' all night."

I look to Jenny, who nods her approval. I pick up her hand and kiss the back of it. "I love you."

She grins, weary but joyous. "I love you too."

I walk down the hallway, through the security doors to the waiting area. There, I find a dozen of the closest people in our lives wearing varying masks of anticipation and impatience.

Before I can get a word out, my little brother, Marshall—the non-idiot one—demands, "Well? What is it?"

I crouch down eye level with him and I smile. "*It . . .* is a she."

• • •

Two days later, I strapped the car seat into my pickup—checking it four times, to make sure it was in right—and I brought Jenny and Presley home.

Home to her parents' house.

And just two months after that, I left them. Traveling twelve hundred miles away to Columbia University, New York.

2

One year later

S he was too precious, Stanton," Jenny laughs. "She didn't want to touch the icing at all, didn't like it stickin' to her fingers, so she just planted her whole face right in the cake! And she was so mad when I took it back to cut it. I wish you could've seen her—this child's got attitude that puts Nana's to shame!" She dissolves in a fit of giggles.

Could've seen.

Guilt rides me hard. Because I *should've* seen the way Presley tore into her first birthday cake. The way she squealed over the bows and was more fascinated by the wrapping paper than any present it covered. I should've been there to light the candles, to take the pictures. To be *in* the pictures.

But I wasn't. Couldn't. Because it's finals week, so the only place I can be is here—in New York. I force a smile—trying to infuse my tone with enthusiasm. "That's great, Jenn. Sounds like it was an awesome party. I'm glad she enjoyed it."

Try as I might, Jenny can still tell. "Baby, stop beatin' yourself up. I'll email you all the pictures and the video. It'll be like you were right here with us."

"Yeah. Except I wasn't."

She sighs. "You wanna say good night to her? Sing her your song?"

In the short time I spent with our daughter after she was born, and the weeks I was able to have with her over Christmas break, we discovered that Presley has an affinity for the sound of my voice. Even over the telephone, it soothes her when she's teething, lulls her when she's fussy. It's become our ritual, every night.

"Dada!"

It's amazing how two tiny syllables can have so much power. They warm my chest and bring the first genuine grin I've had on my face all day.

"Happy birthday, baby girl."

"Dada!"

I chuckle. "Daddy misses you, Presley. You ready for your song?" Quietly, I sing,

You are my sunshine, my only sunshine.
You make me happy when skies are gray . . .

In her sweet, adorably garbled voice, she tries to sing the words with me. After two verses, my eyes are misty and my voice cracks. Because I miss her so much.

I miss them.

I clear my throat. "Time for bed. Sweet dreams."

Jenny comes back on the line. "Good luck with your exam tomorrow."

"Thanks."

"Good night, Stanton."

"Night, Jenn."

I toss the phone to the foot of the bed and stare at the ceiling. From somewhere down below, there's raucous laughter and calls to chug—most likely from the marathon beer-pong game that started two days ago. In my first week at Columbia I learned that careers aren't just built on *what* you know. They're built on *who* you know.

So I pledged a fraternity—to make those lifelong connections. Psi Kappa Epsilon. It's a good frat, filled with white-collar majors—business, economics, prelaw. Most come from money, but still good people, boys who work hard, study hard, and play hard.

Last semester a member graduated early, then got shipped abroad by his Fortune 500 company. My fraternity big brother lobbied strongly for me to get a room here in the house. A big brother is the guy you're paired with when you're pledging a frat. He's the guy who gives you the hardest time. You're his bitch—his slave.

But after you become a brother he's your best friend. Your mentor.

As self-loathing threatens to swamp me, my big brother just happens to walk past my open door. Out of the corner of my eye I see his dark head pass, pause, and back up.

Then Drew Evans strolls into my room.

Drew is like no one I've ever known. It's as if there's a spotlight on him that never dims—he demands your notice. Claims your full attention. He acts like he owns the world, and when you're with him? You feel like you own it too.

Deep blue eyes that all the girls go stupid for look down on me disapprovingly.

"What's wrong with you?"

I wipe my nose. "Nothin'."

His eyebrows rise. "Doesn't look like nothing. You're practically crying into your pillow, for Christ's sake. I'm fucking embarrassed *for* you."

Drew is relentless. Whether it's pussy or answers he's going after, he doesn't let up until he gets his way. It's a quality I admire.

My phone pings with incoming email—the pictures Jenny sent me of the party. With a resigned sigh I sit up and access the photos. "You know my daughter, Presley?"

He nods. "Sure. Cute kid, hot mom. Unfortunate name."

"Today was her birthday." I flash him one particularly endearing shot of my little angel with a face full of cake. "Her *first* birthday."

He smiles. "Looks like she had fun."

I don't smile. "She did. But I missed it." I scrub my eyes with the palms of my hands. "What the fuck am I doin' here, man? It's hard . . . harder than I ever thought it'd be."

I'm good at everything I do—always have been. Football, school, bein' a kick-ass boyfriend. In high school all the girls envied Jenny. Every one wanted to screw me and all the guys wanted to be me. And everything about it was too easy.

"I just feel . . . I feel like I'm failin' . . . everythin'," I confess. "Maybe I should throw in the towel, go to a shit community college back home. At least then I'd see them more than three times a year." With anger I bite out, "What kind of father misses his child's first fuckin' birthday?"

Not all guys feel like I do. I know boys back home who knocked up girls and were perfectly content to walk away and never look back. They send a check only after their asses get hauled into court, sometimes not even then. Hell, neither of Ruby's kids' fathers have seen their children more than once.

But that could never be me.

"Jesus, you're a mess," Drew exclaims, his face horrified. "You're not going to start singing John Denver songs, are you?"

I stew in silence.

He sighs. And perches himself on the edge of my bed. "You want the truth, Shaw?"

Evans is big on the truth—the harsh, crude, dick-in-your-face truth. Another quality I respect, though it's not much fun when his critical eye is aimed at you.

"I guess," I reply hesitantly.

"My old man is the best father I know, no contest. I don't remember if he was at my first birthday party, or my second . . . and I really don't give a shit either way. He put an awesome roof over my head, he's proud of me when I deserve it, and kicks my ass when I deserve that too. He took us on fantastic family vacations and pays for my tuition here—pretty much setting me up for life.

"What I'm saying is: any asshole can cut a fucking cake. You're here—working on the weekends, carrying a full class load, busting your balls—so one day your kid won't have to. That's what a good father does."

I think about what he's saying. "Yeah. Yeah, I guess you're right."

"Of course I'm right. Now dry your eyes, take some Midol, and stop with the premenstrual pity party."

That earns him the flip of the bird.

Drew raises his chin toward my pile of notes for Statistics 101, the first-year requisite final I'm taking tomorrow morning. "You ready for Windsor's final?"

"I think so."

He shakes his head. "Don't think—know. Professor Windsor's a dick. And a snob. He'll bust a nut if he gets to fail a redneck like you."

I flip through the stack of papers. "I'll look it over one more time, but I'm good."

"Excellent." He smacks my leg. "Then be ready to leave in an hour."

I glance at my watch: 10 p.m. "Where are we goin'?"

Evans stands. "If I teach you only one thing before I graduate let it be this: before any big exam, you go out for a drink—*one* drink—and you get yourself laid. Standardized test-prep courses should add that to their rule book. It's infallible."

I rub the back of my neck. "I don't know . . ."

He holds out his arms, questioning, "What's the problem? You and your baby mama are doing the whole open relationship now, right?"

"Yeah, but . . ."

"That was a brilliant move on your part, by the way. I'll never understand why any man would tie himself down to one woman when there's so many to choose from."

I don't tell him it wasn't my idea. That Jenny insisted on it after we talked—argued—when I was home for Christmas break. I don't tell him the only reason I agreed is because the horny bastards in my hometown know Jenn is *my* girl, the mother of *my* daughter. I may only come home two or three times a year, but when I do I'll happily rearrange the face of anyone who makes a move on her.

I also don't tell him that I haven't taken advantage of the new open-door policy in the five months since.

Not once.

Instead I explain, "I've never tried pickin' up women in a bar before. I don't know what I'd say."

Drew chuckles. "You just drop a few *y'all*s, a few *darlin'*s—I got the rest covered." He points at me. "One hour. Be ready."

And he cruises out of my room.

• • •

Ninety minutes later, we walk into the Central Bar—a favorite student hangout. It has good food, a dance floor with a DJ upstairs, and no cover charge. Even though it's finals week the place is wall-to-wall drinking, laughing bodies. "What are you having?" Evans asks as we make our way to the bar.

"Jim Beam, neat." If I'm only allowed one drink, better make it count.

I catch my reflection in the mirror behind the bar. Nondescript blue T-shirt, stubbled jaw 'cause I couldn't be bothered to shave, and a thick blond head of hair that needs cutting. It's practically immune to gel, so I'll be pushing it back from my forehead all night.

Drew passes me my bourbon and takes a sip of his own—looks

like whiskey and soda. Wordlessly we survey the room for a few minutes. Then his elbow nudges me and he cocks his head toward two girls in the corner, by the jukebox. They're good-looking in the way that appears effortless but in reality takes two hours of primping to achieve. One's tall, with long, straight blond hair and even longer legs, wearing ripped denim jeans and a cropped tank top that shows off a lacy black bra and a twinkling belly-button piercing. Her friend is shorter, with curly jet-black hair, a pink halter top, and dark jeans so tight they look like they're painted on.

Drew walks purposefully toward them and I follow.

"I like your shirt," he says to the blonde, gesturing to the writing across her chest: Barnard Women Do It Right.

After looking him up and down her lips stretch slowly into a flirty smile. "Thanks."

"I've got one at home just like it," Drew reveals. "Except mine says Columbia Guys Do It All Night."

They giggle. I gulp my bourbon while the dark-haired girl checks me out—and seems to like what she sees.

"You guys go to Columbia?" she asks.

Drew nods. "Yep. Go Lions."

Even though I have no real idea what the hell I'm doing, I try to follow Drew's instructions, asking the most unoriginal question ever. "What are y'all majorin' in?"

The brunette giggles again. "*Y'all*? You don't sound like you're from around here."

"I'm from Mississippi."

She eyes my bicep appreciatively. "How do you like New York?"

I think for a second . . . then it comes to me. With a lopsided grin I answer, "Right now, I'm likin' it a whole lot."

Drew nods almost imperceptibly—approvingly.

"We're art majors," the blonde offers.

"Seriously? Art?" Drew smirks. "Guess you have no interest in making an actual contribution to society." He raises his glass. "Here's to graduating without a marketable skill set of any kind."

I know he sounds like an insulting ass, but trust me, it works for him.

"Oh my god!"

"Jerk!" The girls laugh, like they always do, eating up his cocky attitude and sarcastic humor with a spoon.

I take another drink of bourbon. "What kinda art do you do?"

"I paint," Blondie answers. "I particularly like body painting." She trails her hand up and down Drew's chest. "You would be an amazing canvas."

"I sculpt," her friend tells me. "I'm really good with my hands."

She finishes the pink drink in her hand. Even though I'm not twenty-one and don't have an ID that says I am, I hook my thumb toward the bar. "You want me to get you another round?"

Before she can answer, Drew intercedes. "Or we could get out of here? Go back to your place?" He makes eye contact with the blonde. "You can show me your . . . art. I bet you're extremely talented."

The girls agree, I down the rest of my bourbon, and as easy as that, the four of us head out the door.

• • •

Turns out the girls are roommates. I'm quiet as we walk the three blocks to their apartment—distracted by the uneasy feeling churning in my stomach like butter gone bad. It's a mixture of nervousness and guilt. I imagine Jenny's face in my head, smiling and sweet. I picture her holding our daughter in the rocking chair my Aunt Sylvia gave us when Presley was born. And I wonder if what I'm doing—what I'm about to do—is the right thing.

Their apartment is a lot nicer than what two college girls could afford alone. A doorman, third floor, a spacious living room with unstained beige couches and gleaming hardwood floors covered by an

Oriental rug. A full-size kitchen with oak cabinets and granite countertops is visible from the living room, separated by a breakfast bar and three white bar stools.

"Make yourselves at home," the dark-haired girl says with a smile. "We're just going to go freshen up."

After they disappear down the hallway, Drew's head whips to me. "You look like a virgin on prom night. What's the matter?"

I wipe my sweaty palms on my jeans. "I don't know if this is a good idea."

"Did you not see the brunette's tits? Getting a closer look at those bad boys could never be anything *but* a good idea."

My lips tighten with indecision, then . . . I spill my guts. "The thing is . . . I've never had sex with anyone except Jenny."

He rubs his forehead. "Oh Jesus."

With a sigh he drops his hand and asks, "But she's good with you hooking up with other people? I mean, she agreed?"

I lift my shoulder and explain, "Well yeah—she's the one who suggested it in the first place."

Evans nods. "Sounds like my kind of girl. So what's the problem?"

I rub the back of my neck, trying to relieve some of the tension that's taken up residence there. "Even though we talked about it . . . I'm not sure . . . this doesn't feel . . . I want to do right by her."

Drew's voice loses its edge of irritation. "I admire that, Shaw. You're a stand-up guy. Loyal. I like that about you." He points at me. "Which is why I think you owe it to yourself, and your Jenny chick, to have hours of dirty, sweaty sex with this woman."

Not for the first time, I wonder if Drew Evans is the devil—or a close relation. I can picture him offering the fasting Christ a loaf of bread and making it sound completely acceptable for him to take a big ole bite out of it.

"Do you actually believe the horseshit that comes out of your mouth?"

Drew waves me off. "Pay attention, you're about to learn something. What's your favorite ice cream?"

"What the hell does that have to do—"

"Just answer the fucking question. What is your favorite ice cream?"

"Butter pecan," I sigh.

His eyebrows rise sardonically. "Butter pecan? I didn't think anyone under seventy liked butter pecan." He shakes his head. "Anyway. How do you know butter pecan is your favorite?"

"Because it is."

"But how do you *know*?" he presses.

"Because I like it more than—"

I stop midsentence. Understanding.

"More than any other flavor you've tried?" Drew finishes. "Better than vanilla, strawberry, or mint chocolate chip?"

"Yeah," I admit softly.

"And how would you have known that butter pecan was the flavor for you—not just your default choice—if you were too afraid to ever taste anything else?"

"I wouldn't have."

He waves his hand, like a magician. "Exactly."

See what I mean? *The devil.*

Still . . . it's similar to what Jenny said, the questions she raised. Can we really mean it when say we love one another if all we've known is each other? Are we strong enough to pass that kind of test? And if we're not, what kind of future do we have together anyway?

A slap to the arm snaps me from my introspection. "Look, Shaw, this is supposed to be fun. If you're not having a good time, if you'd rather take off, I won't think any less of you."

I snort. "Sure you will."

The corner of his mouth twitches. "Yeah, you're right, I will. But . . . I won't tell the guys you pussed out. It'll stay between you and me."

Before I can answer him the girls walk back into the room. They've changed into loose-fitting, strappy pajamas, shiny in satin. I can smell the mint on her freshly brushed teeth when the blonde leans over and says to Drew, "Come on, there's something in my room I want to show you."

He stands smoothly. "Then there's something in your room I want to see." Before they advance to the hallway, he glances my way. "You good, man?"

Am I good?

The curly haired brunette stares at me expectantly—waiting for me to make my move. And the realization finally sets in that . . . there's not any reason to say no.

"Yeah. Yeah, I'm good."

Drew takes the blonde's hand and she leads them into the room at the end of the hall.

Left alone with my dark-haired companion, I take a minute to look at her—really look at her. She has breasts larger than I'm used to, a tiny waist, and a firm bubble bottom that balances out the whole package nicely. The kind of ass a man could hold on to, knead with his fingers and guide forward and back, up and down. Her legs are smooth and toned, her skin flawless and tanned.

For the first time tonight, genuine attraction unfolds low in my gut, stirring my poorly underused dick from his five-month hibernation.

I don't ask her name and she hasn't requested mine. There's a thrill in anonymity, a freedom. I'll never have to see this girl again—what we do and say tonight won't leave this apartment, won't come back to haunt me, won't find its way to judgmental ears in a small town far, far away. A thousand fantasies, each more deviant than the last, flit through my brain like smoke coming off a campfire. Acts I'd never dream of asking Jenny to perform—things she'd probably smack me for even suggesting.

But a beautiful, nameless stranger . . . why the fuck not?

"You want to see my room?" she asks.

My voice is deep, rough like my thoughts. "Okay."

Her room is a swirl of dark reds, browns, and burnt orange, not overly feminine. I sit on the edge of her bed, feet on the floor, knees spread.

Any trace of indecision has left the building.

As she closes the door she questions, "What's your major? I meant to ask earlier."

"Prelaw."

She moves in front of me, standing an arm's length away, regarding me with an angled head and hooded eyes. "Why do you want to be a lawyer?"

I smile. "I like to argue. I like . . . provin' people wrong."

Taking a step closer, she picks up my hand. Then she turns it over and traces my palm with her fingertip. It tickles in a stimulating kind of way that gets my pulse hammering.

"You have strong hands."

There are no soft hands on a farm. Tools, rope, fences, saddles, lifting and digging makes for tough palms and hard muscles.

"You know what I like best about sculpting?" she asks on a breathy sigh.

"What?"

She drops my hand then lifts a dark, daring gaze to mine. "I don't think at all while I'm doing it. I don't plan, I let my hands . . . do whatever they want. Whatever feels good."

She grasps the bottom of her top and slides it over her head. Her breasts are pale and ripe and gloriously new to my eyes. She stands just inches away, bare and proud. "You wanna give it a try?"

She puts her hands over mine, skimming them up the warm velvet of her rib cage. When she places my callused palms on her breasts, I take over. Cupping their weight, massaging gently, brushing my thumbs across the peaks of her nipples. They tighten and darken from pink to dusty rose and I scrape my lip with my teeth to stave off the immediate urge to latch on, lick, and bite.

My last coherent thought is six quick words:

I could get used to this.

. . .

Three weeks later

"You lying, cheating sonofabitch!"

Jenny's hands fly out, wild and whipping, striking my face, shoulders, and anywhere she can reach.

Slap.

Slap, slap.

Slap.

"Jenny, stop!" Finally I get a grip on her forearms, holding her still. "Fuckin' stop!"

Hot, angry tears cover her cheeks and her eyes are puffy with betrayal. "I hate you! You make me sick! I hate you!"

She pulls out of my grasp and runs up the porch, slamming the screen door behind her as she disappears into the house. I'm left standing on the lawn—shredded. Feeling like I've been flayed open, my heart not just broken but ripped out. And there's something else—more than regret—there's fear. It makes my palms sweat and skin prickle. Fear that I've messed up, terror that I just lost the best thing that will ever happen to me.

I push a hand through my hair, trying to keep it together. Then I sit on the porch steps and brace my elbows on my knees. I keep an eye on Presley, on the blanket twenty feet away where she plays with her cousins near the swing set. Her white-blond curls bounce as she giggles, thankfully, completely unaware.

Out of nowhere, Ruby, Jenny's older sister, appears on the steps next to me. She smooths her denim miniskirt then pushes her wavy red locks off her shoulders.

"You certainly got yourself locked in the shithouse this time, Stanton."

Normally I wouldn't go to Ruby for any kind of advice—least of all about relationships. But she's here.

"I . . . I don't know what happened."

Ruby snorts. "You told my sister you fucked another girl, that's *what happened.* No woman wants to hear that."

"Then why did she ask?"

She shakes her head, like the answer is obvious. "'Cause she wanted to hear you say no."

"We agreed to see other people," I argue. "We said we'd be honest with each other. Mature."

"Sayin' and feelin' are two different things, lover boy." She picks at her manicure. "Look, you and Jenny are eighteen, y'all are babies . . . this was bound to happen. Only a matter of when."

I can barely get the words past my constricted throat. "But . . . I love her."

"And she loves you. That's why it hurts so bad."

There's no way I'm giving up, no way I'm goin down—not like this. It's the fear that pushes me to do something, say anything. To hold on like a man clinging to a boulder in a current.

I walk up the oak staircase to the room Jenn shares with our daughter and through the closed door that tells me I'm not welcome.

She's on the bed, shoulders shaking, crying into her pillow. And the knife sinks deeper in my gut. I sit on the bed and touch her arm. Jenny has the smoothest skin—rose-petal soft. And I refuse for this to be the last time I get to touch her.

"I'm sorry. I'm so sorry. Don't cry. Please don't . . . hate me."

She sits up and doesn't bother to wipe the evidence of heartache off her face. "Do you love her?"

"No," I tell her firmly. "No, it was one night. It didn't mean anythin'."

"Was she pretty?"

I answer like the lawyer I'm trying to become. "Not as pretty as you."

"Dallas Henry asked me to go to the movies with him," Jenny tells me quietly.

Any remorse I feel goes up in smoke and is replaced with blue flaming anger. Dallas Henry was a receiver on my high school football team—he was always a raging asshole. The kind of guy who made a play for the drunkest girls at the party—the kind who would've slipped something into their drinks to get them drunk faster.

"Are you shittin' me?"

"I told him no."

The fury cools a notch—but only just barely. My fist is still gonna have a nice long chat with Dallas fucking Henry before I leave.

"Why didn't you say no, Stanton?" she accuses quietly.

Her question brings the guilt back full force. Defensively, I get to my feet—pacing and tense. "I did say no! Plenty of times. Shit, Jenn . . . I thought . . . it wasn't cheatin'! You can't be mad at me for this. For doin' what you said you wanted. That's not fair."

Every muscle in my body strains—waiting for her response. After what feels like forever, she nods. "You're right."

Her blue eyes look up at me and the sadness in them cuts me to the bone. "I just . . . I hate picturing what you did with her in my head. I wish I could go back to when . . . when I didn't know. And I could pretend that it's only ever been me." She hiccups. "Is that . . . is that pathetic?"

"No," I groan. "It's not." I drop to my knees in front of her—aware that I'm begging, but not having the will to care. "It *has* only ever been you—in every way that matters. What happens when we're apart, only means somethin' if we let it mean somethin'."

My hands drift up her thighs, needing to touch her—to wipe this from her mind—wanting so badly for us to be *us* again.

"I'm home for the summer. Two and half months and all I want to do for every second of that time is love you. Can I, darlin'? Please just let me love you."

Her lips are warm and puffy from crying. I brush at them gently at first, asking permission. Then firmer, spearing her mouth with my tongue, demanding compliance. It takes a moment, but then she's kissing me back. Her small hands fist my shirt, gripping tight, pulling me to her.

Owning me. The way she always has.

Jenny falls back on the bed, taking me with her. I hover over her as her chest rises and falls—panting. "I don't want to know ever again, Stanton. We don't ask, we don't tell—promise me."

"I promise," I rasp, willing to agree to just about anything at this moment.

"I start school in the fall," she presses. "I'm gonna meet people too. I'm gonna go out—and you can't get angry. Or jealous."

I shake my head. "I won't. I don't want to fight. I don't . . . I don't want to hold you back."

And that's the crazy truth of it.

There's a part of me that wants to keep Jenny all to myself, lock her away in this house, and know she's doing nothing else but waiting for me to come back. But stronger than that is the dread that we'll burn out, end up hating each other—blaming each other—for all the living we missed out on. For all the things we never got to do.

More than anything, I don't want to wake up ten years from now and realize the reason my girl hates her life . . . is because of me.

So if that means sharing her for a little while, then I'll suck it up—I swear I will.

My eyes burn into hers. "But when I'm home, you're mine. Not Dallas fucking Henry's—no one else's but mine."

Her fingers trace my jaw. "Yes, yours. I'll be who you come home to. They don't get to keep you, Stanton. No other girl . . . gets to be who I am."

I kiss her with rough possession—sealing the words. My lips move down her neck as my hand slides up her stomach. But she grasps my wrist. "My parents are downstairs."

My eyes squeeze closed and I breathe deep. "Come to the river with me tonight? We'll drive around until Presley falls asleep in the back."

Jenny smiles. "A truck ride knocks her out every time."

I kiss her forehead. "Perfect."

I lie beside her and she curls into me, playing with the collar of my shirt. "It won't be like this forever. One day, you'll be done with school and things will go back to normal."

Yeah.

One day . . .

3

Ten years later
Washington, DC

The work of a criminal defense attorney isn't as exciting as you probably imagine. It's not even as exciting as law students imagine. There's a lot of research, case law referencing to back up every argument in pages and pages of legal briefs that are filled with enough semantics to give a layman a migraine. If you're part of a firm, when you're eventually entrusted to represent your clients at trial, there are rarely any dramatic cross-examination revelations, no big *Law & Order* moments.

Mostly it's just laying out the facts for the jury, piece by piece. One of the first rules you learn in law school is: *never ask a question you don't already know the answer to.*

Sorry to piss on your parade, but it really doesn't get less exciting than that.

In the United States of America, defendants get to pick who'll decide their fate: a judge or a jury of their peers. I always advise my clients to go with the jury—it's a miracle to get twelve people to agree on where they're having lunch, let alone the guilt or innocence of a defendant. And a mistrial, which is what happens when they can't agree, is a win for the defense.

Have you ever heard that old joke about juries? *Do you really want to be judged by twelve people who weren't smart enough to get out of jury duty?* Yes—that's exactly who you want judging you. Because juries are people unfamiliar with the letter of the law. And those are people who can be swayed—by lots of elements that have absolutely nothing to do with facts.

If a jury likes a defendant, they'll have a harder time convicting them of a charge that could keep their ass in a prison cell for the next ten to twenty years. It's why an accused thief shows up to court in a nicely pressed suit—not prisoner oranges. It's precisely why Casey Anthony's wardrobe and hairstyle were carefully chosen to appear sweetly demure. Sure, juries are supposed to be impartial, they're supposed to base their judgment on the evidence presented and nothing else.

But human nature doesn't quite work that way.

Likeability of the defendant's legal counsel also carries weight. If an attorney is sloppy, grumpy, or boring, the jury is less inclined to believe their version of the case. On the other hand, if the defending lawyer appears to have their shit together, if they're well spoken—and yes— good looking, studies show juries are more likely to trust that lawyer. To believe them—and by extension, believe their client.

It's important not to look like you're trying too hard. Not to appear shifty or sneaky—the last thing you want is to give off a "used car sales- man" vibe. People know when they're being lied to.

But, here's the most important thing: whenever possible, you want to show them a good time. Give them something to watch. They're expecting objections and out-of-orders, the pounding of tables and banging of the gavel. They're hoping for a live reenactment of Tom Cruise and Jack Nicholson in *A Few Good Men*. The system may be boring, but you don't have to be. You can be entertaining. Show them you've got a big swinging dick and you're not afraid to use it.

My dick is the swingingest of them all—juries can't take their eyes off it.

Figuratively . . . and literally.

"You may proceed with closing arguments, Mr. Shaw."

"Thank you, Your Honor." I rise to my feet, buttoning the jacket of my tailored gray suit. That color is a big hit these days with the ladies— and ten out of these twelve jurors are female.

I meet their collective gaze with a contemplative expression, drawing out the pause, heightening the dramatic tension. Then I begin.

"The next time I fucking see you, I will cut your balls off and shove them down your throat."

Pause. Eye contact.

"When I find you, you'll be begging me to kill you."

Pause. Finger point.

"Just wait, asshole, I'm coming for you."

I step out from behind the defense table and position myself in front of the jury box. "These are the words of the man the prosecution claims is the"—air quotes—"victim in this case. You've seen the text messages. You heard him admit under oath that he sent them to my client." I click my tongue. "Doesn't sound like much of a victim to me."

All eyes follow me as I slowly pace, like a professor giving a lecture. "They sound like threats—serious ones. Where I come from, threatenin' a man's balls . . . words don't get more fightin' than that."

A series of low chuckles rises up from the jurors.

I brace my arms on the railing of the jury box, glancing at each occupant just long enough to make them feel included—readying them for the divulgence of a dirty little secret.

"Over the course of this trial, you've heard things about my client, Pierce Montgomery, that are unflattering. Abhorrent, even. I'm bettin' you don't like him very much. To tell you the truth, I don't like him much myself. He had an affair with a married woman. He posted pictures of her on social media, without her permission. These are not the actions of an honorable man."

It's always best to get the bad out of the way. Like tossing out a bag of rancid garbage—acknowledging then moving on makes the stench less likely to linger.

"If he were being judged on human decency, I can assure you I would not be defending him here today."

I straighten up, holding their rapt attention. "But that is not your task. You are here to judge his actions on the night of March 15. We as a society do not penalize individuals for defending their lives or their bodies from physical harm. And that is precisely what my client was doing on that evening. When he came face-to-face with the man who had threatened him relentlessly, he had every reason to believe those threats would be carried out. To fear for his physical well-being—perhaps for his very life."

I pause, letting that sink in. And I know they're with me, seeing the night in their heads through the eyes of the rotten sonofabitch who's lucky enough to have me for a lawyer.

"My old football coach used to tell us a smart offense is the best defense. It's a lesson I carry with me to this very day. So, although Pierce threw the first punch, it was still in defense. Because he was acting against a known threat—a *reasonable* fear. That, ladies and gentlemen, is what this case is really about."

Standing in front of the jury box I take a step back—addressing them as a whole. "As you deliberate, I am confident that you will conclude my client acted in self-defense. And you will render a verdict of not guilty."

Before taking my seat at the defense table, I put the finishing touch on my closing argument. "Thank you again for your time and attention, you have been . . . delightful."

That gets a smile from eight of the ten—I'm liking those odds.

After I'm seated, my neutral-faced co-counsel discreetly writes on a legal pad, passing it to me.

Nailed it!

Lawyers communicate with notes during trial because it's bad form to whisper. And a smile or a scowl could be interpreted by the jury in a way you don't want. So my only visible reaction is a quick nod of agreement. My internal reaction is a schoolboy snicker. And I write back:

Nailing things well is what I do best.
Or have you forgotten?

Sofia's the consummate professional. She doesn't crack a smile. And I've never seen her blush. She just writes:

Cocky ass.

I allow myself the barest of grins.

Speaking of asses, mine still has your nail marks on it.
Does that make you wet?

It's inappropriate, totally unprofessional—but that's why it's so damn fun. The fact that our dickhead client or anyone sitting front row in the gallery behind us could glance over and see what I've written just adds to the thrill. Like fingering a woman under the table at a crowded restaurant—also fun—the potential for discovery makes it all the more dangerous and hot.

A mischievous sparkle lights her hazel eyes as she scribbles:

You had me wet at "Ladies and gentlemen." Now stop.

I scribble back:

Stop? Or save it for later?

I'm rewarded with a simple, subtle smirk. But it's enough.

Later works.

• • •

After the rebuttal and an hour's worth of instructions from the judge, the jury filed into the guarded back room for deliberations and court was recessed. Which gave me the opportunity to meet up for lunch with a certain old fraternity brother at a local watering hole that serves the best sandwiches in the city. Between demanding work schedules and family, we only have time to get together once or twice a year—when we happen to land in each other's cities on business.

Drew Evans hasn't changed all that much from our days at Columbia. Same scathing wit, same arrogance that draws women to him like moths to a blue-eyed bug light. The only difference between then and now is Drew doesn't notice the flurry of female attention that follows him. Or, if he does notice, he doesn't reciprocate.

"Are you sure you wouldn't like anything else? *Anything* at all?" the twentysomething waitress asks hopefully—for the third time in fifteen minutes.

He takes a drink of his beer, then dismisses her with, "Nope. Still good—thanks."

Shoulders hunched, she scurries away.

Drew is an investment banker at his father's New York City firm. He's also my investment banker—the reason two years of Presley's college tuition is already sitting pretty in a 529 fund. Mixing money and friendship may not seem like a smart move, but when your friends are as talented at making money as mine are, it's brilliant.

His phone chimes with an incoming text. He glances at the screen and a goofy smile spreads across his face—the kind of smile I've only seen him wear one time before: at his wedding, eight months ago.

I wipe my mouth with my napkin, toss it on the table, and tilt my chair back on two legs. "So . . . how is Kate these days?"

Kate is Drew's wife.

His extremely beautiful wife.

His extremely beautiful wife whom I danced with—briefly—at their wedding reception. And my buddy didn't seem to like that one bit.

What kind of friend would I be if I didn't mess with him about it?

He glances up with a smirk. "Kate's fantastic. She's married to me—what else could she possibly be?"

"Did you give her my card?" I prod. "So she can contact me for legal services . . . or *any* service she may need?"

I grin as he scowls.

"No, I didn't give her your card. Asshole." He leans forward, suddenly smug. "Besides, Kate doesn't like you."

"Is that what you tell yourself?"

He chuckles. "It's true—she thinks you're shady. You're a defense attorney, Kate's a mother. She believes you enable child molesters to walk the streets."

It's a common misconception, and completely inaccurate. Defense attorneys keep the legal system honest—healthy. We advocate for the individual, the little guy, and we're all that stands between him and the unconstrained power of the state. But people forget that part—it's all pedophiles and Wall Street retirement fund thieves.

"I have a daughter," I argue. "I wouldn't defend a child molester."

Drew finds my reasoning lacking. "You're trying to make partner—you defend who the powers that be tell you to defend."

I shrug noncommittally.

"Speaking of your daughter," he segues. "How old is she now? Ten?"

As always, the topic of my baby girl brings an immediate surge of pride to my chest. "She turned eleven last month." I whip out my phone and pull up the pictures that account for most of the memory. "She just made the competition cheerleading squad. And in the South, cheerleading's a real sport—none of that 'rah-rah' pom-pom horseshit."

Jenny and Presley still live in Mississippi. After Columbia, while I was going to law school at George Washington University, we talked about them coming to live with me in DC, but Jenny didn't think the city was any place to raise a child. She wanted our daughter to grow up like we both did—swimming at the river, riding bicycles down dirt roads, running barefoot through the fields, and Sunday barbecues after church.

I agreed with her—I didn't like it—but I agreed.

Drew lets out an impressed whistle when I show him the most recent shots of her decked out in green and gold team colors. Her long blond hair curled into ringlets and pulled up high, shining sky-blue eyes and a breathtaking pearly white smile.

"She's a beauty, Shaw. Lucky for her she takes after her mother. Hope you've got a baseball bat ready."

Way ahead of him. "Nah, man, I got a shotgun."

He nods with approval and slaps my arm.

"Hey, stranger, long time, no see." My eyes are drawn to the sumptuous form of Sofia Marinda Santos, my co-counsel—among other things—as she walks up to our table.

Clothes don't just make the man—they make a statement for a woman. They speak particularly rapturously for Sofia. She dresses as she is—impeccable, sharp, classy, yet so damn sexy it makes my mouth water. Her red silk blouse is tastefully buttoned, revealing only a few inches of bronze skin below her collarbone—not even a hint of cleavage. But the material accents the God-given bounty of her ample breasts—

full, firm, and fucking gorgeous. A short, gray tweed jacket covers long, elegant arms, and the matching pencil skirt hugs the rounded swell of her hips before revealing toned legs that go on for days.

"Where were you hiding?" I ask, then point to an empty chair. "You want to join us?"

Naturally ruby lips smile back. "Thank you, but no, I just finished having lunch with Brent in the back."

I gesture while making the introductions. "Drew Evans, this is Sofia Santos, a fellow child molester liberator according to your wife." Sofia's dark brow arches slightly at the description, but I continue. "Soph, this is Drew Evans, my old college buddy, my current investment banker, and just an all-around rude bastard."

Ignoring my dig, he extends his hand. "Nice to meet you, Sofia."

"Likewise."

She checks the time on her Rolex and teases, "You should finish up here too, Stanton. Don't want to miss the verdict."

I'm shaking my head before she's done speaking. Because we've been debating this since the trial started. "I've got all the time in the world, darlin'. Hell, we may even order dessert—that jury isn't coming back until Monday, at the earliest."

"You may be the Jury Charmer." Her manicured fingers swirl in a circle, like she's conjuring a crystal ball. "But I'm the Jury Seer. And I see those housewives wanting to scratch this trial off their to-do lists for the weekend."

"The Jury Charmer?" Drew comments dryly. "That's adorable."

I give him the jerk-off sign with my hand while insisting to Sofia, "Your vision is off this time."

Her mouth purses. "Care to make a wager on that, big boy?"

"What are your terms, sweet thing?" I counter with a daring grin.

Evans watches our exchange with unconcealed mirth.

She braces her hands on the table, leaning forward. And I have a whole new esteem for gravity—because it's that force that causes her blouse to pull away from her body, giving me a delectable view of her stunning tits encased in delicate black lace.

"The Porsche."

Caught off guard, my eyes widen. She's not messing around.

She knows my silver 911 Carrera 4S Cabriolet convertible is my prized possession. The first thing I bought myself when I was hired at the prestigious Adams & Williamson law firm four years ago. It's pristine. It doesn't come out in the rain. It doesn't get parked where a bird could shit on it. It doesn't get driven by anyone but me.

"*When* the jury comes back today, you let me take your Porsche out for the ride of its life."

She stares me down, waiting.

I rub my knuckles along my jaw, debating.

"It's a stick shift," I warn in a low voice.

"Pft—child's play."

"What do I get if—when—you lose the bet?"

She straightens up, looking pleased with herself, even though she hasn't heard my terms. "What do you want?"

The image of Sofia's curves barely covered in a tiny red bikini, damp and soapy with suds, infiltrates my brain. And I can't hold back the lewd smile that graces my face. "You have to wash the Porsche, by hand, once a week for a month."

She doesn't hesitate. "Done."

Before we shake on it, I look into her eyes and spit deliberately on my palm. Our grasp is sliding and slick. Her nose crinkles, but her eyes—her eyes simmer with an amused heat only I can read.

She likes it.

After I release her grip, she wipes her hand with a napkin. Then Brent Mason walks out from the direction of the restrooms to join us. Brent is an associate at our firm, started the same year as Sofia and me, though he looks much younger. His round blue eyes, wavy brown hair, and carefree personality invoke protective, little brother–like feelings. The limp that accompanies his gait adds to the boyish impression, though in reality it's the result of the prosthetic on his left leg, the consequence of a childhood accident. The event may have taken his limb, but Brent's jovial good humor remains fully intact.

Like all the associates at our firm, Brent and Sofia share an office. They're close, but in a strictly platonic, friend-zone sort of way.

He also has more money than God—or at least his family does. Old money, the kind of wealth so abundant his relations don't realize that not everyone "summers" in the south of France or is able to retreat to their country estate on the Potomac when they need a break from the city. Brent's father has political aspirations for his only child and believed an impressive record as a prosecutor would lay the foundation for those ambitions.

Which is precisely why Brent went out and became a criminal defense attorney.

"Hey, Shaw," he greets.

I nod. "Mason." I gesture once again to Drew. "Brent Mason, this is Drew Evans, an old friend." My eyes fall to him. "Brent's another lawyer at our firm."

They shake hands firmly, then Drew remarks, "Jesus, is anyone in DC not a lawyer?"

I chuckle. "Most per capita in the country."

Before he can respond with what I'd bet my life on would've been an insult, Brent pipes up. "You ready to go, Sofia? I have a client coming in twenty minutes."

"I'm all set. It was nice meeting you, Drew. Stanton, I'll see you at the courthouse soon."

I feign confusion. "You mean the office?"

With a shake of her head, she lets Brent lead her out the door.

I watch her go. And I enjoy every damn second of it.

Which does not go unnoticed. "Do you really think that's wise?"

My attention drags back to him. "What's that?"

"Screwing your coworker," Evans clarifies. "Do you think that's wise?"

I pause a moment, wondering how he knew . . . and then I laugh at myself for wondering . . . because of course he'd know.

"This coming from the man who *married* his coworker a few months ago?"

Drew leans back, resting one arm on the chair beside him. "That's completely different. Kate and I are special."

I sip my water. "What makes you think Soph and I are screwing?"

"Ah . . . because I have eyes. And ears. And nothing about the sexual tension I just witnessed was unresolved. You sold yourself short on the bet, by the way. My terms would've been *fucking* her on the hood of the car first—*then* she washes it." He shrugs. "But that's just me. Now back to my original question . . ."

There's really no point in denying it. "Sofia is without a doubt the wisest woman I've ever done—pun intended."

He doesn't approve. "That's a dangerous path you're walking, Shaw. A minefield of awkwardness and female scorn."

I understand his concerns, but they're not necessary. Sofia's a woman in all the important places, but with the practicality of a man. There are no minivans or white picket fences in her future, just corner offices and billable hours. She's frank, direct, but also fun. A woman I consider a friend—someone I enjoy going out with as much as I enjoy going down on.

Our arrangement started six months ago. The first time was spontaneous, reckless. I'd known I wanted her, but didn't realize how much until the night we were alone in the firm's basement library. Both working late, tense and tight for time—one minute we were discussing the finer points of Miranda v. Arizona and the next we were tearing each other's clothes off, up against the stacks of thick, leather-bound volumes, rutting like wild animals.

Sounded just like them, too.

I get turned on every time I think of the noises Sofia made that night, a symphony of gasps, whimpers, and growls as I made her come three times. A trifecta. And when my orgasm finally flooded me—shit—I couldn't feel my legs for five full minutes.

Afterward, when we were sweaty and disheveled as soldiers after battle, we talked. We agreed that it was something we both wanted to do again—and again—a needed stress reliever that would fit perfectly into our mutually packed schedules.

It's not as cold as it sounds. But it is . . . easy.

I grin. "Nah, man, Sofia's like . . . one of the guys."

"You're screwing one of the guys?"

I frown. "It doesn't sound nearly as hot when you say it like that. What I mean is—she lives for the job, like me. Trying to make partner doesn't leave a whole lot of time for anything else. She's convenient and fucking beautiful. I know you're married and all, but you'd have to be half-dead not to notice. And even then, her tits would coax an erection from a corpse."

"Oh, I noticed, believe me," he says. "Does she know about your Mississippi booty call?"

"Jenny's not my booty call," I grumble. "Dick."

"Well, she's not your girlfriend or your wife. She's the chick you bang when you happen to breeze into town. Hate to break it to you, but that's the definition of a booty call."

At times Drew's propensity to call 'em like he sees 'em puts his nads in grave danger of getting punched.

"Sofia knows all about Jenn and Presley."

"Interesting." Then comes the patented advice. "I'm just saying a situation like this could get . . . complicated for you. Regret is a bite in the ass that stings like a motherfucker. I've been there—it's not fun."

"Thanks for the warning. But I can handle it."

"Famous last words. Just remember, by the time you realize you can't handle it, it's too late." He checks his phone and stands. "And on that note, I have to take off—gotta catch my train."

I stand up and smack his arm. "Hey, why don't you stay in DC tonight? I'll set up a poker game with the boys—it'll be like old times."

He lifts his hands, weighing the options. "Let's see . . . take Shaw's money . . . or go home to the stunning wife who's been sexting me all afternoon? No contest. I like you, man, but I'll never like you that much."

We hug briefly, slapping each other's back, both pledging to do this again soon.

That's when my cell phone chimes. I pick it up from the table, read the message, and curse.

As Drew retrieves his briefcase from under the table, I hold my phone out.

"Jury's back."

He laughs at me. "For your sake, I hope she's as good with a stick as she claims." He pauses, then grins. "But I guess you already know she is."

With a final smack to my arm, he heads toward the door. "Later, man."

"Give Kate my best," I call after him. "And my card!"

He doesn't turn around, doesn't break his stride, but just raises his hand, with his middle finger extended loud and clear above his head.

4

Sofia

There's an energy in a courtroom just before a verdict is read, a static that crackles in the air. It's a shared, breathless tension, the same the Romans must've felt at the Colosseum as they waited to see what direction Caesar would point his thumb. Your pulse pounds, your blood hums, and the adrenaline surges. It's exciting.

As addictive as really fantastic sex. The kind that leaves you marked, sore, and exhausted—and you can't wait to do all over again.

I always knew I wanted to be an attorney. As I was growing up, I watched shows like *L.A. Law*, where female litigators possessed rapier wits, wore stylish suits with impeccable hairstyles, and worked in glass and chrome offices in the sky.

Education was the highest priority for my parents, because they had had such limited access to it themselves. My mother left the poverty of her home village in Pará for the relative opulence of Rio de Janeiro when she was a young girl. But she escaped illiteracy only after meeting my father, who taught her to read when she was sixteen years old. Together, they emigrated to the United States and became the very definition of the American Dream—building a thriving business, rising through the ranks of the middle class to prosperous wealth. Keenly aware of the opportunities their hard work afforded their children, they impressed upon each of us—myself and three older brothers—that education was the key to unlocking all doors. It was a treasure that could never be stolen, the most durable safety net. It's no accident that we each went on to pursue professional fields: my eldest brother, Victor, became a doctor; the next, Lucas, a CPA, and Tomás, just a year older than me, an engineer.

"Madam Forewoman, have you reached your verdict?"

Our client Pierce Montgomery's simmering attention is blatantly *not* on the woman who's about to announce his judgment, but instead trained squarely on my chest. It makes me feel dirty in an unenjoyable way.

There's a nice hot shower in my future—to rinse off the sleaze.

"We have, Your Honor."

Going in to criminal defense, I knew the high probability of having to work with scumbags like Montgomery, but that didn't deter me. Because I was the youngest in my family, and the only daughter, they were highly protective. But instead of restricting me, that protective instinct drove my parents to make sure I was capable and prepared for whatever life may throw at me.

Opportunities, my father would say, *have to be seized with both hands, because you never know if they'll come again.*

He's the one who taught me to be fearless.

Opportunity is all he's ever wanted for me. More than a husband or children, he wanted me to have the chance to go anywhere. Do anything.

Being raised in Chicago gave me an edge. It's a beautiful city, but like all urban areas, it has its dangers. I learned early to move fast but stand my ground, to be on guard and generally distrust unfamiliar people until they prove otherwise.

In short, a leering, skeevy son of a senator like Pierce Montgomery doesn't intimidate me. If he ever tried to touch me with more than his eyes, I could bring him to his knees with the turn of my wrist.

Simple as that.

"What say you?"

Here we go. Moment of truth.

From the corner of my eye I see Stanton's broad shoulders rise ever so slightly as he inhales . . . and holds his breath.

Just like I do.

The forewoman rattles off the case number and the charges, and then she utters the magic words: "Not guilty."

Hell to the yes! Whoot fucking whoot! Let the mental fist pumping commence!

Much like with touchdown-scoring NFL players, excessive celebration in the courtroom is frowned upon, so Stanton and I restrain ourselves to glowing, congratulatory smiles. But both of us know this is huge, a win that's a stepping stone to the kind of notoriety enjoyed by Cochran, Allred, Geragos, Abramson, and Dershowitz—the League of Everybody Knows Your Name.

Montgomery thanks Stanton with a handshake, yet manages to make even his gratitude sound supercilious. He turns to me with open arms—expecting a hug of course.

Because I have a vagina.

And like so many, he functions under the belief that penises shake hands, vaginas hug.

Not this one, buddy.

I extend an unyielding arm, which makes my point and keeps him out of my personal space. He settles for the handshake, but adds a leering wink.

And the hot shower beckons louder.

When we step outside the courthouse, reporters are waiting. Local, not national. Not yet. Like I said, stepping stone.

Stanton, being first chair, fields the questions with a well-practiced mixture of charm and egotism—lawyers don't do modest. But he gives me my due, referring to "our" defense, mentioning how "we" were confident of the outcome from the very beginning, highlighting our firm like a good little soldier, and stressing that every client of Adams & Williamson would receive equally stellar representation.

While he speaks, I take a moment to admire him—because he's so easy to admire. His jade eyes glitter with excitement and afternoon sun, framed by dense, surprisingly dark lashes that women would kill to have. A few rebel strands of thick, golden hair—Robert Redford, *Legal Eagles* kind of hair—fall over his intelligent brow. A Roman nose and high cheekbones give him a strong, noble look, but Stanton Shaw's all man—not a hint of pretty boy here. I think my favorite part is his jaw. It's porn worthy. Rugged and square with the perfect amount of scratchy, blond stubble to conjure images of sexy late mornings and warm beds.

He stands at six foot two—just four inches taller than I am—and his long legs and broad torso are a tailor's dream. It's the kind of body that was made to wear a suit. His voice is deep, a melodic baritone with the barest hint of southern lilt that during cross-examination can slash like a scalpel or mesmerize with the comfort of a bedtime storyteller. But it's his smile that draws you in, that disarms. Expert lips that make you want to laugh when they do or provoke the dirtiest of thoughts when they slide into that lazy, lopsided smirk.

The smirk and I are well acquainted.

". . . isn't that right, Ms. Santos?" he asks, and the reporters' gazes fall to me expectantly.

Shit. I have no idea what he's asking. I was too busy staring at the jawline—*damn you, jaw*—remembering how its bristles scraped my inner thigh, making me purr with the satisfaction of a feline enjoying her favorite scratching post.

But I recover smoothly. "Absolutely. I couldn't agree more."

The reporters thank us, and while our client climbs into his chauf-feured car, Stanton and I decide to walk the few blocks back to the office.

"Where'd you go back there? You zoned out," he says with a ring of amusement that tells me he's already guessed.

"I'll give you detailed instructions later on," I reply as Stanton opens the door to our building for me.

Abrams & Williamson is one of the oldest law firms in DC. The building itself is only ten stories, adhering to the Height of Buildings Act of 1910, which prohibited construction of any new structures that would be taller than the Capitol dome, save for a few limited exceptions. But what the building lacks in stature it makes up for in historical grandeur. Polished mahogany gleams beneath overhead lighting, designed to highlight the handcrafted moldings that decorate every wall. A restored marble fireplace welcomes visitors with its perpetual light as they walk to the huge walnut receptionist's desk.

The longtime receptionist, Vivian, is in her fifties, her flawless white suit and blond updo providing the perfect first impression of experienced elegance to all who enter.

She smiles warmly. "Congratulations to you both. Mr. Adams would like to see you in his office."

News travels fast in DC, making high school gossip grapevines look as slow as dial-up Internet. So it's no surprise that word of our win has already reached our boss's desk. However, impressive win or not, Jonas Adams, founding partner of our firm and direct descendant of our second president, would never descend from his top-floor perch to offer congratulations.

He summons us to him.

On the elevator ride up, the same eager excitement bubbling inside me emanates from my colleague in crime. We're immediately ushered into Jonas's office, where he stands behind his desk, speedily sliding folders into a worn leather briefcase. His resemblance to his founding father ancestor is nothing short of uncanny—a bulging midsection accessorized by the gold chain of an antique pocket watch, round spectacles balanced on a pointy nose, and white tufts of hair combed over in an attempt to cover the bald crown of his head, which is as shiny as the hardwood floors we're standing on.

If he ever retires, historical reenactment companies will be tearing each other to pieces to have him.

Jonas has lectured at the finest legal institutions and is considered one of the most brilliant minds in our field. But like many gifted intellectuals, he exhibits a busy, scatterbrained temperament that makes you think he's forever losing his car keys.

"Come in, come in," he calls as he pats his pockets, relieved to discover the items he was obviously hoping were still there. "I'm leaving momentarily for a conference in Hawaii, but I wanted to congratulate you both on the Montgomery case."

He shuffles out from behind his desk and shakes our hands. "Excellent work—not an easy win, that one. But Senator Montgomery is sure to be grateful."

"Thank you, sir," Stanton replies.

"What's that for you now, Mr. Shaw? Eight wins under the proverbial belt?"

Stanton shrugs, immodestly. "Nine, actually."

Jonas nods as he removes his glasses and cleans them with a monogrammed handkerchief. "Impressive."

"It's all about the jury, Mr. Adams," Stanton crows. "Never met one that didn't like me."

"Yes, very good, very good. And you, Miss Santos? Still undefeated, eh?"

With a smile, I lift my chin proudly. "Yes, sir—six for six."

Professional women have come a long way—our feet are now firmly in the door of the previously dominated boy's club of political, legal, and business fields. But we still have a long way to go. The fact remains that more often than not, when it comes to promotions and professional opportunities, we're the afterthought, not the first consideration. In order to get to the forefront of our bosses' regard, it's not enough to be as good as our male counterparts—we have to be better. We have to stand out.

It's an unfair truth, but a truth all the same.

Which is why when Jonas's driver enters the room to retrieve his luggage, wheeling out a luxury brand golf bag whose contents are worth more than Stanton's Porsche, I comment, "I didn't know you were a golfer, Mr. Adams."

That's not true—I totally knew.

"Yes, I'm an avid player. Relaxing, you know, helps with the stress. I'm looking forward to a few rounds during the conference. Do you play?"

I smile like the Cheshire Cat. "I do, as a matter of fact. Just shot a seventy-seven at East Potomac."

He replaces his glasses over widened eyes. "That's remarkable." He wags his finger. "When I return from Hawaii, you'll be my guest at my club, Trump National, for a few rounds."

"That would be lovely. Thank you."

Jonas's jowls jiggle hypnotically as he nods. "My secretary will have your assistant add it to your calendar." Then he turns his attention back to Stanton. "Do you play, Shaw?"

Because I know him, I notice the nanosecond of hesitation. But then his face splits into a wide grin. "Of course. Golf is my life."

Jonas claps his hands. "Excellent. Then you'll join us for the day."

Stanton swallows hard. "Super."

After Jonas takes his leave, Stanton and I are back in the elevator heading to our own respective offices on the fourth floor.

" '*Golf is my life*'?" I quote, watching the lighted numbers descend.

His amused eyes turn to me. "What the hell was I supposed to say?"

"Ah, you could have said what you said to me three months ago: '*Golf is not a real sport.*' "

"It's not," he insists. "If you don't sweat, it's not a sport."

To which I respond, "Golf requires a tremendous amount of skill . . ."

"So does Ping-Pong. And that's not a fucking sport either."

Stubborn, stupid man perspective. Having grown up with brothers I'm familiar with it, yet I still laugh at the absurdity.

"So what are you going to do? Jonas returns from Hawaii in two weeks."

"Plenty of time for you to teach me to play," he answers, elbowing me softly.

"Me?" I sputter.

"Sure, Ms. Seventy-Seven at East Potomac. Who better?"

I shake my head. This is how Stanton operates. Like my niece uses her quivering lip against my oldest brother, Stanton uses his damnable charm.

It's impossible to resist—especially when you don't really want to.

"Two weeks isn't much time."

He puts his hand on my shoulder, rubbing his thumb against the bare skin at the nape of my neck. The action scorches a path down my spine, making all the muscles below my waist clench.

"We'll start this weekend. I have total confidence in you, Soph. Plus"—he winks—"I'm a fast learner."

As the elevator doors open, he removes his hand, and for a quick moment, I mourn the loss. "That'll be the perfect time to settle up on our bet. Your car owes me a drive."

"I don't think I should be held responsible for bets I made under duress."

My heels click on the wood floors as I scoff, "What possible duress were you under?"

Stanton stops a few feet from our office doors. He lowers his voice and leans in to whisper against my ear. "You underestimate the power of your miraculous tits. They were in my face—thinking clearly was not possible."

I fold my arms skeptically. "Miraculous?"

He holds his hands up, palms out. "Made me want to stand up and shout amen . . . or drop to my knees and do other things."

A small laugh escapes me. "If all breasts distract you so easily, you've got bigger problems than me driving your baby."

Stanton looks me over for a moment, and his eyes grow warm. Almost tender.

"Not all breasts, Soph. Just yours."

I've heard the expression 'my heart skipped a beat,' but I didn't realize it can actually happen. Until this moment.

Still, I feign indifference. "Nice try. Request to be excused denied. I don't give golf lessons to jilters."

"Can't blame a man for trying."

Brent steps out of our office, on his way into Stanton's. He stops when he sees us and raises his arm in salute. "Ah, the returning victors. Just the two people I wanted to see."

We follow him into Stanton's office, which he shares with Jake Becker, who's reclined in his desk chair, perusing an open case file on his lap. With barely a glance our way Jake says, "I hear congratulations are in order. My compliments on proving that justice is dumb as well as blind."

Stanton and Jake have known each other since law school, when Stanton was in dire need of a roommate to offset the rent and Jake was in dire need of sleeping somewhere that wasn't his mother's living room couch. Jake Becker doesn't look like a lawyer. He reminds me of a heavyweight boxer or the muscle from a black-and-white mobster movie. Black hair, eyes the color of cold steel, full lips that rarely smile and utter the most caustic remarks. His frame is large and dangerously powerful, with hands that swallow mine whole when we shake. Brick-like hands that would make you pity his foolish opponent in a brawl.

Despite his intimidating appearance, Jake is the perfect gentleman. He has a dry sense of humor and he's unwaveringly protective of those he counts as friends. I feel lucky to say I'm one of them. I've never seen him lose his temper or raise his voice, but I suspect his is the kind of anger that strikes with a lethal vengeance—without any warning at all.

Stanton puts his briefcase on his desk and sits down.

"Don't get too comfortable," Brent warns him. "We're not staying long. It's Friday, and your victory gives us the perfect justification for cutting out early."

I didn't know Brent when he was young, but he has all the makings of an epic class clown . . . or a child in desperate need of Ritalin. Always upbeat, with a joke at the ready and an endless supply of energy. He rarely sits still; even if he's reading, he's on his feet pacing or balanced on the edge of his desk, a file in one hand and a grip strengthener in the other.

Oh, and he doesn't even drink coffee. Some Monday mornings I want to strangle Brent.

"I have to finish the Rivello brief," I explain, but his head shake cuts me off.

"You can finish it tomorrow, Miss Go-getter. You're already Adams's new pet—don't need to show the rest of us up that much. Besides, we have cause for celebration, and I make it a rule never to pass those up. Time for happy hour."

I look at my watch. "It's three o'clock."

"Which means it's five o'clock somewhere." He hooks his thumb toward the door. "Let's go, kids—find your buddy. First round's on Jake."

Jake's already standing, packing his briefcase with take-home work. He twirls his finger in the air and says flatly, "Sure. Water for everyone."

With a chuckle, Stanton loops his arm over my shoulders. "Come on, Soph. There's a Tequila Sunrise with your name on it. We've earned it."

I have an enduring love/hate relationship with Tequila Sunrises—I love them at happy hour and hate them in the morning.

With a sigh, I give in. "Okay, what the hell."

5

Stanton

By the time happy hour officially rolls around, Sofia and Brent are way past happy. Not Jake, though—Jake's the original designated driver. He enjoys a single-malt scotch as much as the next guy, but I've never seen him drink to get drunk. Unlike everyone else around him at this moment. Six o'clock on a Friday night in Washington, DC, the streets are a ghost town—because anyone who's still here is already inside the bars.

Politicians don't actually live in the city. If Congress isn't in session, they go back to their home districts. Those who are married with kids head back to the suburbs. That leaves the rest of us—hungry, hardworking, and horny. And there's no better way to blow off a whole lot of steam from a long-ass week at the office than having a nice drink in a noisy tavern. Sofia calls it the "*Grey's Anatomy* effect."

"Air bubble in the IV," Brent suggests in a diabolical voice, leaning his elbows on the wood table cluttered with empty glasses. "Hard to trace, impossible to prove beyond a reasonable doubt—unless there's video cameras in the patient's hospital room, quick, efficient . . ."

"And totally unreliable," Sofia quips, tapping him on the nose. "The amount of air to cause an embolism varies, plus the victim would already have to be in the hospital. Then there'd be a record of visitors . . ."

The perfect murder. It's an ongoing discussion. Knowing the ins and outs of the criminal justice system, I'm actually surprised more people in the legal field don't commit major crimes.

Or, how's this for a mind fuck—maybe they do? Cue the creepy music.

"I still say poison is the surest bet," Jake offers from the head of the table. "Something like ricin or polonium."

His suggestion is met with taunts and heckles.

"Amateur."

"Postmortem forensics is too advanced," Brent argues.

"And where the hell would you find polonium?" Sofia adds. "Know many Russian spies, do you?"

"Remind me never to take you on as a client," I tell him, pointing with my bourbon. "You'd ruin my winning streak."

The dance floor in the adjacent room is filled to capacity with bodies, pitifully short on rhythm. Not many things are as funny as watching people who can't dance but think they can.

Elated arms rise as the song "Oh What a Night" pours from the speakers. Sofia stands excitedly. "That's my cue. Come on, Brent, let's go shake what your momma gave ya."

He rises. "Can't, sweetheart, my date just walked in."

"You have a date tonight?" Sofia asks.

"I do now." He winks. "She just doesn't know it yet."

As Brent walks off, Sofia looks to Jake. He sounds like Dirty Harry asking a punk if he feels lucky when he says, "Do you even need to ask?"

She saves me for last, 'cause she knows full well I don't dance.

Still she tries, running her hand up my arm. "Want to show me your moves, Shaw?"

I chew on the toothpick between my lips. "Darlin', I'll show you every move I've got—just not on a fuckin' dance floor."

She giggles, then prances over to the swinging, shaking bodies. And I watch her with the gaze of a man who's sure he's going to get laid—and knows it's going to be good.

Her rounded hips swivel in perfect time to the quick beat, confident and practiced. I imagine those hips straddling me—riding me—with the same fast rhythm. And I'm instantly hard.

Throbbing with remembrance and expectation.

It's how she moves moments before she comes, tight and rapid, feeding off sensation, chasing that blissful grinding friction.

I suck hard on the toothpick in my mouth as she lifts her arms, circling her pelvis. Sofia likes her arms above her—pinned by my palms—against a bed, a wall, a hard oak desk. Fucking her is phenomenal on any given day, but screwing when she's like this—just drunk enough—is particularly fantastic. She's wilder, rougher—she pulls my hair just a little harder.

Begs just a little sweeter.

The bourbons I've downed have loosened my muscles and my mind. I'm not intoxicated, but relaxed enough to forget any worries—to give very little shit about anything. I pull at my tie as her foreplay show continues, content to watch unhurried, to let this anticipation build.

But then she turns around.

Her dark hair fans out, and I'm caught in those hazel fucking eyes. Large, almond-shaped eyes that practically glow with hunger.

She's not just dancing in front of me, she's dancing *for* me.

Her hands skim down her sides slowly, cradling her hips, squeezing. But it's my hands she's imagining, my grip she's feeling. Sofia's full lips are parted, breathing heavy, the gloss of moisture beading on her upper lip.

And I want to lick it off.

But that'll just be the start—devouring that mouth—before licking down and around, until I've tasted all of her. Until every inch of her skin is branded with the feel of my tongue, my lips.

My teeth.

Twirling the toothpick against the roof of my mouth, I stand. And stalk her way. Before I reach her, Sofia turns her back, ass still swiveling.

Taunting.

Over her shoulder, she keeps her gaze trained on me. I don't stop until I'm flush against her, my palm on her stomach, pulling her back. So she can't have any doubt about how she's affected me. Every hot, hard inch of effect is pressed against her ass.

"Change your mind?" she teases. "Want to dance after all?"

"I want to fuck," I breathe against her ear, making her shiver. "You. In case there was doubt. Now."

She thrusts back, trapping my dick between us, then sliding up and down, rubbing with sublime pressure. I swallow a groan.

"Then I guess we're leaving."

· · ·

On the cab ride to my apartment, I make it a point not to touch her—no casual brushes of her thigh or a hand to help her exit the taxi. Because I know the waiting will key her up even more.

And because once I start, I don't plan on stopping.

After a tense, torturous elevator ride, we stand in the hall outside my apartment door. As I put the key into the lock, Sofia's body is close—not pressing—but near enough behind me I can smell her perfume. A clean, sweet floral scent; gardenia maybe.

We walk through the door, then I turn, using her to close it, slamming her back. Trapping her between the door and me. Hands grasp at air as I hold her wrists in one hand, high above her head, stretching her out, making her back bow. Straining for contact.

She gasps as I run my nose up her cheek, her breath escaping in tiny puffs. "You want to be fucked?" I rasp.

She moans. Squirms. "Yes."

Sofia likes it rough—hard words, bruising fingers—and I'm all too happy to please.

I skim my free hand up her thigh, bunching her skirt as I go. "You want to come?"

She once told me one of her favorite parts of screwing me was that she can just let it all go. No worries, no stress, no shots to call. It's the one area of her life where she's happy to let someone else—me—do all the work.

Her chin rises, scraping soft skin against my stubble. "Please," she begs.

"How bad?" I taunt, rubbing over her silk panties where she's soft and hot. Her hips gyrate against my hand as I push the fabric aside and slide my fingers through her smooth, slick lips. My dark chuckle rumbles. "Feels like you want to come pretty bad."

"Stanton . . ." She groans in an impatient plea.

And then my mouth is on hers, taking her words, sucking those plump lips that I watch all fucking day. She tastes so sweet—grenadine with a tang of tequila, making my head swim. She gives me her tongue, moist and warm. I move my lips over hers, plundering firmly, barely allowing for breath, and capture her lower lip with my teeth.

Her arms push against my grip, wanting to grab, to pull me closer, but I hold her steady. I press the length of my body against hers, feeling every soft, full curve against my hard angles. She moans, grateful for the contact while I ravage that mouth. Then I slide my lips down her jaw, leaving a wet trail, to her neck, feasting on her sweet skin like a starving man. She gasps and lifts her chin higher, giving me better access as I slip lower, to the top buttons on her blouse.

One-night stands, sex without feelings, stranger screwing—I've done them plenty of times before. Sometimes it's good, sometimes it's just—mechanical—fulfilling a base physical need. But this, here with Sofia—there's never been anything mechanical about it. It's scorching flames, licking at our limbs, pulling us together from a space deep inside—making us clash like magnets separated too far for too long.

My mouth sucks at her tits, over her blouse, leaving a dark, wet mark on the silk. There aren't any thoughts—just feelings and sensations. I release her wrists, grip the delicate fabric with two hands and yank, ripping it open, baring the gorgeous flesh that fascinates me.

I'll replace the blouse—I don't have time for fucking buttons.

I pull the cup of her black lace bra down and her hands sink into my hair, massaging my skull as I devour her breast. *So warm, so soft.* I place long, open-mouth kisses along the mound, suctioning the skin until Sofia cries out—leaving my mark—punishing it for distracting me. Then I run my tongue around the dusky circle of her nipple—flicking and laving. When I engulf it with my mouth, she bucks, then sighs with relief as I suckle.

Her head rolls on her neck. "Oh yes . . . oh God yes . . ."

As I move to the other stunning tit and ply it with equal attention, I slip my fingers back into her panties, wanting to make her come, make her scream just like this. Her thighs spread, making room for my hand, as my fingers circle her opening. Her hips rotate in opposite circles to mine, her nails scour my back over my shirt. With my teeth trapping one peaked, sensitive nipple, I plunge two fingers into her tight wetness.

"Fuck . . ." she whimpers.

Sliding my fingers in and out, pumping, I wiggle my thumb down to her waiting clit and rub. Her voice rises, becoming desperate, because release is so fucking close. Then I lift my head and take in the sight of her face. Eyes closed, dark lashes fanned out against bronze skin, parted, panting lips calling my name. If I had any talent for painting, this would be the masterpiece I'd capture. This pure, unguarded moment, when she's completely bare before me—trusting me to give her hard, pounding pleasure, but leave her unbroken.

I have to kiss her.

Gently now, I coax her lips to mine, while my fingers pump faster, thumb rubbing harder.

And then she explodes. I taste her beautiful moan, as her arms clasp and her thighs squeeze, and her pussy traps my fingers in fantastic pulsating contractions.

When her limbs loosen and her hands are cupping my jaw and she's kissing me slow and sweet and grateful, I slip my fingers out of her. I rear back, and she watches with burning eyes as I taste the wetness that coats them. Better than grenadine or tequila or fucking bourbon—Sofia's juice is the elixir of the gods, and I'll be sucking on that delicious pussy before the night is over.

But first it's time for her to have her fun.

With a sharp grin and an almost evil spark in her eye, she grips my tie and pulls me back in for a kiss. I let her spin us around, so my back is against the door. As our mouths dance, I push my hands into her hair—gripping—pulling the way I know she craves. Then I'm pushing her down.

Down on her knees.

She looks up at me, those fucking eyes alight and hungry, as her open palms slide over my pants, up my thighs, unbuckling my belt with a clang. I watch, my hand running across her head, through her hair, as she tugs them and the boxers underneath down to my ankles. I step out of them and lose eye contact as she rubs up my legs, toned and solid with muscle.

"These legs," she admires aloud. "They were made to be kneeled at."

I chuckle darkly. "Thanks for the compliment, darlin'. But no more talkin' now—I have much more interesting uses for that mouth of yours."

She smiles and runs her tongue across her lips. My thick cock jumps, 'cause it knows what's coming next. I grip my dick firmly, pumping slow, then trace the tip over Sofia's lips, spreading the moisture already there across them.

I look into those eyes, eyes a man could drown in if he's not careful—and I tell her, "Open."

I don't mind a woman who's eager, and I've been more than happy to lay back and let a girl have her wicked way with me. But here—now—with Sofia, there's a rush from her submission. A thrill at being above her, in charge of her. And I want to take my time, let her feel every inch of what I'm giving—instead of just allowing her to take.

Like the saying goes, giving really is better.

Her lips are swollen, rosy from my rough kisses. They spread as she opens wide, and I guide my dick into that wet, hot heaven. I push in slow, breathing hard, until I hit the back of her throat with a moan. And I sink into the fucking sensation of her snug, warm mouth wrapped around me. *So goddamn good.*

I look down, watching as I slide back out, her lips tightening, like they don't want me to go. Then I push back in, a little harder, a little farther. I hold myself inside, feeling her throat constrict around me.

"Fuuuuck," I groan.

It's delicious torture—perfect agony that I want to last all night.

But I pull back out, just to have the chance to push in again.

Cradling her head, I tell her, "That's it, baby. Just like that. Keep that mouth open, take it all in . . . fuck . . ."

I can't hold back. Eyes rolling closed, I start to thrust. I don't want to come, not yet, but I also don't want to stop. *Just a little more, a bit longer.*

Sofia moans with excitement—loving it almost as much as I do—and the vibration goes straight to my balls, making them tighten, readying for the rapture that's just so fucking close. Right on the edge, I grip her hair and pull her off. Then I guide her up to her feet and kiss that perfect mouth.

Now where to? The floor, the couch, up against the wall?

The bed just isn't an option—way too far away.

I pick up my pants, retrieving the condom from the pocket, tearing it open and rolling it on with an expertise born of practice and desperation. Watching me, Sofia slips out of her skirt and panties, not bothering with the blouse that's little more than hanging, torn scraps.

The floor it is.

Pulling her into my arms, fucking her mouth with my tongue, I descend to my knees, taking her with me, then lay her down, cushioning her head from the hardwood with my palm.

"Hurry, Stanton," she begs. Screwing is the only time I'll ever hear Sofia beg, and it's awesome. "I need it. Oh God . . ."

She lifts her hips, rubbing against my stomach, her pussy even wetter now. We both groan as I push inside—stretching her stunning tightness—burying to the hilt.

Fuck, yeah.

Exquisite, harsh sounds come from her throat as I thrust hard, pummeling, building us both back up. Her nails dig into my back, making me hiss, and I grip her shoulders for leverage. I grind against her, my hips circling when I'm deepest, pelvises clashing.

"You want it harder?" I rasp, breathless against her ear.

Her legs tighten around me, heels digging into my ass in answer.

"Give me your mouth," she pleads.

I lower my lips to hers, nipping and licking, fusing us together. Tingling sparks dance along my spine and I pump faster, giving her everything I've got, everything I'll ever have.

I feel her flutter around me, tiny spasms gripping my dick, gaining intensity. "That's it, baby, come with me . . . right there . . ."

Dots of light dance behind my eyes, and I bury my face against her neck. Her hips surge up one final time and hold, as I thrust forward and magnificent pleasure swells in my veins. Beyond the blood rushing through my ears, I hear her chanting my name as we spike together, coming at the same time—sharing that perfect fucking space where all that exists is her and me and bliss.

Breath against my shoulder, like the flutter of a bird's wings, is the next thing I'm conscious of. It takes some effort, but I lift up and look into Sofia's dazzling eyes. Her smile, tender enough to break my heart.

I brush the hair back from her face and press a delicate kiss to her lips. Without another word, I slip out of her and stand. Sweeping her into my arms, I head for the bedroom.

Because the night's not over yet—not by a long shot.

• • •

Sofia collapses onto her back, laughing breathlessly. I peel off the second well-used condom of the night and toss it into the trash can beside the bed. We lay side by side, in comfortable quiet until a loud grumble from her stomach breaks the silence.

She tries to hide behind her hand, but I enjoy watching the embarrassed flush that spreads from her tits to her cheeks.

"We skipped dinner, didn't we?" I say.

"Unless you count the fruit garnish on the Tequila Sunrises."

I tap her leg. "Come on. Let's see what we've got in terms of sustenance."

I walk down the hall. Naked. I happen to like being bare ass. It feels good, natural. Sure I live on a busy city street and we don't have curtains, but if people want to look up at my window, might as well give them something to look at.

Sofia follows, my blanket wrapped around her shoulders—I assume for warmth. We left modesty in the dust a ways back—around the first time she played jockey on my face.

She sits at the kitchen table while I get a bowl from the fridge and put it in the microwave to heat. I set two plates on the table, then two glasses of cold water. I feel Sofia's undivided attention follow me as I move—enjoying the view.

When the microwave chimes, I take the bowl out—and burn the holy hell out of my fingers in the process.

"Shit!" I wag my hand, then suck on the injured digits.

"Careful," she warns in an amused voice, "don't singe any good parts."

Using a towel, I carry the steaming bowl to the table. "Thanks for your concern."

I dish us out two gooey, heaping servings of homemade macaroni and cheese. Sofia moans on the first bite, and my dick—no longer in fear of injury—takes notice.

"This is so good, Stanton. Did you make it?"

"Nah, I don't cook. And neither does Jake usually, but his momma's macaroni and cheese is the one meal he committed to memory. He can't go a week without it. It keeps well in the freezer, which is convenient."

We're quiet for a few minutes, focused on the food. Then Sofia muses, "Today was a good day."

I watch her hair fall over the bronze skin of her collarbone, the soft, languid glow in those hazel eyes. And it's nice—just being here. With her.

"Sure was."

After our plates are empty, I venture, "Can I ask you a question?"

"Of course."

I push the blanket off her shoulder, revealing the stunning swell of her right breast, heavy in its natural fullness. Her breath catches as I trace my finger down the side, to her rib cage, over the jagged eight-inch scar that mars otherwise flawless skin.

"How'd this happen?"

When I first noticed, it didn't feel right to ask—not my place. Our early encounters consisted of getting each other's clothes off as quickly as possible, staying hard as long as possible, and coming as many times as possible—without risking dehydration or unconsciousness. Didn't leave a whole lot of time for talking.

But now . . . lately . . . I've found myself wanting to know more than how Sofia likes to be sucked or fucked. And more than the rudimentary stuff Brent or Jake would know.

I want her fantasies . . . a few of her secrets.

There's no painful clouding of her features, no flinching at the mention, and for that I'm eternally grateful.

"Plane crash," she says matter-of-factly.

"You're shittin' me."

"I'm most certainly not shitting you," she mimics with a smile. "When I was eight, we were coming back from visiting family in Rio, and the landing gear malfunctioned. We had to land belly first—hard." Her voice takes on an airy quality—remembering. "It was loud, that's what I remember most. The crunch of metal on metal, like a car accident . . . times a thousand. The armrest of my seat sliced through the skin—broke two ribs—but didn't damage anything major. We were lucky, as far as plane crashes go. No fatalities; everyone recovered."

"Damn," I mutter, not sure what I was expecting—but it sure wasn't that.

She gives me a small smile. "My second oldest brother, Lucas—he's the philosopher in the family—he thinks it was a sign. A reminder that life is short. Precious. And that there must be great things for us to accomplish, because we all could've died, but we were spared. For a reason."

I cover the mark with my hand, thinking of the pain she must have endured, wanting to somehow absorb it. But at the same time, it's a part of her—made Sofia into the woman she is today. And there's not a thing I would change, 'cause she's fucking incredible.

My hand slides upward, cupping the warm softness of her breast, feeling the vibration of her heartbeat beneath. The sound of her breath—full and high pitched—spurs me on. Her pulse throbs quickly as I lean in.

She whispers my name, and I don't think it's ever sounded quite so damn sweet.

Before I can press my lips to the hollow of her throat, the rattle of keys in the door jars us both. We straighten up, like two teenagers in the beam of a policeman's flashlight, and dash back to my bedroom. I close the door, both of us chuckling.

With a yawn, I flop down onto the bed, pulling the remaining comforter over me. Sofia watches me for a moment, then drops her own blanket and reaches for her clothes.

"I should get going."

This is how it works. We screw, we dress, we leave: have a good night, see you at the office.

I glance at the clock showing 3 a.m. "It's late," I point out with another yawn. And the steady patter against the window pane registers. "And it's rainin'. Why don't you just stay?"

We don't have set rules—nothing we've ever agreed to out loud anyway. We've just gone with it, done whatever works, whatever feels good. If we have rules, unspoken ones, there's a fair chance sleepovers break them.

But I just can't make myself give a shit.

I rub my face against the cushiony pillow and crack open one eye. Sofia stands there—beautifully bare—holding her bra in her hand. Looking at me.

Debating.

I throw back the covers, revealing the empty space in front of me. "It's cold out there, warm in here. Don't overthink, Soph."

It doesn't have to mean anything. And Sofia's soft and smooth—having her to rub against is sure to bring on some sweet dreams.

She drops the bra and crawls in beside me. Her back presses against my chest, her ass cradles my cock, giving me new perspective on the benefits of cuddling.

My hand rests on her hip, the other under my pillow. After shifting around to get comfortable, Sofia whispers, "Did you know when you're tired, your accent comes out more?"

Her hair tickles my nose, making me sniff. "Does it?"

"Yeah," she says softly. "I . . . like it."

Just as I'm about to drift off, a pounding thud fills the room, like an unwelcome drummer boy.

Bang, bang, bang. It's the sound of wood meeting Sheetrock— headboard against wall. Accompanied by a whiny, feminine voice. "Yes, yes, yes!"

I lift my head and yell at the wall. "Hey! Do you mind—some of us are tryin' to sleep here."

Jake's uncaring voice calls back. "Do *you* mind? Some of us are trying to fuck over here."

The banging resumes, but thankfully, not the whine of affirmation.

Sofia giggles as I yank the blanket up over our heads, drowning out some of the sound.

"Christ," I grumble. "I really need to get my own place."

6

Sofia

At some point before morning, I'm awakened by the steady brush of Stanton's pelvis against my backside. His large hand slides up my stomach, squeezing my breast then tracing my hardened nipple with the tip of his fingers, in a way that makes my back arch—press into his touch. His teeth scrape my shoulder, and it feels feral and dangerous.

He's not waiting for permission, but I moan it just the same.

Then those magical fingers are between my legs, sliding and spreading the wetness already there. He takes my hand and presses my own fingers against my clit, rubbing delicate circles.

His voice is gravelly with sleep as he directs, "Keep doin' that."

The warmth of his chest disappears from my back, and the bed vibrates with his movement. The sound of ripping foil pierces the otherwise silent air and then he's back—hot skin pressing, lips blazing a trail up my neck to the sensitive flesh behind my ear.

My breath comes in quick gasps and my fingers press harder, spiking pleasure that tightens my stomach. Stanton's panting breath tickles my shoulder blade as he grips my knee and lifts my leg.

Yes. This. Now.

Please now.

I don't realize I've spoken aloud until I feel his chuckle. "We must've been havin' the same dream."

And then he fills me. Fully. Perfectly. Spearing my pussy with his hard, heavy thickness. My head tilts back, chin rising with an excited moan. Air escapes his lips in a long, whistling stream as he thrusts slowly.

I feel his cock against my fingers and reach lower, caressing him where he strokes in and out in a steady rhythm. *Jesus, God,* I love how he moves—how he knows just the right angle, the right speed to drive me straight to the brink. I don't have to say a word, do a thing. Unless I want to—unless *he* tells me to.

His hand squeezes my leg harder and I reach around to the back of his thigh—the firm swell of his ass—pushing him into me deeper.

Making him groan.

Stanton sucks on my earlobe, his voice scraping. "Goddamn, Sofia, I love doin' you like this. Being able to look at every inch of you. So fuckin' beautiful."

He plunges harder, his pelvis slapping loudly against my ass.

"You love it, too?" he pants.

He releases my leg, but I keep it elevated—feeling too good to let it drop. Then his fingers pinch and tug on my nipples, torturously exquisite.

"Show me," he grunts. "Show me how good it feels. How much you love it."

With a cry I push back into his thrust, meeting his every move. I bend forward at the waist for leverage, grinding back as he surges forward. Faster. Building. More.

"Fuck, that's it, baby."

And we've become a pulsating, writhing mass of pleasure. Moans and gasps, clutching limbs and contracting muscles. My nails dig into the skin on his leg when I come, my mouth open against the crisp bed sheet, silently screaming.

Stanton pushes me onto my stomach, stretching out over me. Three more powerful shoves of his hips and he's grunting against my back in the sexiest way. I feel him swell inside me—pulsing hard and hot—as he comes. The sensation, his sounds, make me want to start all over again.

We're still for several moments, all panting breaths and pounding hearts. Even before his weight rolls from my back, I'm sinking—effortlessly sliding into that mindless exhaustion that comes after blissful exertion. Movement is the last thing that registers, being dragged into a strong embrace, surrounded by the spicy fragrance of after-sex mixed with the comforting scent of warm man.

I sigh, snuggling closer to his chest. And one final thought floats through my brain before oblivion takes me:

I could get used to this.

• • •

The sunlight streaming through Stanton's bedroom window is what wakes me—bright and warm on my face. The smell of coffee is in the air and there's an empty space beside me. I don't sit up right away, but indulge in a few extra minutes of basking—in the softness of his bed, the masculine scent that still clings to the sheets, and the tantalizing memories that dance behind my eyes.

Spending the night is a new development. A spontaneous choice that . . . probably wasn't my smartest move.

Because, guilty as charged, I liked it.

I liked everything about it. His arms around me, his chest under my cheek, his late-night cock deep inside me. My internal muscles clench with remembrance and I flinch slightly with blessed soreness—the best kind of ache. I wonder if Stanton liked having me here too. He enjoys "having me," that's obvious, but I wonder if he'd want—

No.

Objection.

Out of order.

Cease and desist.

We all know what happens when we play with matches—but I will not get burned. I'm like . . . the hand that passes through the flame of the candle *without* getting burned.

I'm fireproof.

Because I'm prepared. Voices that sound suspiciously like my brothers' echo in my ears. Overheard conversations about "friends" who wanted more benefits than they were willing to give. Strategies for disentangling themselves from the needy tentacles of women who'd become too attached. Adjectives to describe those women that started with "cool" "awesome" "casual" but changed into "annoying" "clingy" "awkward."

Friendships that never recovered.

Because boundaries were breached.

Not me.

I don't need that kind of distraction. Don't want that type of complication. My career is right where it's supposed to be—the fast track—and come hell or high water, or orgasms that make me forget my social security number, that's where it's going to stay.

Now I spring out of bed, purposefully, and start to dress. Until I get to my blouse. I didn't get a good look at it last night, but it's in tatters. Ripped at the buttons, with a hole big enough for my hand—or my boob—to fit through. It looks like a red flag that dared to tease a horny bull and took the punishment doled out by his long, thick horn.

Which isn't too far off the mark, I guess.

Then I notice the T-shirt folded at the end of the bed, placed beside my clothes. Gray with bright yellow writing: Sunshine, Mississippi.

Thoughtful.

I pick it up and guiltily press the cotton against my face, inhaling deeply. It smells predominantly of fabric softener, but there's the detectable trace of Stanton hidden in its threads.

I shake my head. *Eye on the prize, Sofia.* And no matter what my clitoris might believe, the prize is *not* Stanton Shaw's glorious, golden penis.

I pull my hair up into a ponytail. I shove my ruined blouse and jacket into my purse, thanking the fashion gods that big bags are in style. Then I give myself the once-over in Stanton's dresser mirror. Tired eyes, hair that even in a ponytail sticks out like wings on my head, a gray T-shirt that reaches to my hips with a tweed pencil skirt peeking out from beneath it.

This is why they call it the walk of shame.

Steeling myself, I open the door and step down the hall.

He's at the kitchen table, shirtless in navy-blue sweats, his tousled blond hair annoyingly sexy. He's Skyping on his laptop. Judging from his almost empty coffee cup, it seems like he's been Skyping for a while. He meets my eyes with a welcoming smile and points to the pot of coffee on the counter. A silent offering I eagerly accept.

Though the screen is facing away from me, the young girl's voice that emanates from the speakers tells me exactly whom he's speaking to.

". . . and then Ethan Fortenbury said I had man hands."

Stanton looks at the screen, his brow wrinkled with consternation. "Man hands? Well that wasn't very nice of Ethan Fortenbury."

Maybe it's just because I know who he's talking to, but his voice sounds lower, smoother—calm and protective. I could listen to him talk like this all day.

I hear the crunch of cereal being chewed, and then she answers, "No, he's not nice, Daddy. I'd like to call him a jackass, but Momma said that's impolite, so instead I call him a horse's anus—because he is."

Stanton laughs.

And Jake walks into the kitchen, dressed for the day, wearing jeans and a blue button-down shirt. He passes behind Stanton's chair, glancing into the screen.

"Hey, Jake!" the happy voice squeals.

He gives her a rare grin. "Good morning, Sunshine." Stanton says

Jake calls Presley Sunshine because that's where she's from . . . and because that's what she is.

Jake joins me at the counter, pouring himself a cup of black coffee and looking me up and down. "Nice outfit."

I stick my tongue out at him.

A lithe, leggy blonde comes striding out of Jake's room, looking better in a camel-colored dress and matching shoes than any woman has the right to after a late night of drinking and sex.

Loud sex.

She barely glances Jake's way as she heads for the door. "Bye."

Jake appears equally invested. "See ya around."

I take another sip of my dark morning drug. "She seems pleasant."

He chuckles. "She showed herself out. Definitely pleasant in my book—I might even see her again."

With that, Jake takes his coffee mug and retreats back from whence he came.

"So what happened next with Ethan Fortenbury?" Stanton asks his daughter.

"Oh! I told him if he didn't stop pickin' on me, I was gonna wrap my man hands around his throat. He hasn't bothered me since."

The rumble of laughter from Stanton is low and smooth and brimming with pride. "That's my girl."

"I gotta go find my sneakers for practice, Daddy. Here's Momma. Mwah! I love you!"

Stanton blows a kiss to the screen. "I love you too, baby girl."

And it's possible my panties just disintegrated. A not-unpleasant ache throbs in my womb—a sudden, passionate desire to procreate with this man. It's purely instinctual, evolutionary, and thankfully I think with my brain, not my ovaries. But I have to admit . . . it's not easy.

I sip my coffee as the voice from the speakers changes—more mature but still heavily accented. "Mornin', Stanton."

"Mornin', darlin'."

"So . . . there's somethin' . . ." There's a nervous-sounding pause, and then she begins again. "Somethin' I've been meanin' to talk to you about . . ."

With my thumb over my shoulder, I gesture to Stanton that I'm going to catch a cab home.

He holds up a pausing finger. "Jenny, could you hold on for one second?"

He closes the laptop. "Don't take a taxi home, Soph, I'll drive you."

I brush him off with the wave of my hand. "No, you're busy—it's not a big deal."

"It's a big deal to me. Just wait—I'll be done in two minutes."

Then he returns to Jenny. "Sorry. What were you saying?"

She hesitates. "Is now a bad time, Stanton?"

"No," he reassures her. "Now's fine—a friend just needs a ride home. Go ahead and tell me your news."

He waits. And I swear I hear her take a big breath . . . right before she chickens out.

"You know what? It can wait . . . you have company . . . I have to get Presley to practice."

"You're sure?"

"Yeah, it's all right," she insists. "I'll . . . um . . . I'll call you later. It's not . . . it's nothin' urgent."

His eyes darken with uncertainty. But he still replies, "All right. Have a good day, then."

"You too."

With a few taps of the keys he disconnects. And that devastating smile falls on me.

"Morning."

Stanton and I have never done a morning-after. It doesn't feel awkward, just . . . new. Different.

I raise my cup of coffee in salute. "Morning."

"I'll just grab a shirt and my keys and then I'll get you home."

• • •

We pull up outside my townhouse and Stanton leaves the car run-ning—apparently not planning on coming in. Which suits me fine. I push a loose strand of hair out of my face.

"Thanks for the ride."

He nods. "Sure. And you too—thanks for the ride." He winks. "Last night."

I chuckle. "Ass."

As I exit the car and close the door behind me, he says, "Hey, don't forget. Our game's at three. At the Turkey Thickett Field on Michigan."

Almost every firm has a team in the DC Lawyers Coed Softball League, and ours has a shot at the championship this year. I'm good at sports—my brothers made sure I was—but I also work at it, because sports like golf, tennis, and racquetball can open career doors that might otherwise be closed. It's all about the networking.

With a wave, I step back. "I'll be there."

As Stanton pulls away, I stand on the street, watching until his car disappears from sight. A twinge of . . . something blooms in my chest. And I find myself sniffing the T-shirt. Again.

Not good.

A run—that's what I need. To sweat out the last drops of alcohol and get that addictive rush of endorphins surging through my brain. I text Brent, who lives down the block, to see if he wants to join me. Then I walk into my townhouse and am greeted by 150 pounds of black and caramel love—my Rottweiler, Sherman.

Like the tank.

My mother carried a fear of dogs with her her whole life, so we didn't have any growing up. But when I got a place of my own, I ful-filled my childhood dream by getting the biggest, brawniest dog I could. Because of my late hours, I employ a dog walker who takes Sherman for his much-needed sprints three or four times a day, and staying out all night isn't a problem. But he's my baby and I'm his mommy—so even though his physical needs have been met, his heartbreakingly adorable brown eyes light up when he sees me.

I spend a good while scratching his ears and rubbing his belly.

Then I connect my phone to the speaker system and turn the volume up loud. Because I need something upbeat. Something snappy. "Still Standing," by the great Elton John—on repeat. Unlike my mother's fear of dogs, her taste in music *was* passed on to me. She heard "Tiny Dancer" for the first time as a teenager on her first day in the United States, and she's loved Elton John's music ever since. It played background while I grew up, the soundtrack of my childhood. I go to see him in concert any chance I get.

By the time the first chorus is complete, I'm already feeling better, bouncing to the beat as I change into a sturdy pink sports bra and snug black running pants. I'm stretching in the living room when Brent walks in the unlocked door, suited up for a run himself—a blue Under Armour T-shirt that highlights the sharp swells of muscle that make up his upper body, black shorts, and the metal arc of the prosthetic leg he uses for jogging.

Though I know about Brent's accident and what it took from him, there's always a moment of shock when I see the harsh metal below his left knee. It's difficult to imagine the struggles he must've faced, all the challenges he had to overcome, and yet he still came out of it with such an awesome, dynamic personality.

He appraises me for a beat, then tilts his head, lifting his ear. " 'Still Standing,' huh? Someone needed a pick-me-up this morning."

Brent knows me well.

"Get in late . . . or . . . not get in at all?" he says.

I grab my keys and we head out the door to Memorial Park, the best spot to run in the city. After last night's rain, the air is warm but dry—a gorgeous summer day.

"I stayed at Stanton's," I tell him casually.

His round eyes widen. "Really?"

"It was late," I explain.

"Uh-huh."

"I was tired," I offer.

"Mmm . . ."

Then, with exasperation, "It was raining!"

He nods, his boyish blue eyes seemingly all-knowing. "So it was."

As an attorney, it's important to know how to turn the tables on a witness. How to steer them away from certain topics. So that's what I do.

"And how did your 'date' go?"

Brent smirks deviously. "A gentleman never kisses and tells."

On slow days at the office, he has a tendency to fill the empty sound space with his more outrageous stories. The actress who blew him while a thousand paparazzi swarmed outside her car; the heiress who had a thing for danger and how he screwed her while suspended from the chandelier of a sixteenth-century castle. Not all the stories involve sex—just his favorite ones.

"I don't see any gentlemen here."

He barks out a chuckle. "Good point. Let's just say she left my house walking crooked this morning, and leave it at that."

We start at the Washington Monument, a warm-up pace, side by side but careful to avoid the many other joggers, bicyclists, and in-line skaters on the path. DC is a young city, active and, at least in the area I live, attractive. You can practically see the rivalry in the air, like smog in LA. Everyone wants to be at the top of their game—ready to move up or push someone else out.

If greed is good, in DC, power is king, and everybody's jockeying for position to get a piece of that pie.

Our steps are steady, our breathing deep but even. "What do you think of facial hair?" Brent asks out of the blue.

I look at his smooth, youthfully handsome face that has gotten him into trouble more than once and shrug. "Depends on the face. Why?"

He rubs his jaw. "I'm thinking about growing a beard. Might save me from getting hit on by high school girls."

I laugh at his predicament. "I think you'd wear a beard well."

Several more minutes pass before the Jefferson Memorial comes into view. I believe that when the monuments were being planned, someone didn't like Thomas Jefferson—because his is pretty far out there. Isolated. In terms of visitors, Jefferson got royally screwed.

"So . . . about you and Stanton . . ." Brent hedges.

I catch his expression from the corner of my eye and it makes me stop short.

Concern.

Uncomfortable friendly concern—like he's working up the nerve to tell me something he really doesn't want to have to tell me.

"Did he say something to you? About me?"

Another lesson learned from the promiscuous big brothers? Boys talk.

"No—no, he hasn't said anything. I just . . . you do realize that Stanton is . . . emotionally unavailable?"

"That's one of the things I like best about him. Who has time for available?"

We're walking now, side by side, getting our breath back.

"But you get that he's . . . spoken for?"

"Of course I get it, Brent—he talks about Jenny and Presley all the time. He's got a picture of them on his desk and a bunch at his apartment."

There are pictures of Stanton leaning close to Jenny, in a hospital bed, holding a newborn baby in a pink blanket. Stanton and a little blonde in pigtails, standing next to a shiny pink bicycle after her first ride. Stanton, Jenny, and Presley sitting together on a Ferris wheel, smiling brightly. The three of them are fair-haired and perfect—like the southern version of The Dresden Dolls.

Brent gestures with his hand. "Personally, I think you and Stanton would be great together. And, hey, you wouldn't even have to change your monogram."

With a laugh I shake my head. "You are the only straight guy I know who knows what a monogram is and would use it in a sentence."

"That's how I roll."

Then he shrugs. "I just . . . I don't want to see you get hurt, Sofia. However . . . unintentionally it may happen."

Brent's a playboy, but he's not a shit. He's had casual lovers or girlfriends who were ready to take things to the next level, when he preferred to remain at their current cruising altitude. When those relationships ended, and emotions inevitably bruised, he's always felt bad about it—guilty, even.

I tug at his sleeve affectionately. "I appreciate that, but it's all good. That's the beauty of friends with benefits—no one gets attached."

Brent returns my smile and we're back to jogging. "On a purely selfish note, it'd suck if our unit at the office got screwed up."

"Our unit?"

He nudges me with his elbow. "Yeah—we're kicking ass and taking names. We're like the Avengers. The good ones, anyway."

"Ooh!" I gasp, playing along. "Can I be Thor? I always liked the hammer."

He pats my head. "No, you poor, foolish girl—you're Black Widow, Jake's the Hulk, Stanton's Captain America."

"And who are you?"

The metal of his prosthetic pings as he flicks it with his fingers, grinning. "I'm Iron Man."

I raise a suggesting finger. "Just a thought—you might have better luck not getting hit on by high school girls if you gave up references to comic book superheroes."

He purses his lips, considering. "Yeah, that's not gonna happen."

With another laugh, I concede, "Facial hair it is then."

• • •

On Sunday morning, I get up early and make a big batch of *pão de queijo*—Brazilian cheese rolls. I try to make them every week—with their light flaky outside and warm, gooey middle, they're perfect for breakfast.

I take a hot cookie sheet out of the oven and put it on the counter to cool, when there's a knock on the door. I open it to find Stanton—with a brand-new golf club over his shoulder—and Jake standing on my front steps.

"Hey," I greet them, opening the door wider.

"Ready to school me, hot teacher?" Stanton asks as Sherman rears, trying to lick his face off.

"Ready, willing, and able. Are you coming golfing with us too, Jake?"

"No, I'm just here for the cheese balls."

As I pour coffee for Stanton and Jake, there's another knock at the door—this time it's Brent.

"Hi."

"Good morning."

He walks into my living room, and though I already suspect the answer, I ask anyway. "What are you doing here so early?"

"It's Sunday," he explains, like he's stating the obvious. "Cheese balls."

And this is how traditions become traditions.

We sit around the table, finishing breakfast, when Stanton tosses a roll in the air for Sherman to catch. "Your dog's getting kind of fat, Soph."

I rub Sherman's back and come to his defense. "He's not fat! He's just . . . big boned."

Brent cocks his head appraisingly. "I don't know, I think Stanton has a point. You may want to up his exercise regimen. You don't want the other dogs at the park bullying him—calling him Fatty McChub-Chub."

I frown at them both. "I have a dog walker come by three times a day."

Jake chimes in. "I don't think you're paying her enough."

Men are harshly straightforward. Mean, even. In a courtroom, these three guys are capable of being the epitome of tact and charisma. But among friends—they're sledgehammers. Maybe it's because I grew up with brothers, maybe their thought process rubbed off on me, but there's something about that honesty that's appealing. Comfortingly simple.

It's that XY chromosomal directness that brings on Stanton's next comment. "Did anyone else notice that dipshit Amsterdam staring at Sofia's ass at the softball game yesterday?"

"I did," Jake says, raising his hand.

"Like it had the cure for cancer written on it," Brent adds.

Richard Amsterdam is a contract attorney from Daily & Essex, another notable firm whose team we played—and beat—yesterday. He's in his late thirties, successful, attractive, and has a reputation for fucking anything with a pulse.

"Must've liked what he saw." I stand, bringing the dirty plates to the sink. "He asked me out after the game. Dinner and a show."

"Ah." Brent nods. "*Dinner and a show*—classic code words for 'alcohol and an orgasm.'"

"I don't like Dick," Jake says, chewing on the last cheese roll. "He goes through secretaries like I go through condoms—can't trust a guy with such a high turnover rate in this economy. Something's not right there."

"What'd you tell him?" Stanton asks, frowning at me.

"That I was too busy. Which I am, golf lessons notwithstanding."

His eyes brighten. "Oh . . . good."

I can take the direct approach, too. "Why is that good, exactly?"

The corner of his mouth pulls up into a bashful, lopsided grin. It makes me warm and tingly in all the right places. "You can do better, Soph."

7

Stanton

Wednesday morning, I'm in the US Attorney's Office, engaging in the rudimentary but exciting behind-the-scenes activity that prevents the court system from grinding to a screeching fucking halt: negotiating the plea deal. It's a common, everyday responsibility—but where the exciting comes in is the thrill of bargaining. I know my client is guilty, the prosecutor knows it too, but it's my job to convince them to take the easy win—that the time and money saved by the taxpayer is worth the lesser charge and reduced sentence.

I follow Angela Cassello, a short, red-haired firecracker of an Assistant US Attorney, down the bustling hallway. "He connects people with the same interests, people looking for specific physical attributes in a partner, who don't have the time to vet a potential companion," I explain.

Diplomacy at its finest. Also known as a crock of shit.

"He's a pimp," Angela argues. "Just because he's rich doesn't make him any less of a pimp."

"He's a matchmaker."

"Ha!" she counters, not slowing her brisk pace. "And next you'll be telling me drug dealers are pharmacists."

That's actually not bad—I may use that in the future.

"Look." I lean against the wall, forcing Angela to stop beside me. "He doesn't work with underage girls, he doesn't cross state lines, there's no claims of abuse. This is a guppy, Angela—a harmless, victimless fish. You've got sharks to fry. If this were Nevada there wouldn't even be a charge."

"If your client were smarter, he would've set up shop in Nevada."

"He'll cop to the tax evasion," I offer. "But you have to take procuring off the table."

"Ah yes, because financial crimes committed by the obscenely wealthy are socially acceptable. Sex crimes are frowned upon—at least when they get caught."

Sometimes the best answer is no answer. I wait her out.

And she sighs. "You're lucky I like you more than your client, Shaw. We'll take the tax evasion. But I want jail time; he's not skating on probation or house arrest."

"Low-security facility and you've got a deal."

She holds out her hand and I shake it. "I'll have the papers sent to your office this week."

"You're the best, Angela."

She pushes my shoulder playfully. "You say that to all the prosecutors."

"Only the pretty ones."

• • •

Back in my office, I open my briefcase and take out the pimp's case file and yesterday's mail I grabbed from the box on my way out this morning. I sit down, drink my coffee, and sort through it. *Junk, junk, bill, junk* . . . an envelope catches my eye.

Five by seven, white, addressed to me in handwritten calligraphy . . . with Jenny's parents' return address.

I open it and remove the flat ivory card.

And it's like a nuclear bomb goes off in my head.

My brain must've turned to ash—making me illiterate—because I can barely decipher the words.

Honor of your presence . . .

Jenny Monroe . . .

James Dean . . .

June . . .

Wedding . . . wedding . . . wedding . . .

"What in the actual *fuck*?"

That gets Jake's attention. He turns in his chair. "Problem?"

I grasp for understanding, for a theory that makes sense. "Did you do this? Is this a joke?"

He points to himself. "Have you ever known me to make a joke? On purpose?"

He's right. Pranks aren't his style.

Brent, on the other hand . . . This is right up his alley.

I spring out of my desk chair and stomp into Brent and Sofia's office.

"Is this supposed to be fuckin' funny?" I accuse, harsh and desperate.

He plucks the card from my fingers. "I don't know why it would be. Ivory isn't a particularly funny color."

And then he reads it. "Whoa." He glances up to my face warily, then back down to the invitation. And again mutters, "Whoa!"

Sofia stands from her desk. "What? Why are we whoa-ing?"

Brent flashes her the invitation. Comprehension dawns in her eyes. "Wh— *Shit*."

Sweat breaks out on my forehead and my chest squeezes like I'm having a panic attack. I grab the card, and with Brent and Sofia right behind me, trudge back to my office—needing to fucking yell at someone.

And I know just the someone.

I punch the familiar numbers into the phone. But I'm brought up short by the voice that answers.

"Presley?"

"Hey, Daddy."

"Why aren't you in school?" It's an hour earlier in Mississippi, but she should still be in school.

"We got the day off—teacher trainin'."

"Where's your mother?"

"She's gettin' ready for work."

"Put her on the phone."

There's a rustle, muffled talking and then my daughter's back on the line. "Momma says she's late for work, she'll call you back."

I don't think so.

"Presley," I hiss, "tell your momma I said to get on the goddamn phone right fuckin' now."

There's a shocked pause. Then a hushed whisper. "You want me to say that?"

"Say *exactly* that," I urge. "You won't get in trouble."

With a little too much enthusiasm, she yells, "Momma! Daddy said get on the goddamn phone right fuckin' now!"

I can practically hear Jenny stomping to the phone. "Have you lost your mind?" she screeches seconds later. "Tellin' my daughter to cuss at me? I will cut you!"

"You've already cut me!" I unleash. "What the hell am I lookin' at right now, Jenn?"

Obviously she can't see what I'm looking at—not my best opener—but it's hard to be logical when you've been kicked in the nuts.

"I don't know, Stanton, what the hell *are* you lookin' at?"

"Well it looks like a fuckin' wedding invitation!"

She sucks in a mouthful of shocked air. "Oh my lord." Then in a growl not directed at me, "Momma!" An inaudible argument ensues with sharp tones and angry pitches. Then she comes back to me. "Stanton?"

My grip on the phone tightens. "I'm here."

Jenny swallows with a gulp. "That news I was gonna tell you about this weekend? I'm gettin' married, Stanton."

It's like she's speaking another language—I hear the words but they make no sense.

"Sonofabitch!"

"I was gonna tell you . . ." she rushes out.

"When? When the golden anniversary rolled around?"

She tries to soothe me. "I know you're angry . . ."

But I'm gone. "I passed angry so far fuckin' back it's scary!" I look over the card again. "Who in the holy hell is James Dean? And what kinda name is James Dean anyway?"

Brent chooses this moment to comment softly. "The same as one of our finest American actors. *Rebel Without a Cause, Giant* with Elizabeth Taylor . . ."

"Elizabeth Taylor," Jake pipes up. "She was hot when she was young."

I ignore the idiot ramblings and focus on what Jenny is saying.

"We've been seein' each other for a few months now. He asked me three weeks ago."

An unsettling thought occurs to me and goes straight out my mouth.

"Are you pregnant?"

Offense rings clear in Jenny's tone. "Why would you ask that? You think bein' pregnant is the only way I could get a man to marry me?"

"No, but between you and your sister—"

"Don't you talk about my sister!" Now she's yelling too. "Not when you got a brother livin' in a trailer sellin' marijuana to high school kids!"

I kick my desk. "I don't want to talk about fuckin' Carter or Ruby! I want to talk about this ridiculous notion that's runnin' in your head."

Then another, worse thought flashes through my brain. "Has he . . . been around Presley?"

She breathes slowly, whispers guiltily, "She's met him, yes. He comes to the park with us sometimes."

"He's a dead man!"

Dead. Gone. Done. I think of every perfect murder scenario that's ever been suggested simultaneously, and plan to inflict each one on James fucking Dean.

"Stop yellin' at me!" she screeches.

"Then stop bein' stupid!" I rail.

I pull the phone away from my ear, as Jenny's volume threatens to rupture my eardrum.

"Fine! You wanna yell? Let's both yell real loud, Stanton, 'cause that'll solve everything!"

Sofia rushes to the desk and furiously scribbles on a legal pad.

Stop! Take a breath. You're badgering—that will get you nowhere.

My nostrils flare and my face feels like stone. But I close my eyes and do as directed—swallowing down the arsenal of insults that were locked and loaded on my tongue.

"I'm sorry for yellin'. I'm just . . . this is a shitload to try and take in." But I get a little louder with each word. "And the idea that some fucker, that I don't know, has been around my *daughter* . . ."

"You do know him!" Jenn replies quickly, as if that makes it better. "He went to high school with us, a year younger. But back then he went by the name Jimmy. Jimmy Dean—he was the manager for the football team."

Her words sink in, conjuring the image of a skinny, dark-haired little shit with Coke-bottle glasses.

And we're back to the yelling.

"The *water boy*? You think you're marryin' the fuckin' *water boy*?"

On the periphery of my rage, I hear Brent say, "He's losing it."

Jake watches me, fascinated. "Total meltdown."

"Shh!" Sofia scolds.

But I'm on a roll.

"We used to call him Sausage Link cause his pecker was so small! He used to pick up the jock straps from the locker room floor! You were the homecomin' queen, for Chrissakes! Homecomin' queens do *not* grow up to marry the fuckin' water boy!"

"I can't talk to you when you're like this! You've lost your mind!" Jenny fires back.

"You've made me like this! Packed up my balls in your purse and driven my mind right over the edge into Bat-Shit-Crazy Town!"

Sofia sticks another note in my face.

Get a grip!!! Make a plan!! State your points or you'll lose her.

It's the last words that slap me in the face—right on point. I scrub my hand over my face and breathe deeply, feeling like I've run a marathon.

Jenny's voice is cold as ice. "I have to go to work. We'll discuss this later."

"I'm coming home, Jenn," I tell her.

She turns panicky. And I can almost see her flailing her arms, the way she does when she's upset. "No! No, Stanton—you stay in DC and just . . . cool off. I'm workin' twelve on, twelve off for the next three days. I won't have any time to see you . . ."

"I'll be home tomorrow," I insist. "That gives you twenty-four hours to tell James Dean you've made a terrible mistake."

"Or what?" she challenges.

"Or I'll kill him," I tell her simply. "I swear on Jesus, either break it off or you'll spend your weddin' night with a goddamn corpse."

"Necrophilia is *so* 1987," Brent comments.

And Jenny hangs up on me.

I slam the phone down and fall into my chair.

"Shit." I push a hand through my hair. "Motherfucking shit! My girl . . . my girl's gettin' *married*."

It's only then, when I say the words calmly and aloud, that they sting. But before the pain rises, Sofia makes a disgusted sound in the back of her throat.

"What in God's name was that?" she asks with derision.

"That was the Iceman melting," Jake answers.

She ignores him, stepping closer, arms folded, eyes hard. "You are a criminal defense attorney, Stanton. A professional arguer. And that was the most pathetic display of arguing I've ever seen."

"This isn't a case, Sofia! This is my fuckin' life."

She spreads her arms. "The whole world is a court case . . . and we're all . . . defendants."

Brent squints. "I don't think you're using that quote correctly."

"Did you really think calling her up and yelling at her would score you any points? If anything, you just set yourself back. If you called *me* stupid, I'd tell you to go fuck yourself."

"I don't know what I was thinkin', okay!" And with more scorn than I intend, I throw out, "And Jenny's not like you."

But Sofia's not perturbed. "Obviously she's a little like me, since she hung up on your sorry ass. But the question you have to ask yourself is—what are you going to do about it?"

She's right. I have to get out in front of this—make my case, hold my claim, get my shit together. I have to talk to Jenny—better this time—and convince her not to get married. And I can't do that from Washington, DC.

"I have to go home. I have to see her—face-to-face. Find out what the hell's been going on. I have to fix this."

Sofia puts her hand on my shoulder. "Take it one step at a

time—build your case. Win her over to your side. Be charming. Be . . . you."

I stand up. "I'm going to human resources, to get time off." I look at the three of them. "You'll cover for me?"

"Sure."

"Of course."

Jake nods.

Before I step out through the door, Sofia's voice stops me. "Stanton."

I turn back. Her eyes are encouraging, but her smile seems . . . forced. "Good luck."

I nod. And without another second of hesitation, I get ready to go home.

8

Sofia

I haven't lifted my head from my laptop since I walked through the door. My heels lie discarded beside the entrance, my damp beige trench coat is strewn across the floral armchair where I tossed it, my umbrella is propped in the corner, dripping. Sherman's stretched out in front of the picture window, his big browns eyeing the raindrops that pour down the window pane. Elton's *Greatest Hits 1970–2002* has been playing as I draft one motion to suppress evidence, another asking for change of venue, and still a third—a response to the district attorney's attempt to charge my seventeen-year-old client, the son of an esteemed lobbyist, as an adult for drug possession with intent to sell.

The back of my neck aches as I roll my head, trying to loosen the protesting muscles. I set the computer on the couch cushion beside me and rub my shoulders as Elton croons "I Want Love."

And it's then I finally let myself think about all the things I was using work to avoid.

Stanton is leaving. Going to Mississippi to fight for "his girl." There was no uncertainty—letting Jenny Monroe marry someone else was never a consideration. He was adamant, bold, determined as I've ever seen him. And I have no doubt he'll march down there and remind her of everything she's obviously forgotten.

I imagine him bursting through her door, lifting her with those strong, sculpted arms—like Tarzan claiming his Jane—and convincing her, with his irresistible smile and shrewd charm, to give him another chance.

And when she does—and I'm sure she will—my arrangement with Stanton will be over.

I close my eyes. Because my stomach is tight and there's a heaviness on my chest—like the feeling you get after swimming in a pool for too long.

This isn't my first trip around the block. I'm a twenty-eight-year-old single woman. I've had several one-night stands. In law school they're about all you have time for. They fill a need, leave you in a good mood, and help you focus.

One hand literally helping the other.

That's why I said what I did this afternoon—snapped him out of his shocked funk. Got him on the right track. Because before anything else, Stanton is my friend. I wouldn't say I'm self-sacrificing—but I'm loyal. And that's what good friends do. They help each other.

What we have—what he and I do together—is fun. Physical and convenient. And above all else, it was supposed to be simple.

But the sick feeling in my stomach, the tinge of sour jealousy on my tongue—there's nothing simple about that.

I shake my head at myself, determined to shake off this melancholy right along with it. I'm not one of *those* girls, the kind ruled by emotions. I'll just put it aside, like last season's handbag. Maybe Stanton going away for awhile is the best thing. It'll give me the space I need to clear my head. Because falling for your "friend with benefits" would be a dumb move, and I'm no dummy.

Sherman lifts his head a moment before there's a brisk knock on the door. He gets to his feet, but stays silent like the good watchdog he is, as I cross the room. I open the door, and there—his saturated arms braced on the frame—stands a panting, dripping Stanton Shaw. Raindrops cling to his thick lashes as he looks up at me, bent at the waist. A translucent white T-shirt sticks to his torso, outlining ridges of solid muscle and the path of hair that leads lower beneath his drenched running shorts, leaving little to the imagination of what he's packing beneath. His golden locks lay flat on his forehead, dark and wet.

There's a Latin phrase—*omne trium perfectum*—that means everything that comes in threes is perfect. This stands in direct contrast to the commonly held belief that deaths and catastrophes also comes in threes.

It seems only fitting that Stanton utters three words. He's said those same words to me before in a raspy plea, as a harsh order—each time with his hands grasping my slick body and the air between us heavy with desire.

And in this moment, just as all the ones before it, they're my undoing.

"Come with me."

• • •

Dripping in the middle of my living room, Stanton takes my offered towel, rubbing it over his head and down his tan arms.

"Explain it to me again?" I ask, because I just can't wrap my head around his plan.

"I want you to come with me to Mississippi. I've got one shot at this—I can't afford to screw it up. If I go off like a rocket on Jenn like I did this afternoon, she'll shut down. That girl's as stubborn as a whole pack of mules. You can help keep me calm—focused—just like we do in court. Plus, you can give me pointers on how to show her she's making the biggest mistake of her life."

"I don't even know Jenny."

He shakes his head. "Doesn't matter—you're a woman. You know how they think. She's obviously not satisfied with our relationship, so I need to pull out all the stops. Big romantic gestures. You can be my resource—my wingman."

His wingman—great. Like Goose in *Top Gun*. The less-than-attractive sidekick. The little buddy. The Expendable.

His shirt makes a wet, sloshing sound as he peels it from his body. I soak in the sight of his deliciously wet, warm skin that tastes like salty heaven on my tongue.

That's just not fair.

I close my eyes—he's not the only one who needs to work on his focus.

"Stanton," I begin with a sigh. "Don't you think it'll be weird bringing me home with you while you're trying to win back your ex?"

He actually takes a moment to consider the question. But doesn't get it.

"Why would it be weird? We're friends."

And I'm forced to point out the obvious. "Friends who have sex!"

Wild, sweaty, unforgettable sex that leaves me exhaustedly, wonderfully sore. Sex we could be having at this very moment . . . if an envelope hadn't arrived that shot it all to shit.

Rubbing the towel across his ridged torso, he agrees. "Exactly. We're friends who fuck—that's nothing like what me and Jenn are."

The breath is knocked from my lungs—but he doesn't notice. And I want to punch him in his stupid boy mouth, so he can't say any more stupid words.

But it's his expression that stops me from doing it. Innocent, bewildered curiosity shines in his wide green eyes, making him look young and guiltless. Sherman gave me the same look after he mauled a pair of six-hundred-dollar shoes.

A look that says: *Huh? What I'd do?*

I switch tactics. "I can't possibly take off from work. My schedule's packed."

He doesn't believe me, because he knows my schedule as well as his own.

Damn him.

He steps closer, grabbing my cell phone off the table behind me. "What's your code?"

I tighten my lips deliberately.

He just rolls his eyes and punches in a few numbers. He gets it on the first try.

Bastard.

"Your birthday?" he says with a mocking snort. "You should take your security more seriously."

He accesses my calendar. "You don't have any court dates. You have one deposition and one client consultation. Brent and Jake could cover those for you."

Stay strong, Sofia.

"I don't want them to cover for me."

Stanton changes tactics too. "You grew up in Chicago, went to school in Boston, and now you live in DC—you've never been to the country, never been to the South. You'll love it—it'll be like a vacation."

I snort. "Mississippi in June? It'll be like a vacation in hell." Before he can counter, I add, "Besides . . . I don't fly."

He wasn't expecting that. "What do you mean?"

I point to my right side, where the jagged scar adorns my rib cage. "The plane crash, when I was a child? No one in my family has stepped foot in a plane since."

He gazes off to my left with squinting eyes, reevaluating his plan, and hopefully my role in it. Then his jaw clenches with conviction. "We'll drive. We'll get there in two days—later than I'd wanted, but still enough time. And hey, you can drive the Porsche! I'll be able to make good on that bet: two birds, one stone."

All out of excuses, I tell him softly, "I think me coming home with you is a really, really bad idea."

Stanton holds my stare for a moment . . . then he lowers his chin, breathing deep. And he looks . . . defeated. Sad. Completely not like himself.

And there's a pull—the desire to put my arms around him and tell him it'll all be all right. To see him smile that beautiful smile again. The part of me that really is his friend wants to help him.

Unfortunately, the part of me that wants to keep being his lover votes to drop-kick her on her ass.

"I know I'm asking a huge favor," he says in a low, scratchy voice. "But I'm only asking because this is hugely fucking important to me. And you're the only one who can help. Please, Sofia. I need you."

Three words. Again. The only ones he really needed to say.

Damn it.

This time I lower my head with a defeated sigh.

"Okay."

9

Stanton

Some ideas hit you like a flash of lightning—a quick shock of brilliance. Like that story in grade school of how gravity first occurred to Sir Isaac Newton—with a knock to the head by an apple. Other ideas aren't as obvious or immediate. They stew in the back of your mind, simmering slowly, then eventually boil to the forefront. And when the proverbial lightbulb goes off, you wonder why it took you so long to see it.

I went for a run to burn off the frustration of my conversation with Jenny. And somewhere along the path in front of the Lincoln Memorial it occurred to me what going home would entail. Clients would need to be passed off to other attorneys at the firm, extensions might have to be requested, Jake could take care of the apartment . . . and Sofia would be back here. In DC. Without me. Surrounded by a whole town of Richard Amsterdams who would swarm her like bears on an unclaimed honey pot.

The thought was . . . bothersome.

Sofia's a grown woman, she can take care of herself—and she has no obligation or commitment to me. I understand this. But I'm allowed to care about her—I'm her friend. The idea that she could take up with an

Amsterdam, that she may replace me with someone so fucking unworthy, because of a physical need, didn't sit right with me at all.

Then I recalled my talk with Jenn. I went over it in my head the way a quarterback reviews last game's tapes. And I saw clearly the tone I should've taken, the words I shouldn't have said. All the worse things I would've said if Sofia hadn't been there to set me straight, to pull me back from the brink. That's when the notion occurred to me—the solution.

And the more I thought about it, the smarter it seemed. The best course of action for both of us.

When I looked up, I was outside Sofia's townhouse. Like my feet had led me there on their own. My dick does that on occasion, and he's never steered me wrong before.

So here we are. Bright and early Thursday morning, in front of the same townhouse, carrying Sofia's bags out to load up the Porsche for our covert operation.

Sofia's many, many bags.

"I think I just gave myself a hernia," Jake complains, dropping a Louis Vuitton duffel that sounds like it's filled with bricks. Next to five matching—and equally weighted—bags. "Are you going for a week or a year?"

Sofia emerges from the house, wearing a black sleeveless jumpsuit, loose but elegant, with a low-cut V-neck that pushes it to the front of my favorite-outfits lineup. A boxy yellow purse is slung over one arm, a floppy white-straw sunhat sits on top her shiny dark head, and big round sunglasses cover half her face. In the light of the early morning June sun, she's nothing short of breathtaking.

Brent walks beside her holding Sherman on his leash, listening as she rattles off a litany of instructions. Her dog walker's still going to take care of the mammoth beast during the day, but his nights will be spent in Brent's care.

"I really appreciate this, Brent," she says, leaning down to give the jowly dog a few hugs, a bunch of kisses, and two *be a good boy*'s. Then she feels Jake's and my stare. She looks between the two of us. "What?"

I hold up a member of the luggage gathering. "Did you get Porsche confused with Winnebago?"

She takes off her sunglasses, revealing eyes clouded with genuine confusion. "Are you suggesting I overpacked?"

"I'm suggesting you need to narrow it down, Soph. Take only what you need."

Her hand circles over the bags. "This *is* narrowed down."

Pointing to rear of the car, I counter, "We've got one compact trunk and a backseat that's not big enough to fit a . . . Sherman."

"Woof."

It sounds to me like the dog's on my side.

Sofia frowns at him, then insists to me, "I need all of it."

"Do you want to see what I'm bringing?" I march around and pull a battered old gym bag out from behind the driver's-side seat. "This is my luggage."

"And I should change my packing habits because you choose to live like a hobo? I don't think so." She rolls up imaginary sleeves and looks from the car to her bags then back to the car.

"These will totally fit."

Jake shakes his head. "No way."

Sofia grins. "Sure they will."

"They're not gonna fit," I reiterate.

"Watch and learn, boys."

Fifteen minutes later . . . they fit. Each bag strategically placed, stacked in just the right order—like one of those riddle puzzles that you can't ever get back together again once it's taken apart.

I'm pretty damn impressed.

"Now," Sofia sighs, smile glowing. "Keys, please."

She holds out her hand for the aforementioned keys. And I start to explain—to argue why it would be best for her to not actually drive my car. I'm good at the arguing.

But before I can utter a single word, her open hand turns into a single finger.

"No."

I close my mouth. Then open it again to convince . . .

And the finger strikes again.

"Nooo." When I scrape my teeth across my lip instead of speaking, Sofia goes on. "You asked for my help—I agreed. If I'm going to the Middle-of-Nowhere, Mississippi, I'm driving there."

She's good at arguing too.

I hand over the keys.

And like the Griswolds in a German car, we buckle in for the road trip.

Jake reminds us, "Drive safe. Watch out for assholes," while Sherman barks and Brent waves.

Then, in an accented voice, Brent shouts, "Bye-bye—have fun stormin' the castle."

And we hit the road.

• • •

Within the first twenty-five miles, Sofia's driving takes about ten years off my fucking life. It's not that she's a bad driver—the opposite, actually. She drives like a female Dale Earnhardt. I just wish it wasn't *my* car she's playing NASCAR with.

"Whoa!" I yell, bracing my hands on the dash as she rides straight up the ass of the truck in front of us, only to change lanes at the last minute, almost nicking the front bumper of a minivan already there.

"You're like an old woman!" she complains, yelling above the noise of the open top, her hair whipping around like Medusa's snakes on methamphetamine.

"And you're like a soccer mom late for practice!" I yell back. "Slow down and enjoy the driving experience—because believe me, after today you'll never have it again."

Her mouth opens wide in an unrepentant laugh. Then she messes with the buttons on the steering wheel, activating her phone's playlist that's wirelessly connected to the speakers. And out pours Elton John's "I Guess That's Why They Call It the Blues," one of Sofia's favorites.

I can't help but watch her and chuckle as she belts out the song, loud and shameless, swerving her head and bopping her shoulders. I've seen Sofia fired up, stubborn, determined, and turned on. But adorable—that's a new look for her. And I like it. Very much.

Her expression turns sultry as she meets my eyes quickly while singing, "*Rolling like thunder, under the covers . . .*" I don't have to wonder what images she's seeing in her mind—*whose* images, because I know it's snapshots of us.

When the song ends, I slide my own phone into the jack, hooking it up to the speakers.

"Hey," she objects. "Driver picks the tunes!"

"Actually," I correct, "shotgun controls the music, but I was being benevolent. We'll take turns—quid pro quo."

She nods and I scroll through my songs until I find the one. "Now *this* is a song to cruise down the highway to."

And the unmistakable voice of Elvis Presley fills the car, singing "Burning Love." I nod my head in time to the beat and snap my fingers—as close to dancing as I'll ever get.

Sofia laughs. "You can take the boy out of the South, but you can't take the Elvis out of the southern boy."

I point my finger her way. "That's very true."

I feel her smiling eyes watching me as I sing, " *'Cause your kisses lift me higher, like a sweet song of a choir . . .*"

Pushing the hair away that threatens to strangle her, Sofia asks, "Did you name your daughter after Elvis?"

I grin, remembering. "We just liked the name—thought it was different, but pretty for a little girl."

"Did you have a boy's name picked out too?"

With a nod, I explain. "Henry, after Jenn's granddad, or Jackson, after mine."

She's quiet a moment, shifting quickly and not holding back on the gas pedal. Then she asks, "Family's important to you, isn't it, Stanton?"

"Of course. When it comes down to it, family's the only thing you can really count on. Don't get me wrong—there've been days I wanted to bury my older brother alive. You'll meet him, you'll understand why. But . . . he'll always be my brother." I pause, then voice the thought that's been tickling my brain since I opened that envelope. "That's why I'm surprised about Jenny. She's always been solid, you know? True north. I can't believe she's being so . . . fickle."

Sofia's voice is soft, but loud enough to make out above the wind. "Maybe she just really missed you."

Before I reply, the speedometer catches my eye. "You better slow down, Soph."

She brushes me off. "Don't worry, Granny, it's all under control."

"The highway patrol might disagree with you, Speed Racer."

No sooner have the words left my mouth than a siren screams from behind us, flashing lights on our tail.

Sighing but unworried, Sofia pulls over to the shoulder.

"I don't want to say I told you so, but . . ." I let that hang while Sofia busies herself in the mirror—patting her hair, pulling her top down a bit, and pushing her tits together. "What the hell are you doing?"

"Getting us out of a ticket." She pinches her cheeks and bites her lip, making them plumper, rosier.

I smirk. "You think it's that easy?"

She bats her long-lashed eyes. "Please. Men are the simplest of all creatures. They're mesmerized by the boobage 'cause they don't have any. Turns their brains to mush. I'll have us out of here in five minutes."

My smirk spreads into a wide, smug grin when I catch sight of the officer of the law before Sofia does. Sofia turns to her left, eyes wide and innocent. "Is there a problem, Off— Oh. Damn."

The police*man* is actually a police*woman*.

Step aside, boobage: this is a job for the Jury Charmer.

I lean across the seat, smiling seductively, my voice as smooth and persuasive as The King's. "Good morning, Officer. What can I do for you?"

• • •

After a sincere apology and my promise to not let my overzealous companion anywhere near the wheel gets us out of the speeding ticket, we spend the next twelve hours making good time on the road. It's after dark by the time we check into a Motel 6, dusty, dirty, hungry, and tired.

I have every reason to be presumptuous, so I get us one room with a nice king-size bed. Sofia heads straight for the shower, while I venture out to pick up a pizza, a six-pack for me, and a bottle of wine for her.

I walk into the room just as she's coming out of the bathroom, running a brush through her long, wet hair, a silk dark green nightshirt clinging to her curves. Her face is free of makeup, giving her a more innocent, younger look than I'm used to seeing on her. Protective warmth unfurls low in my stomach.

She lights up when she spots the pizza. "God bless you!"

Three slices later, we sit at the cramped, round table. Nibbling a piece of crust, she asks, "So, what's the plan? Who am I?"

I swallow a mouthful of beer. "What do you mean?"

"I mean . . . am I the new girlfriend? Your date for the wedding? Have you never seen *My Best Friend's Wedding*?"

I scoff. "No, thankfully, I haven't."

"Should I be making Jenny jealous? A man is never as attractive as when he's got his arm around another woman. Or I could flirt with her fiancé. Test his faithfulness. That would give you some serious ammo against him."

I'm not sure what bothers me more—hearing a man referred to as Jenny's fiancé, or the thought of Sofia flirting with him. "I don't like head games. They're too manipulative. Undignified, you know?"

Sofia shrugs. "If you want to win, sometimes you have to play dirty."

I shake my head. "I prefer a different kind of dirty." I drink my beer, then explain why the idea leaves such a bad taste in my mouth. "A few years ago, I was seeing a woman named Rebecca. We met at a conference."

She chuckles. "Professional conferences are as fertile mating grounds as swinger parties."

I laugh, agreeing with her. "I didn't go into details with her about Jenny, but I made it clear we were strictly casual."

"Of course you did."

"Anyway, she said she was fine with that. We hooked up twice— and then she started pulling all kinds of sneaky shit. Dropping hints about other guys she was seeing, making plans with me, then break- ing them—trying to play hard to get—while at the same time finding excuses to randomly drop by the apartment. She became clingy and her games were annoying. The whole thing just made her seem . . . pathetic. I ended it real quick."

"Did it bother you that she disrupted the 'strictly casual' by falling for you, or that she tried to manipulate you into returning her feelings?" Sofia asks.

"Both, I guess."

Sofia nods with understanding. "The direct approach it is, then. So I'm there to . . ."

"You're there to make sure I don't stick my foot in my mouth or up someone's ass. To keep me on track. Jenn and I have a long history together, and we have Presley. She said she's only been seeing James Dean for a few months, so I can't believe that any feelings she has for him could be anywhere as strong as what she feels for me. I think this whole thing is her cry for help, really."

"You think she's feeling neglected?"

"Exactly. So I'll show her she's got my attention."

She takes a long swig of her wine, draining half the glass. "And after that? Do you think you'll . . . propose to Jenny?"

I'd be lying if I said the thought hadn't crossed my mind. I rub the back of my neck. "It's complicated. I don't want her marrying anyone else, that's for damn sure. But . . . Presley's still in school; I don't know if they'd want to move to DC now. I always pictured Jenny and me getting married . . . later. When we're older."

Her brows rise to her hairline. "Have you looked in the mirror lately? You *are* older."

"I'm in my prime."

"That's kind of my point."

I stand up. "The bottom line is, everything's on the table. If proposing to Jenny keeps her from marrying Sausage Link—then I'll do what I have to do."

"Wow." Sofia snorts. "You're so romantic. How could any woman resist that?"

I flip her the bird and smirk. "The romance is in the doing—not the talking."

With that case closed, I hit the shower.

• • •

When I emerge from the steamy bathroom, Sofia's already under the covers. The light of the late-night news muted on the television casts the room in a quiet, shadowy glow. I drop the towel from around my hips on the floor and slide between the sheets.

She's facing away from me, her brown hair fanned out across the pillow. And it occurs to me that we had dinner—but no dessert.

Dessert was always my favorite.

I slip down the bed, taking the covers with me, and come eye level with the silk-covered swell of Sofia's ass. I skim the material up to her waist, baring smooth skin unhindered by panties. My heart beats faster, pumping blood lower, and I press my lips to one cheek, nipping playfully with my teeth.

"Stanton."

It's not an urging moan, but a crisp statement. A no.

I pull back. "What's wrong?"

She pushes her nightshirt back down, covering herself, and turns my way. I slide back up, resting my head on the pillow, just inches from her beautiful face.

"I don't think we should have sex while I'm home with you."

Disappointment crashes in, like the roof of an abandoned house. "Why not?"

The possibility that Sofia might be uncomfortable about my feelings for Jenny flickers briefly, but I discount it. She's always known about Jenn, even before we hooked up that first time, and it's never bothered her before. Plus, the way I see it, Sofia has nothing to do with Jenny—they're like two completely different rooms. Buildings, even. Like a barn and a house. Both important but unconnected, serving totally separate purposes.

In the dim light of the room, her eyes look darker, shiny. She opens her mouth to say something, but then closes it. She thinks for a few beats and then starts again. "You should . . . save up that passion, you know? Like a quarterback before the big game?"

I push her hair behind her ear. "And what about you?"

Sofia's sex drive is as healthy and demanding as my own. We've been screwing three to four times a week for the last six months. Doesn't seem fair that she should have to go cold turkey for the next two weeks.

Her ripe lips stretch into a smile. "I can . . . take care of myself."

The visual that statement brings with it has my cock straining.

"You're killing me, darlin'," I groan.

Her hand rests on my collarbone, then slides up to my jaw, caressing the stubble. "Sorry."

I mimic her actions, not yet ready to give up on dessert—not entirely sure she wants what she's suggesting. I cup her cheek, then slide down to where her pulse throbs under my palm.

"Aren't you going to miss it?" I ask.

"Miss it?"

I take her hand from my jaw and scrape the sensitive tip of her finger with my teeth before sucking it into my mouth, swirling with my tongue. I slide it out with a pop. "Aren't you going to miss my mouth on you? The way my tongue licks you? The way I spread your legs wide, so I can slide my cock in slow—inch by inch—and you dig your nails into my leg 'cause you need it just that bad?"

She breathes heavy and quick. And she stutters, "Um . . . yes, I guess I'll miss it."

"What if I told you I just wanted one last kiss?" I lean closer and run my tongue across her lower lip. "One last taste of your mouth? Could I have it?"

Her eyes glaze over, seeing us behind them, entranced by my words, remembering each moan we've shared. Every touch.

"Yes. I'd let you have one more kiss."

I nip at her chin, her jaw. And whisper, "What if I told you I needed one last taste? One last lick of your sweet, tight cunt? I wouldn't make you come if you didn't want me to . . . or I could. Would you let me?"

"Oh God . . ." she moans, but it's all pleasure. All yearning desire. "Yes . . . yes . . . I'd let you."

I move down her body, heating the silk with warm breath. I kiss the taut skin on her stomach, I lick the soft flesh at her inner thigh. Then I look up at her—watching her watch me.

And when I speak, there's a desperate edge to my soft voice.

"What if I told you I had to have you again? Feel you clamping down around me so hard I see heaven. That I can't stand the thought of not fucking those hot, breathy sounds out of you, until you scream my name? Would you let us do that one more time, even if it's the last?"

Before I finish, her fingers are running through my hair. Tenderly pushing it back, on the brink of pulling me up to her. "Yes, Stanton, I want that too."

I smile. "Good. 'Cause we're not even close to home yet—so we've got lots of time."

Sofia's smile turns into a relieved giggle. She crooks her finger at me—beckoning. "Get up here and kiss me."

• • •

Hours later, my hands grasp Sofia's hips, my fingertips dig into her ass, helping her ride me. I suck on her tits, 'cause they're beautiful and because they're in such close proximity to my mouth.

"That's it, baby . . . ride my cock," I tell her, loving how it makes her gasp. I slide my hand down the tight crevice between us, to her clit—swollen and slick. I rub it slow, with just enough pressure to keep her teetering on that edge, to make her hotter, wetter all around me. Her breath hitches, and her hips thrust against my hand.

"Harder," I order with smooth authority that doesn't leave room for argument—even if she'd want to. I raise my hips, meeting her more than halfway. "Fuck me harder . . ."

My head presses back into the mattress as Sofia does what she's told. For a woman who likes to be top dog at the office, she takes directions amazingly fucking well.

With her fingers in my hair, she pulls my lips up to meet hers. Then, looking into my eyes, she asks, "Is it like this with her?"

"What?" I ask, mindless, as she squeezes around my dick.

But then she stops, stills, seems more serious, tracing my jaw with her fingertip. "Is it like this with Jenny? Do you look like this?"

She places her palm on my chest, where my heartbeat goes wild.

"Do you feel like this when you're with her?"

There's something about the dark that makes honesty easier. And something about being surrounded by a woman, filling her, lost in her—that makes lying impossible.

"No. Not like this."

She waits a second. The corners of her mouth pull up ever so slightly.

"Good."

Then she starts moving her hips again, and everything else fades to black.

10

Sofia

"I really have to go." I wiggle in my seat like a child who . . . well, who has to pee.

Stanton grumbles. "We'll be at the house soon."

"*Soon's* too long—stop at the next Starbucks."

He looks at me like I suggested going for a dip in the ocean—on the moon.

"We don't have a Starbucks here."

I look from left to right, suspecting he's messing with me. "What kind of godforsaken place is this?"

Over the course of our two-day cross-country trek, the strip malls and tall buildings have come fewer and farther between, replaced with cornfields and lonely houses set back from the road. A few miles back, Stanton pointed out the Welcome to Sunshine sign, but all that I've seen since are trees and empty fields. Soon I'll be desperate enough to use one of the trees.

We pull onto a quiet street, sparse with cars. "A restaurant then," I plead, trying to think of anything besides the incessant pressure on my bladder. "When we pass through the business district."

That has him laughing, but I don't get the joke.

"Ah, Soph? We're in the business district."

I look around. There's only a few two-story buildings. The rest are small, one-story structures—a post office, a pharmacy, a barber shop, a bookstore—each with quaint awnings, not a chain name in sight.

"How can you tell?"

Stanton points to the red stoplight we're waiting in front of. "The stoplight."

"*The* stoplight?"

He smiles broader. "Yep . . . just the one."

We drive down the street and I'm struck by how empty it seems, especially on a Saturday morning. I shiver as I think of *Children of the Corn*, an eighties flick that scared the shit out of me when I was ten years old.

I didn't eat corn again for months.

Stanton pulls into a parking spot and motions to the door in front of us. "Diner. You can piss here."

I get out of the car before he makes it around to open my door. "I'll wait out here," he tells me. "If I go in with you, we'll get stuck in a dozen different conversations and it'll be fucking ages before we get to my house."

I rush through the door, a bell above my head chiming a welcome. And the eyes of every patron stare. At me.

There are a few middle-aged men in trucker caps, a few in cowboy hats, two little old ladies in floral dresses with thick glasses, and one young brown-haired woman—struggling with two toddlers bouncing in a booth.

I arch my hand in a wave. "Howdy, y'all."

Most greet me with a nod, and I ask the short-haired brunette behind the counter where the restroom is. She directs me to the one unisex bathroom in the back.

Feeling the sweet relief of being five pounds lighter, I wash my hands, pull off a sheet from the paper towel roll to dry them, and toss it into the coverless garbage can. I exit the bathroom door and run smack into the person waiting to enter.

A tall guy with a beer belly, black T-shirt, and cowboy hat, smelling of stale cigarettes, with dark gunk under his fingernails. He grasps my arms, to keep me from bouncing back like a pinball after colliding with the gelatinous mass of his midsection. A lifetime of city living has me automatically uttering an insincere "Sorry."

But as I go to step around him, he matches my move, blocking my way.

"Slow down there, honey. What's your hurry?" he drawls, looking me up and down before his gaze gets too well acquainted with my chest.

"Hey—cowboy," I snap. "Lose something? My eyes are up here."

He licks his lips slowly. "Yeah, I know where your eyes are."

But he doesn't look at them.

"Nice. So much for southern hospitality."

He tips his hat back, finally looking up. "You passin' through? Need a ride? My backseat is mighty hospitable."

"No . . . and ew."

Using my shoulder, I force my way past the randy cowboy and walk back out onto the sidewalk. I find Stanton by the car, chatting with a diminutive older woman with poofy gray hair. Well . . . listening may be more accurate, as Stanton's just nodding—seemingly unable to get a word in edgewise.

He looks relieved when I step up, but his face has a pink tinge that wasn't there before and the tips of his ears are glowing red. "Miss Bea," he introduces, "this is Sofia Santos."

"Hello."

"It's so nice to meet you, Sofia. Aren't you pretty!"

I smile. "Thank you."

"And so tall. It must be nice to stand out in a crowd—I've never known that feelin' myself."

"Haven't thought about it like that but, yes, I guess it is."

Stanton clears his throat. "Well, we should get going."

"Oh yes," Miss Bea agrees. But then keeps talking. "Your momma is goin' to be so happy to see you. I have to be on my way also, stoppin' by the pharmacy to get Mr. Ellington the laxative. He's constipatin' somethin' fierce. Hasn't moved his bowels in four days, the poor dear. He's grumpy as an ole bear."

Stanton nods. "I bet."

"It was nice meetin' you, Sofia."

"You too, Miss Bea—hope to see you again."

She gets about three paces away, then turns back around, calling out, "And Stanton, don't forget to tell your momma I'm bringin' roast chicken to the card came on Wednesday."

"Yes, ma'am, I'll tell her."

Once we're both in the car, I ask, "What's with your face? Are you . . . are you blushing?"

I didn't know a guy who used his dirty mouth as well as Stanton was capable of blushing.

He nods his head, confessing, "Miss Bea was my schoolteacher, in ninth grade."

"Okay."

"One day, someone pulled the fire alarm and she went into the boy's bathroom to make sure it was clear—looking under all the stall doors to be sure."

I think I know where this is going. But I'm hilariously wrong.

"And I was in one of those stalls . . . jerkin' off."

My jaw drops. "No!"

He groans. "I haven't been able to look at her since without turning red as a baboon's ass."

I cover my mouth, laughing. "That's hysterical!"

He chuckles, scratching his eyebrow. "Glad I amuse you. My momma thought it was hysterical too—when Miss Bea called that afternoon to tell her all about it."

And I laugh louder. "You're kidding."

"I wish I was."

"Oh no!" I laugh, running my hand down the back of his head, rubbing his neck in sympathy. "You poor thing. You must be so scarred."

He smirks my favorite smirk. "Welcome to Sunshine, Soph—the place where privacy comes to die."

Stanton backs out and as we resume our journey to his parents' farm, I see the skeevy cowboy strutting down the sidewalk. "Who's that?"

Stanton's eyes harden and his jaw clenches.

It's pretty hot.

"Dallas Henry," he growls before looking me over from head to toe. "Did he bother you?"

"He groped me with his eyes—nothing I couldn't handle."

With a curse he tells me, "He comes near you again, just tell him you're with me. He won't look at you again after that."

"Friend of yours?"

Shrugging, he tells me, "I broke his jaw a couple years ago."

"Why'd you do that?"

Stanton's jade eyes look into mine. "He tried taken somethin' that didn't belong to him."

• • •

When Stanton told me he grew up on a farm, I had a certain picture in my head. A big farmhouse, a red barn, trees. But that mental image pales in comparison to the real thing—to the sheer size and grandeur of the Shaw family ranch. The Porsche kicks up dirt as we cruise up the tree-lined driveway that's so long, you can't see the house from the road. The white house is large, with a pointed roof, a welcoming porch, green shutters, and huge windows. Ten red outbuildings are scattered out behind it, interspersed with large pens of brown wood fencing. Up the gentle slope from the house, farther than I can see, are pastures covered with a blanket of lush, emerald grass.

I stand next to the car, turning in a slow circle. "Stanton . . . it's beautiful here."

There's a breathless pride in his voice when he answers. "Yeah, it is."

"How many acres do your parents have?"

"Three thousand seven hundred and eighty-six."

"Wow." My brothers could barely remember to trim the potted hedges my mother grew on our balcony. "How do they take care of it all?"

"From sunup to sundown."

Together we walk up the gravel path to the front door. Before we reach it, a young man comes around the side of the house, intercepting us. "Looks like someone remembers where we live after all."

During our trip, Stanton talked about his family—we both did. This blond, handsome boy would be Marshall, one of the twins—eighteen years old and a high school senior. I smile as they hug and laugh and smack each other on the back.

When Stanton introduces us, his younger brother squints shyly, greeting me with a simple "Hey."

The resemblance is shocking—the same bright green eyes, the same strong jaw and thick golden-blond hair. Marshall's not as broad in the shoulders, his neck is thinner with youth, but if he wants to see what he'll look like in ten years, he doesn't have to look any further than the man beside him.

Stanton lifts his chin, asking, "Where's my truck?"

Marshall rests his open hand on his own chest. "You mean *my* truck?" Then pointing near one of the barns to a black pickup with orange flames painted on the rear sides, "She's right there."

Stanton grimaces. "What the hell'd you do to it?"

We walk closer.

"Souped it up, bro. Custom paint, new speakers—gotta have the bass." He demonstrates by reaching in and turning the key—nodding his head in time to the booming music that's vibrating the ground beneath our feet.

"Tha's Jay-Z," he tells us, in case we're too old to know.

Just then, a blue-and-white older pickup rumbles up to the front of the house, with several boys about Marshall's age riding in back. He turns off the music. "I gotta go, I got practice." He taps his brother's arm. "We'll catch up later."

Stanton nods as I call, "Nice meeting you."

After his brother's gone, Stanton looks at the truck another minute, shaking his head.

Then we walk around the house through the side door, into the large, bright kitchen. Butcher-block counters, white cabinets, and sage-colored walls make for a warm but simple room. On the wall there's an antique clock and a framed crocheted piece that reads: Home Is Where the Heart Is.

Stanton's mother is a beautiful woman, thin, tall, and younger looking than I'd imagined. Her honey-colored hair is tied up, a few strands swinging as she scrubs a black pot in the large sink. Her nose is tiny, her chin the point of her heart-shaped face. When she hears us come in and looks our way, I realize Stanton and Marshall must have their father's eyes—their mother's are warm brown.

Her smile is large and wide and she doesn't bother to dry her hands as she engulfs her son in a hug. Stanton lifts her off her feet and spins her around. "Hey, Momma."

When she squeals, he sets her down and she leans back. "Let me look at you." She brushes his forehead, his jaw, and his shoulder lovingly. Then she steps back. "You look good. Tired but good."

"It was a long drive."

Stanton gestures to me. "Momma, this is my . . . this is Sofia."

Before I can extend my hand, Mrs. Shaw wraps surprisingly strong arms around me. "It's so nice to meet you, Sofia. Stanton's talked about you—what a talented lawyer you are, how well you two work together."

"Thank you, Mrs. Shaw, it's great to meet you too. I'm so happy to be here."

And what hits me straight between the eyes is, I truly am happy. Seeing where he grew up, meeting the people who made him into the man he is now, fills me with a joy. A sweet excitement that has my feet tapping and a permanent smile on my lips.

"Call me Momma, everyone does. You call me Mrs. Shaw, I won't even look."

"Okay."

She shoos us to the table. "Sit down, sit down, y'all must be starvin'."

"And so it begins," Stanton whispers, his breath on the back of my neck giving me goose bumps.

As his mother cracks and scrambles eggs, Stanton asks about his father.

"Up in the north field," she explains. "For the rest of the day and then some. Mendin' the fence that was taken out in the last storm."

Within fifteen minutes there are plates of eggs, bacon, and warm biscuits with butter. "This is delicious, Mrs.— Momma," I correct myself with an awkward chuckle.

"Thank you, Sofia."

"Now you've done it." Stanton grins, his mouth full of biscuit. "She's gonna be stuffin' your face the whole time we're here. You've heard the freshmen fifteen? Be prepared for the Shaw twenty."

"Oh my word!" From down the back stairs, into the kitchen skips Stanton's sister, Mary, Marshall's twin. With shoulder length blond hair, and her mother's sherry colored eyes, there's no doubt she's part of the Shaw clan.

Being the youngest with three brothers myself, I feel an immediate kinship with her.

She leans down and kisses Stanton's cheek, teasing, "I'm gonna start callin' you the Grey Ghost, 'cause you played football, and you're never here jus' like a ghost, and 'cause you're gettin' gray in your whiskers."

Stanton pinches her chin sweetly, then rubs his jaw. "There's no gray in my whiskers."

"Not yet," Mary agrees. "You just wait until Presley's my age—she'll have you grayer than Daddy."

Mary introduces herself, then immediately professes her love for my nail polish. And my lipstick. And my silver sleeveless top and black slacks.

"Momma," she whines. "Can we go shoppin'? Please?"

Stanton's mother starts to clear the table. "Do you still have last week's allowance?"

"No, I spent it at the movies."

She gives Mary a shrug. "There's your answer, then."

"I'm goin' to Haddie's," she announces with a pout.

"Not until you feed those calves in the weanin' paddock, you're not."

Mary opens her mouth to complain . . . then bites her lip hopefully. "Unless . . . the best big brother in the whole world would do it for me?"

"Your brother just got home," Mrs. Shaw admonishes. "He's barely eaten; give the man a minute to rest."

She folds her hands and gives him the Sherman eyes.

His mouth twitches. And he cocks his head toward the door. "Go on, then, I'll feed the calves for you."

Mary throws herself at Stanton with a squeal. "Thank you!" Then in a blur she's out the door. "Bye, Sofia!"

After the table is cleared and the dishes are drying, Stanton, his mother, and I finish our coffees.

"After I set Sofia up in my room," Stanton says, "I'm going to drive over Jenn's."

His mother stiffens slightly. Then she nods and sips from her cup.

Stanton worries his bottom lip with his teeth. "It would've been nice to have a heads-up about this weddin' situation. A phone call . . ."

Mrs. Shaw looks her son in the eyes. "That's between you and Jenny, wasn't my place to tell you. Unless it has to do with Presley, her business is *her* business."

Stanton seems satisfied with that. A few minutes later, we grab our bags from the car and head out to Stanton's old room. "Out" because his room is in one of the outbuildings, the top floor of the barn. Heated, sharing a bathroom with the identical bedroom on the other side, wood paneling, hardwood floor, posters and trophies galore—it's a teenage boy's dream.

"My brother Carter and I built these rooms one summer," Stanton tells me, eyes dancing around the room. "My father told us if we finished them right, we could move out here—so we did."

It's then that I notice the pictures on the nightstand—a dashingly young Stanton in a football uniform, with his arm around a tiny Jenny in a cheerleader uniform, and a school portrait of his daughter, wearing a red sweater over a white-collared blouse, her two front teeth endearingly missing.

"Why didn't Marshall and Mary move out here when you and your brother moved out?"

He nods, anticipating the question. "After Jenny got pregnant, my mother wouldn't let either of them. She thought Presley was conceived here and she didn't want any more early grandkids."

With a chuckle, I ask, "Was she conceived here?"

"Nope."

• • •

About a half hour later, I'm unpacked and ready to get some work done on Stanton's queen-sized bed. Since we crossed the Mississippi state line and entered the "friends without benefits" zone, Stanton offered to stay in his brother's old room. He walks out of the bathroom and he's changed his clothes. He's now wearing a pair of jeans, leather boots, a white T-shirt, and a brown cowboy hat. The shirt hugs his arms perfectly, accenting the tight ridges of his biceps. And his jeans mold his ass, his flat stomach, and best of all those strong thighs, in a way that has my mouth watering.

I close my mouth, but he catches me staring. "Take a picture, it'll last longer."

I smirk. "Don't need to, I can just tear an advertisement with the Marlboro Man out of a magazine—you look just like him."

He throws his head back and laughs. I watch the bob of his Adam's apple—something so sexy, manly about it—making me want to pull that T-shirt off, push the jeans down, and let him fuck me with his boots on.

"You'll be okay here for a few hours?"

I throw my hair up in a ponytail while he watches my every move. "Of course. I have emails to return. Oh, I just need the Wi-Fi password."

He looks concerned. "We don't have Wi-Fi, Sofia."

"*What?* What do you *mean*, you don't have Wi-Fi? How can you not have Wi-Fi!"

"We've got radar—to track the weather."

"Radar?" I scream. Then I pick up my laptop and hold it above my head, walking around the room, searching for a signal. How am I supposed to research? Read my emails? I feel so primitive—so cut off.

Like Sigourney Weaver in outer space—no one can hear me scream.

"I'm in hell! You've brought me to dead-zone hell! How could you do this to me? What kind of—"

"Sofia." He says it gently, like a breeze, but it catches my attention and cuts off my rant.

He holds up a small black rectangle, then tosses it to me. I catch it in one hand.

Portable Wi-Fi.

"Thank you."

He winks. Then glances at my feet—still in patent leather high heels. "You didn't happen to bring boots with you, did you?"

"Of course I brought boots." I open his closet and take out a pair of Gucci knee-high black leather boots with three-inch heels.

He lets out a long, disappointed sigh. "All right, here's what we'll do. After I get back, we'll go into town to the co-op and get you a pair of decent boots."

And I just can't resist.

"Really, you just said that? *Into town?* Can Half-Pint and Mary come too, Pa?" I dissolve into a fit of giggles.

"Keep laughin', smartass. Let's see how funny it is when your designer shoes are covered in horseshit and mud."

I rub my lips together, sobering. "That wouldn't be funny."

"It'd be a little funny." With a smile he reaches out and traces my cheek with his thumb, then across my lower lip.

And the action is so intimate—sweet—I almost forget why I'm here.

But then I remember.

I'm Goose. The sidekick. Santa's little helper.

I clap my hands together. "So, last minute advice: Talk *to* her, not at her—no woman likes getting yelled at. Ask her how things went wrong, what she thinks she can get from James Dean that she's not getting from you. Then, tell her how you'll make whatever changes you have to, to give her what she needs."

He nods pensively.

"Remind her of your history—all the years you have together." A drop of sarcasm drips into my voice. "And most importantly, show her what an *amazing* guy you are."

Stanton smirks. "That last part won't be hard at all."

I flick the brim of his hat with more enthusiasm than I'm feeling. "Go get her, cowboy."

He turns, but pauses in the doorway. "Thanks, Sofia. For every-thin'."

And then he's going down the stairs. With a big breath, I sit on his bed and get to work, all the while imagining what it would've been like if he had stayed.

11

Stanton

I pull up the drive, climb out of my truck, and lean back against it, arms folded, taking it all in.

Jenny's parents' place is like the land that time forgot—it never really changes. The white paint on the house is forever peeling in the exact same spots. The big oak tree on the side still hangs the same swing I used to push her on—and still has that one perfect branch that reaches just close enough to Jenn's window to climb through.

Her family—like mine—has worked these acres for generations. But where cattle ranching is slightly more lucrative and dependable, crop farmers like the Monroes have a tougher time. You can harvest a thousand acres of corn, but if all you're getting is pennies a pound, there won't be much to show for it.

"Jenny!" Nana calls from her perch on the porch. "That boy is here again."

That boy.

Nana was never exactly my biggest fan. She always eyed me with a certain suspicion—and annoyance. The way you'd watch a fly buzzing around your food, knowing exactly what his intentions are, just waiting for him to land.

So you can smack his guts out with a newspaper.

After Jenny got pregnant—after we *didn't* get married—all bets were off. Nana became downright hostile. But the shotgun that's lying across her lap as she rocks back and forth in her wicker chair—that's not for me.

Well . . . it's not *just* for me.

Nana's husband died when Jenn was still in diapers. Thrown from a pissed-off horse, old Henry just happened to land the wrong way at the wrong time. Nana's kept Henry's shotgun with her ever since—she even sleeps with it. Should the day come that robbers, hooligans, or Yankees drop from the sky, Nana's determined to take out as many of them as she can. It's not loaded, and every member of Jenny's family does their damnedest to keep it that way.

Some say Nana has dementia, but I don't believe that for a second—her mind's as sharp as her forked tongue. I think instead of walking softly and carrying a big stick, Nana just feels better stomping loudly and carrying a goddamn shotgun.

Jenny pokes her head out the screen door—hair tied up in a messy bun, still wearing pink hospital scrubs from the night shift she just got off working. She stares at me for several moments before the worry on her face slips into a small smile.

Friendly—a little guilty—but not surprised.

Now that we've both had a few days to cool off from our telephone conversation, she knew I'd come. I hold up the six-pack of Budweiser, raising my brows in question.

She nods, then jerks her head toward the inside of the house. "Let me just go get changed."

This is our tradition. Since we were sixteen years old, whenever I'd come home, when we wanted to be alone or if there was something big we had to talk about—it was a six-pack of Bud and a ride to the river.

A blanket on the bank is our therapy couch. Hasn't failed us yet, and I have no intention of letting it fail us now.

After Jenny disappears from the doorway, I climb slowly up the porch steps—the way you'd approach a hibernating, crotchety old bear. You're fairly certain it's safe, but it's best to be ready to bolt just in case it has one good swipe of its claws left.

I tip my hat to Nana in greeting. "Ma'am."

Her eyes thin to razor-sharp slits. "I don't like you, boy."

"Yes, ma'am."

Her crooked finger juts out at me. "You're a Satan. Slitherin' in to trick Eve out of Paradise."

"Yes, ma'am."

"My great-grandbaby is the best thing you ever done."

One side of my mouth pulls up in a smirk. "Can't say I disagree with you about that."

"Shoulda shot you years ago," she grumbles.

I take the seat beside her, bracing my hands on my spread knees— like I'm giving her statement its due consideration. "I don't know . . . if you shot me, there'd be nobody left to bring you your favorite drink."

I lift my shirt, flashing the small bottle of Maker's Mark Cask Strength hidden beneath, like a drug dealer on a corner. Citing her health, Jenny's mother cut Nana off from the bourbon years ago—or at least tried to. But Nana's a sneaky, crafty old bird.

Like a vulture.

She stares at the bottle, licking her thin lips the way a man who's sighted an oasis among miles of desert would do. It might seem unbecoming to bribe an old woman with liquor. Tasteless to pump her for information. But this isn't about manners, or respect, or doing the right thing.

This is about fucking winning.

Plus . . . I would've brought Nana the revered Cask Strength anyhow. I've been sneaking her bottles of top-shelf brands for years. And she still hates me.

"Tell me about Jimmy Dean."

She tilts back with confusion. "The sausage? We got some in the freezer."

I roll my eyes. "No, the guy Jenny thinks she's marrying—James Dean."

And it's like I've spoken the magic words. Years fade from Nana's countenance as her scowl falls away and a dreamy smile takes its place. The first one I've seen in decades.

"You mean JD? Mmm-hmm, he's a fine specimen of a man. If I were forty years younger, I'd make a play for him myself. Handsome, polite . . . he's a good boy." Then the familiar glower is back in place. "Not like you—Satan."

I just chuckle. "What's good ole JD do for a livin'?"

"He teaches at the high school. Chemistry or such . . . He's a smart man. And talented—only been there this past year and he's already assistant football coach. When that Dallas Henry gets booted from the head coachin' position, I imagine JD'll take his place."

Mmm . . . old Sausage Link is coaching football at the same school where he used to be the jock-strap collector. There's irony for you.

Nana eyes my hand as it rubs the bottle of bourbon, like a genie might spring out of it.

"What else?" I push.

She sighs, mulling it over. "His daddy passed on a few months ago. JD sold their farm and is havin' a great big house built, brand new, in that fancy development out on 529. That's where he's takin' Jenny to live . . . and Presley."

My boot hits the porch with an angry thud. Over my dead fucking body.

Nana reads me well. "Don't you take that tone with me, boy. You got no one to blame but yerself." She folds her arms and straightens with a haughty sniff. "You're not a bad daddy, I'll give ya that much. But . . . Jenny needs a man . . . a man who's here."

"I *am* here," I tell her softly.

"*Humph*. And from what I hear told, you're not alone. Brought a pretty little city girl with ya. A La-tina."

Jenny's mother's voice hollers from inside the house, proving once again that a small town is a lot like the Mafia—ears everywhere.

"Momma! Be nice."

Nana gives as good as she gets. "Don't you tell me how to be!" Then she offers me a pearl of wisdom. "One good thing about dyin'—you don't need to be nice to no one."

Oh yeah—Nana's dying. For as long as I can remember. She's just taking her time actually getting to the dead part.

"I did bring someone," I confess. "A friend—Sofia. You two will get on real well—she doesn't suffer fools any more than you do."

I tap the bottle of Maker's Mark with my finger. "Now tell me somethin' . . . uncommon about JD. Somethin' the whole town's not privy to."

She looks at me thirstily. And admits, "Well . . . he don't drink much. Can't hold his liquor. But I don't think that's a bad quality in a man—nobody likes a drunk."

That's interesting.

"Anything else?" I nudge.

She strains her memory for a moment. "Oh—he's allergic to peppers. His face blows up like an overfed tick if he tastes just one."

And that's even more interesting.

Satisfied, I hold the bottle of bourbon out to Nana, keeping my hand low, out of the view of the window behind us just in case Jenny's momma is looking. She snatches it from me like a spoiled child takes candy, slipping it under the blanket across her lap.

Jenny steps outside, dressed in cutoff denim shorts and a simple white T-shirt, as toned and fresh faced as she was at eighteen. I may be pissed at her, but that doesn't change the fact that she's sexy as hell, and sweet, and . . . I've missed her.

"Ready?" she asks.

I stand and tip my hat to Nana. "Always a pleasure, ma'am."

Her only farewell is a frown.

Jenny walks to her grandma and kisses her cheek. Then I hear her whisper, "Don't let Momma smell that bourbon on your breath. She'll send you to bed without supper."

Nana cackles and taps Jenn's cheek with love.

We walk toward the truck, but pause at the bottom of the porch steps when Jenny's momma comes out. Despite the deep laugh and worry lines that wrinkle June Monroe's face, she's a good-looking woman—attractively full figured, long blond hair with streaks of silver.

She gives me a tight, forced smile. "Stanton. You're lookin' well."

"Thanks, June. It's good to be home."

June doesn't hate me as much as her mother does, but I wouldn't say she particularly likes me either. Unlike Wayne, Jenn's daddy—I've always been the son he never had. But I doubt either one is thrilled to have me back, disrupting the grand wedding plans. Ruby still lives with her parents too—five kids and counting—so I imagine the Monroes would be happy to have at least one of their daughters married off and out of the house.

"Jenny," her mother says, high pitched with warning, "we have the dress fittin' this afternoon. Can't be late."

"Don't worry, I'll be back before Presley gets home from practice."

I hold the truck door open. Shutting it behind Jenn, I climb into the driver's seat and we head to the river.

• • •

On the drive, I go over in my head what I'm going to say, like I do the night before a closing argument. Jenny sits on the plaid blanket, cross-legged, while I stand, thinking better on my feet, both of us holding open cans of beer.

"You could've sprung for bottles," Jenn says, squinting at the can in her hand.

"I was being nostalgic."

She lifts her shoulder. "Nostalgia tastes better from a bottle."

She turns her face, catching the sun, and I spot her freckles, scattered across the bridge of her nose, along her cheeks, so tiny and pale they can only be seen when the light is just right. And it feels like yesterday that I was counting them, here, after a long swim and an even longer screw, while she was asleep, covered in nothing but my shadow.

She raises her hand to take a sip and the small diamond twinkling on her left hand stomps on my memory like a big motherfucking elephant.

Splat.

"Did you forget to give him the ring back? After you told him you made a mistake?"

Her eyes tighten. "Is that how you want to do this, Stanton?"

I can almost see Sofia's notes on her yellow pad, telling me to treat this like a case, and Jenny just any other witness. I need her talking—to know how this happened so I can tear it apart piece by piece.

"No, it's not," I relent with a sigh. "Why didn't you tell me?"

A small smile comes to her lips. Just a little sad. "Because I knew you'd try to talk me out of it."

Hit the bull's-eye on that one, didn't she?

Jenny licks the beer from her lips, and in a regretful voice says, "I should've told you. You deserved to hear it from me. My momma mailed out your invitation because she said I was draggin' my feet—and I was." Fair-lashed blue eyes move over my face before meeting my gaze. "I'm sorry, Stanton."

I pick up a stone, bouncing it in my hand. "Apology accepted—as long as you don't go through with it."

She tilts her head, watching as I skip the rock. "I heard you brought someone home with you."

I can visualize the chain of communication that sent that tidbit to Jenny's ear in record time. Miss Bea telling Mrs. Macalister, who works

at the pharmacy. Mrs. Macalister whispering to old Abigail Wilson
when she drops off her heart medication, because Abigail's half-blind
and can't drive anymore. Abigail Wilson phoning her cousin Pearl, who
just happens to be best friends forever with none other than June Monroe. I wonder if June let Jenny walk in the door before telling her, or if
she called her while she was driving home from work.

"She's a friend."

Jenny scoffs. "What kinda friend?"

"The kind who comes home with me when my girl says she's marrying someone else."

With the flick of my arm, another stone skips across the water. "I
told you mine, you tell me yours. Who the hell is this guy?"

She plays with the sand, scooping it up then letting it fall between
her fingers. "After high school, JD went to college in California. He
moved back here last year, when his daddy was diagnosed with cancer.
We ran into each other one day at the hospital and he remembered me.
He visited every day, and when I was there we'd talk. Then talkin' turned
into coffee in the cafeteria, then dinner after my shift." She pauses,
thinking back, her voice going soft. "It was bad in the end. When his
daddy passed, JD took it real hard. I was there for him. He . . . needed
me. It felt nice to be needed. After he didn't need me anymore, he still
wanted me. And that . . . felt even nicer."

"Did I cross your mind at all? While you were busy being *wanted*?"
I shoot out.

And she fires back, "Have I crossed *your* mind? While you're busy
fuckin' your way across the capital?"

"It's not like that."

"Of course it's like that—because you think time stands still when
you're not here. You've got me tucked away, raisin' our daughter, just
waitin' on you to come back."

"First of fuckin' all, you're not raisin' our daughter alone, so don't
act like that's the case. Second, this is the deal we made. Do what we

want when we're apart, but this"—I motion between us—"*this* was *ours*. No one else touches it—no one else comes close. If it wasn't workin' for you anymore, you should have told me!"

And she's on her feet. "I'm telling you now! I'm twenty-eight years old, Stanton, and I still live with my parents."

"Is that what this is about? Jenny, if you want a house, I'll buy you a house."

We've never had a formal child support order, because I send her money every month without one. Anything she needs beyond that—*anything*—all she has to do is ask.

"JD wants to make a home with me—a family, a marriage—all the things you never did."

I clench my fists, the muscles in my forearms bulging. And I can't decide if it's better to kiss her or shake the shit out of her. "You and Presley are *my* family. And I would've married you ten years ago. I told you that, right here—in this goddamn spot!"

"*Wanting* and *would have* are two different things."

"*You told me to go!*" I yell, pointing at her. "You told me to leave! For *us*—*our* future, *our* family."

And then there are tears. Rising in her eyes, glistening on her lashes, making them shine like sunlight on the water. "If you love something let it go, if it comes back to you it's yours." She shakes her head. "You never came back."

"Bullshit! I came back every chance I could—"

"Not after Columbia. You changed, then. You started to like it— the work, the women, the city . . ."

"I was killing myself, Jenny! It was law school, for Christ's sake— work, classes, internships, you have no fuckin' idea."

The yellow pad flashes in my head like a neon sign. Fighting isn't fixing. Talk to her, not at her.

I take a few breaths, calming down. Then I step toward Jenny, catching her eyes.

And I *see* her—my sweet girl, my best friend. The love of my life. "My head was there, it had to be, but my heart has always been here with you. It never left."

She sniffs, but still the tears don't fall. "Didn't you ever wonder why it was so easy?"

"Lovin' someone's supposed to be easy."

"I don't mean bein' together. I mean bein' apart." She turns her back on me, staring at the water, watching it run, lapping at the shore. "All that time, all these years . . . bein' apart was easier than it should've been." She crosses her arms, and a smile seeps into her voice. "After JD gets off work, he comes to the house and he runs up the path—because he can't wait a second longer to see me. He *burns* for me. Can't bear the thought of bein' away, leavin' me, for even a day. Have you ever felt that way, Stanton?"

There's a terrible, malevolent voice in the back of my mind whispering that I *have* felt that way—once. But it wasn't for her.

I block it out and step around so Jenny's facing me. "I love you."

"You love a seventeen-year-old girl who doesn't exist anymore."

"That's not true. She's right in front of me."

Jenny tilts her head and gives the littlest of smiles. "I'm not nearly as fun as I used to be."

I step forward and take her face in my hands, stroking her skin. "I look at you and I see a thousand summer days. The best moments of my life."

Emotion chokes me, making it hard to speak. Feelings for this woman crush me, making it hard to breathe. "I have loved you since I was twelve years old, and I will love you until the day I die."

Her face crumbles and the tears fall. She presses my hand to her face, soaking it with her cries, then she kisses my palm. "And I love you, Stanton—I do. What I feel for you, who you are, is so precious to me. I don't want to lose you."

And I think I've done it. I've convinced her—won her over. Jenny belongs to me and all is right with the world. Have to admit, it was easier than I'd anticipated. I knew I was good—but I didn't realize I was *that* good.

Until she puts my hand down, wipes her cheeks, and looks me in the eyes. "But I'm in love with JD."

Fuck.

I shake my head. "You're just lonely. I was gone too long."

"No," she insists. "I'm in love with him. It happened fast, but it's strong and it's real. You need to accept that."

My next words are past my lips before I have time to think them. "I'll come home. I'll quit the firm, Jenn. Set up an office in town. I'll come back."

Her lips part, her voice breathy with surprise at hearing the words she never expected. "There's not much of a need for a defense attorney in Sunshine."

"I can practice other types of law."

Her eyes narrow. "You would hate that."

I cup her jaw. "I'll do it—for you and Presley. If that's what you need, I will."

Her brows pinch together—half with heartbreak, half with anger. She steps away from me, her voice breaking. "I do not want to be the sacrifice you make! I never did! We *both* deserve better than that."

And then she launches herself at me, wrapping her arms around my waist, her soft warmth aligned with mine, burying her face in my chest, refusing to let go. I hold her right back, tight and safe, kissing the top of her head, murmuring gentle words, pressing my nose to her hair because it smells so sweet.

We stay like that for a while, until her tears are all dried up. And it just feels . . . sad. Like the very last minutes of a funeral.

"I'm marrying JD on Saturday, Stanton. I need you to understand."

I grip her arms and lean back, so she can see my eyes. "It's a mistake. I came here for you. I'm not giving up on us. Understand *that*."

"You don't know—" she starts.

But then I get an idea and I cut her off with a comically heavy Alabama accent. "I'm not a smart man, Jen-ney. But I know what love is . . ."

She covers her ears, and squeaks, "Don't do that! Don't you Forrest Gump me! You know that movie makes me cry, you evil sonofabitch."

She punches me on the arm, both of us almost smiling.

"Yeah, I know." I sweep her blond hair back, letting the heat of my hand seep through her T-shirt, rubbing my thumb along the ridge of her collarbone. "Does *he* know that? Does he know you like I do, Jenn?" I step closer, leaning toward her. "Does he know how much you like those long, wet kinds of kisses or how licking that spot behind your—"

Her hand covers my mouth. She peers up at me with patient amusement, like I'm an incorrigible adolescent. "That's enough, you. He knows me—some things better than even you. What he doesn't know, he'll have plenty of time to find out."

I stick out my tongue, licking circles on her palm.

She squeals and snatches it away.

"I want you to meet him, Stanton. He's a good man. You'll like him."

I cross my arms. "If he's breathing, there's no way I'm gonna like him."

Jenny jerks her thumb toward my truck. "C'mon, take me home. Presley will be done with cheerleadin' soon."

"Let's pick her up," I suggest as we walk side by side to the truck. "Together. She'll like that."

"All right."

I reach out to hold Jenny's hand, like I've done a million times before, but she moves it away. I frown. Then I snatch it, not letting her escape, purposely entwining all of our fingers.

She gazes impassively. "You done?"

Holding her eyes, I slowly bring her knuckles to my lips. "Darlin',
I have not even begun to start."

She stares up at my face, looking like she can't decide if she wants
to laugh or burst into tears—maybe both at the same time. Her hand
cups my jaw, her head shaking.

"Oh, Stanton, I know I've turned this whole thing into a shit-
show . . . but I have missed you."

12

Stanton

After I drop Jenny off at her parents' house, I bring Presley to mine. She and Sofia seem to hit it off when I introduce them in my old room. Then the two of us head outside, tossing a football. My throw spirals through the air, arching midway, then comes to rest in her hands. A perfect pass.

It's nice to know I've still got it.

She aligns her fingers on the laces like I've shown her since she was old enough to hold a ball and launches it back. She most certainly has her daddy's arm.

It's not that I want her going out for the football team or anything, but I think there are certain skills every girl should learn—if only so they're not overly impressed when some cocky little prick comes along trying to show off. How to change a tire, throw a football, ride a horse, drive a manual transmission—how to change the oil in a car is important too.

Plus, our catches give us time to talk. To reconnect when I've been away for months at a time. I've always imagined having those chats when she's a teenager—about drinking, smoking, screwing—will be less awkward if there's a football between us.

"So . . . what do you think about this weddin' business?"

She giggles as she catches. "Were you surprised? I was gonna tell you all about it last week, but Momma said to wait—she said you'd be really surprised."

I force a smile. "Oh, I was surprised, alright."

"I get to be the flower girl!" She practically bounces. "My dress is blue and satin, and I feel just like a princess in it. And Granny got me blue slippers to match. Momma said I can get my hair done up and I can wear lip gloss!"

Her enthusiasm loosens my lips into a more genuine grin. "That's good, baby girl."

Presley's next pass is wide, and I jog to grab it as it bounces on the grass. "And this JD guy . . . you like him?"

My daughter nods. "Yeah, he's real nice. He makes Momma all giggly."

Giggly? Wonder if she'll fucking *giggle* when I remove his head from his shoulders.

"What, ah . . . What are you gonna call him . . . if he and your momma get married?"

She holds the ball, her tiny features scrunched in contemplation. "Well, I'll call him JD, o'course. That's his name, silly."

My breath comes out in a quick relieved burst, sounding like a gravelly chuckle. I catch Presley's pass, then ask, "But you're sure you like him?"

She stares at me for a moment.

Thinking.

"Do you not want me to like him, Daddy?"

Times like this never cease to amaze me. All the things we don't say in front of children to preserve their innocence, the words we spell, the actions we hide so they don't copy our bad habits. Like the way my father used to smoke behind the barn, out of view. But we could still smell it on him.

They don't listen to what we say—they look at how we say it, picking up on the undercurrent of emotion like a sixth sense.

And they just *know*.

I don't want to share my daughter's affection with another man. But I also don't want to tear her in half—make her choose between the two people she loves most in the world. It's not her job to protect my feelings or her mother's. It's our job to protect hers.

And I hate myself just a little bit for the fact that she felt the need to ask.

I walk to her and kneel down so we're eye level. "I want you to be happy, Presley—you and your momma. And I want you to tell me if the day ever comes that you're not. But I never want you to feel that you can't like him, or anyone, because of me. Does that make sense?"

"Will you be sad when Momma and JD get married?"

How the hell am I supposed to answer that one? *Well, darling, I'm here to make sure that never happens.*

I tip my hat back and deflect. "Will you?"

Her smile is shy, like she's about to reveal a secret. "When I was little . . ."

"When was that?" I tease. "Last year?"

She pushes my shoulder playfully. "Nooo . . . when I was *little* . . . like five or six. I used to wish on the stars before I went to bed. After Momma tucked me in, I'd climb out, look out the window . . . and I'd wish for you to come home."

A knot twists in my chest, tighter and tighter, until I can barely breathe past it.

"Or that you'd take me and Momma with you to DC and we'd stay there . . . forever."

Jenny and I are good parents, I don't doubt that . . . but it's hard to hear that you've let your child down. To know they wished fervently for something that was actually in your power to give . . . but you just didn't.

"I didn't know you did that, Presley." I avert my eyes and pick at the blades of grass. "Do you still wish that?"

"No." She sighs thoughtfully. "You're happy there. You have your office and the White House . . . and you have Jake. And Momma's happy here. And now she has JD to keep her company."

Great—Momma gets JD and I get Jake the fucking grouch. What's wrong with this picture?

Then she perks up even more. "Plus, this way I get two Christmases—who in their right mind would be sad about that?"

I laugh outright. And pull her into my arms. "I love you, baby girl."

She wraps her arms around my shoulders and squeezes with all her might. "I love you too."

13

Sofia

Presley Shaw was everything I'd pictured she'd be, from the sound of her voice and the photographs that fill Stanton's apartment. Vivacious, sweet, with a mischievous shine in her eyes that reminds me of her father.

I continued to work after Stanton popped in to tell me he was driving her back to Jenny's parents'. I was still drafting a brief as the sunlight outside faded and the orange fireball in the sky slipped lower on the horizon.

I put my laptop away only when Mrs. Shaw came to collect me for dinner. The table was set, with Marshall, Mary, and Carter Shaw Sr., Stanton's dad, already seated—it seems family dinners are a consistent thing, with a regularly set time. Mr. Shaw is a tall, burly man with a handsome, weathered face and stoic disposition. The strong, silent type. He's older than his wife by about ten years, I'd guess, but there's a tenderness in the way he looks at her and a devotion in her voice that tells me theirs is a happy marriage.

I was the center of attention, answering questions about my family, about growing up in Chicago, and regaling them with stories of DC courtroom shenanigans. In between bites of delicious pot roast and potatoes, they told me tales about Stanton—high school football glories, an adolescent prank that almost burned the house down, and how he broke his leg when he was five jumping off the roof because he was sure his Superman Underoos would give him the power to fly.

A place at the table was set for Stanton—but his chair remained empty.

After dinner, back in his room, I call Brent to check in. Apparently Sherman is becoming quite accustomed to his new standard of living, and might not want to come back to me. Ever.

After a shower, I slip into a chocolate-colored nightgown, dry my hair, and open the window before lying on the bed, on top of the covers. It's a cool night and the crisp air feels good on my skin. My eyes get heavier as I watch the window. Waiting to see headlights, the return of a certain black pickup.

No, not just waiting. It's much worse than that.

I'm hoping.

• • •

Ding.

"Shit!"

Bang.

"Damn it!"

Smack.

"Son of a whore!"

I grab for the bedside lamp and shield my eyes when light explodes in the room. Stanton's just inside the door—down on his hands and knees.

He looks up at me, baffled. "The floor tripped me."

I go to him, helping him stand, his weight making us stumble toward the bed. With my face pressed against his collarbone, I smell earth and campfire, underneath the stronger, overwhelming scent of alcohol. Not unpleasant, but possibly powerful enough to get me drunk on the fumes alone.

"It's a good thing I don't have any candles burning—you'd burst into flames."

Stanton laughs as I get him settled on the edge of the bed, his feet braced on the floor for stability. His hat is adorably askew, and his squinting, unfocused eyes look up at me through those dark lashes, drifting over my face. "Wow. You're pretty."

Oh boy. I can't help but smile at his less than suave delivery.

"I'm sorry I left you alone for so long, Soph."

I take a step back, shaking my head dismissively. "It's okay. That's why we're here, right?" But there's a slight stirring of irritation when I realize, "You drove like this?"

He just shrugs. "My truck knows the way."

"That was stupid, Stanton." I swallow hard. "Were you . . . with Jenny this whole time?"

His lips vibrate as he blows out a breath. "Nah, Jenn and her momma, Presley, and her sister went to get their dresses fitted. Wayne—Jenny's father—took me out back to his hunting shed, to show me the buck he got last season mounted on the wall. We started drinkin', talkin' . . . mostly drinkin'."

Raw emotion hits me square in the chest, like a Miley Cyrus swinging wrecking ball. And I'm momentarily speechless when I recognize it for what it is.

Relief.

Gut-wrenching relief—like the feel of cooling balm spread on a scathing burn. It starts in my chest and spreads out through my arms, down my legs, making my fingertips and toes tingle.

Holy shitballs. I didn't realize how tight my muscles were strung, how much I hated the idea that Stanton had spent these hours with Jenny, until he told me he hadn't.

What the hell is wrong with me?

When I glance at Stanton's face, my misplaced emotion dissipates. Because he looks crushed. His shoulders are weighted, eyes downcast, his lips pulled low with mourning.

"I think it's really over," he whispers. "I stayed away too long and . . . I've lost her." His voice rises. "Everyone's so damn fine with it! Wayne, Jenn, Presley, even my own mother—they all think the idea of her gettin' married is fantastic. Was I the only one who thought we were in it for the long haul? I was game, you know? For life."

"I'm sorry," I murmur, stepping forward between his legs, to hug him. His head rests against my breastbone, his breath warm against my chest. Those strong, gentle hands squeeze my waist, then encircle, resting on my lower back.

I put his hat on the bed beside him, running my fingers through his hair comfortingly. His voice is soft, barely audible—lost in the fabric of my nightgown—and my nipples go taut when he adds, "I'm just so fucking glad you're here, Sofia."

One of the perks of being close with a bunch of guys is knowing how they think, understanding the underlying meaning of the words they say.

I roll my eyes. "Of course you're glad I'm here. You've been figuratively kicked in the balls. You're ego's bruised."

And after a man's crashed and burned, nothing soothes that wounded ego faster than climbing into a new, warm welcoming cockpit.

He lifts his head from my chest and gazes up at me looking adorably bleary eyed, yet sincere. "It's not just that. I'm not only glad *someone* is here—I'm glad it's *you*."

Slowly, Stanton's hands slide lower, cupping my ass, squeezing a muffled moan from my lungs. "Of course, if you want to kiss my bruised . . . ego . . . and make it better—I'm on board with that, too."

He wiggles his eyebrows and I laugh. His thick hair is soft against my palms as I continue to push my fingers through it, thinking. Weighing my options.

I want him. I always want him. Why shouldn't I have him? I thought keeping things platonic while I was here would help keep things straightforward. Compartmentalized.

But now, gazing down at that handsome face, those full, grinning lips . . . why shouldn't I enjoy him while I have him? It's not like I'm the other woman—Jenny turned him down.

His hands skim and knead, fingers searching, knowing my body so well. The rhythm I like, the secret touches that make me clench and gasp and want.

Why shouldn't I reap the benefits of what she so stupidly threw away?

It's only sex. Amazing, hot, physical release. I try to think of a reason I should say no.

And can't come up with a single one.

I pick his hat up from the bed, placing it on my own head.

Ride 'em cowgirl.

He smirks. And my knees go weak.

"My hat looks good on you," he drawls.

I stare at his mouth, then smile devilishly. "You know what else looks good on me?"

"What?"

I lean in, close enough to taste him. "You."

He starts to chuckle, but the chuckle turns into a groan when I kiss him. A tongue-probing, lip-sucking kiss that says I mean business. Stanton's hands rise, burying in my hair, caressing my face, fingertips brushing my neck. He pulls me closer, moving his mouth across and over mine. He means business, too.

A tender electricity surges between us, and a new, rough affection presses us together. It's warm and familiar, wild and exciting at the same time and I want to drown in it. I can't get close enough; I need the contact of his skin more than my lungs need the air they're screaming for. I tear my mouth away and lift his shirt. As soon as it's off, he's pulling at the strap of my nightgown, teeth scraping my shoulder, suctioning the flesh of my collarbone, my neck, hard enough to mar.

I pepper kisses across his bronze chest, running my hands over every sculpted crest, loving how his stomach tightens under my touch as I move lower. My tongue pays homage to the hard nub of his nipple along the way—swirling and flicking—making Stanton hiss. I get on my knees and look up into his eyes as I unbuckle his pants.

He watches me with heavy, hooded lids, knocking the hat from my head, petting my hair, smiling like he has a secret.

There's a naughty joy—a dirty fucking thrill from being on my knees in front of him, when he yanks at my hair, when he utters the filthiest words. Because Stanton knows exactly what he's doing—knows what I need. I give him my body, my supplication, and he gives me breath-stealing pleasure in return. He doesn't rely on my direction. I don't have to worry about instruction—he'll get me there gloriously and all on his own.

But I'm not powerless, even on my knees. I give, he takes—but he *needs* me to give. He's desperate for me to give—it's there in the pleading of his eyes, the assertive push of his hand, and the whispered command to fuckin' hurry. We're the perfect balance of passion—a heady, equalized mix of desire and fulfillment.

I peel his pants off and push them to the side. Stanton's cock juts up, thick and ready, exacting all of my attention, waiting to be handled. His dick is a sight to behold—impressive girth, masculine veins, potent length—it deserves to be emulated, sculpted, and revered like a precious piece of art.

I take him in my hand, gripping firmly, stroking slowly from base to tip.

"Fuck, darlin'," he moans.

For a horrifying moment, I wonder if he's imagining it's her fist around him, her blond head bowed at his feet. But then I lick him, up and down, slathering moist desire along the length . . . and it's my name groaning from his lips.

"Sofia . . ."

Liquid heat suffuses my body at the sound of his voice, wetness gathers between my legs, spurring me on. Driving me to give him this pleasure, to make him writhe, to swallow his moans—to swallow *him*.

To make him forget why we came—leaving him fixated only on who's about to make him come.

"I love how hard you are," I breathe against him, making him twitch in my hand. "I love how you taste." I place my lips around the head, bulbous and hot. I suck at it, circling my tongue. Then I descend, taking him all the way down, the way I know he loves. I relax my throat, letting him in, breathing through the gag impulse, and swallow—knowing the reflexive muscles will contract tight around him.

His hips surge up, seeking more depth—more snug, wet heat. Then I slowly withdraw, sucking hard, dragging with my lips and tongue as I go. I lower down on him again, quickening the pace, adding the tiniest scrape of teeth.

His chest rises and falls rapidly—panting and grunting. His fist tightens in my hair, pulling hard enough to give just a bit of pain. And it's rewarding, encouraging, because I know I'm bringing him to the edge of his control.

Yes, Stanton!

I want him to push me, pull me—fucking use me—as long as it's only me he's thinking of. Me he wants.

My head bobs faster. I cup his heavy balls in my warm hand and massage, tug, then gently caress.

"Oh fuck . . . deeper . . . Sofia . . . shit . . . that's it, baby."

His cock hardens even more, a slick, silken rod filling my greedy mouth. I wrap my fingers around him near the base and jerk up and down in harmony with my mouth. Then his hand on my head tugs, holds me steady, as his cock slides in and out of my mouth, with the volition of his thrusting hips. "Fuck . . . I'm coming . . . coming in your perfect mouth . . . fuck . . ."

I feel the flesh expand, swell, and a second later hot, salty streams surge on my tongue, filling my mouth. I swallow every bit he gives me—appreciatively. Because I love that I can do this to him. I love that I gave him this.

Stanton gulps for air as he runs his fingers through my hair softly now, soothingly. When he goes slack in my mouth I release him and immediately find myself pulled up, pressed against him. He holds me as we tumble back on the bed. He kisses my forehead, my closed eyes.

Then his hand slides up my thigh, as his body slides lower, his breath a tickling scrape across my stomach. He settles between my spread thighs, cups my ass, lifting me as he lowers his mouth. The air whooshes from my lungs at the sensation, the first touch of his lips enveloping me. I arch my back, he grips my hips, holding me steady for the onslaught of his tongue.

His tongue licks and probes, rubs against the tight, desperate bundle of nerves between my legs, bringing wet, delicious heat that steals my thoughts and renders me speechless. I look down to watch him, and the sight makes my hands clench in the sheets, my thighs quiver. His eyes are closed in concentration, his face blissful, his mouth hums wordless appreciation as his head swivels. And I feel it build—the pressure, sparks of erotic pleasure spike deep inside me—building, cresting, getting closer.

"Oh God, Stanton, oh God . . ."

He releases my hips from his grasp and my pelvis gyrates shamelessly against him, wanting him deeper, harder, hotter. He slides two fingers into my tightness as his tongue makes firm, relentless circles against my clit. Every muscle in my body goes stiff in anticipation, and for a few beautiful seconds I'm suspended, hanging weightless on that sensual precipice.

And then, with a long serrated moan, I shatter. My shoulders shake with the force of my orgasm, my pussy pulses around Stanton's fingers, as carnal joy wracks every nerve in my body. It goes on and on, spasms of pleasure that force whimpering gasps from my lungs.

After the heated sensations cool to soft embers, I open my eyes. Shining dots of light sparkle on the outer edge of my vision, and in the center is Stanton's face—watching me with tender satisfaction. I feel his hand hold my jaw, and when he kisses me slowly, I taste a pleasing combination of tart alcohol and my own sweetness on his lips.

Drained and boneless, we crawl up the covers, rest our heads on the pillows, and with mingled breaths, close our eyes to the rest of the world.

14

Stanton

There's a body of scientific study on sleep—the benefits, the side effects, how best to fall asleep, how many hours, which position, what kind of bed, what type of pillow, optimal room temperature. Researchers agree it's best to wake up naturally—when your body tells you it's had enough. If you work for a living, that's probably not possible.

Second best is to be woken gradually—which is why there are clocks with crashing waves, classical music, and Tibetan chimes for alarms. But whatever the fucking sound, gentle is always better.

This is not a theory my mother has ever subscribed to.

Ding, ding, ding, ding, ding, ding, ding, ding, ding, ding, ding, ding, ding . . .

Sofia shoots upright, hair flying, arms swinging.

"What? What's happening? Where . . . are we under attack?"

Ding, ding, ding, ding, ding, ding, ding, ding, ding, ding, ding, ding, ding . . .

I barely muster the energy to moan, "It's a triangle dinner bell." My momma's favorite wake-up call. "As for under attack . . . you could say that."

Shit. I feel my forehead, run my hand over my hair—looking for the pickax that's obviously sticking out of my goddamn head—splitting it in two.

Ding, ding, ding, ding, ding, ding, ding, ding, ding, ding, ding, ding, ding . . .

"It's getting louder . . ." Sofia wails before wrapping the pillow around her face like a taco. "Why is it getting *louder?*"

I fumble for my phone on the nightstand and check the time.

Fucking hell.

"It's gettin' louder because it's Sunday." My own whisper grates on my ears. "And because we're in Mississippi."

She lets half the pillow drop, picks up her head, and looks at me through one open eye. "Is that supposed to mean something?"

"Yeah. It means we're goin' to church."

She plants her face right back in the pillow.

And I know just how she feels.

• • •

Not all Southern Baptist churches are the same. There's the contemporaries—with their modern, sometimes "mega" buildings, huge amphitheaters, Christian rock, advanced sound systems, and arm-waving, *amen*ing congregates who sometimes number in the thousands. Then there's the traditionals—like the First Southern Baptist Church of Sunshine, Mississippi, built before the Civil War, no air-conditioning or heat, wooden pews, quiet congregates whose asses are in the seats every week, with the closest thing to a sound system being the organ player, Miss Bea, my old ninth-grade teacher.

We sit in the pew in the back half of the room, flanked by my parents—my sister Mary texting as quickly as she can before my mother sees, and Marshall, who's falling asleep. Sofia caused quite the stir when we first walked in. Not because she's not dressed suitably for church, but because she's a new face—a fucking gorgeous face—with her dark hair piled high, her rich purple dress that highlights her hazel eyes, and strappy sandals that make me think about tying her down to a nice comfy bed.

She'll be starring in the jerk-off fantasies of every teenage boy in this place—and several of their fathers.

Just before the service begins, I catch sight of the back of Jenny's and Presley's heads a few rows in front . . . and the dark-haired man sitting beside them.

Mine. I want to shout, write it on the wall—tattoo it on Jenny's forehead in all capital letters.

He leans over, whispering, and Jenny covers her mouth, *fucking giggling.* My teeth grind and I exhale like a fire-breathing dragon—ready to launch myself across the room, scoop them up, and turn his ass to goddamn soot.

Probably feeling my stare, Presley turns around and gives me a smile that takes up more than half of her face. I blow her a kiss back. Thirty seconds later she's coming over, after getting Jenn's permission. She sits between us, whispering happily with Sofia, the perfect distraction from the man I'm itching to pummel.

When Pastor Thompson begins the service, I hear my daughter inform Sofia, "That's Pastor Thompson—he's a hundred and twenty years old."

I chuckle. "He's ninety-two."

"He looks good for ninety-two," Sofia says, nodding.

Pastor Thompson has been my preacher my whole life—for the entire lives of almost every person in this church. He knows our names, our birthdays, been there to comfort on those terrible, heartbreaking days and led us to rejoice on the amazing ones.

And for the first time in a long time, the thought of my being known so well by so many doesn't annoy me. It feels . . . nice, knowing I'll never have to explain myself. To tell where I'm from, where I've been, where I'm going—it's just not necessary.

I'm one of theirs. They all already know.

Which is why when the preacher gets to his sermon, he looks around the church—and the old bastard winks right at me—then he opens up his Bible and tells the story of the Prodigal Son.

• • •

Outside the church, I spot Jenny and the dark-haired man across the grass. With a better view, I'm able to see he's a few inches shorter than me, thinner, but still in shape. He's average looking with a straight nose, heavy brow, puffy girly lips. And he's got that cleft in his chin like John Travolta.

A heinie chin.

From this moment on, I'll forever think of him as Ass Face.

"That him?" Sofia whispers, her eyes trained in the same direction as mine.

"That's him," I growl. Like a dog that spots his favorite bone in the jaws of another canine.

"Wow," she exclaims quietly. "He's gorgeous! He could model for Calvin Klein or Armani."

Frowning, I turn to her. "Why would you tell me that?"

She looks back, grinning. "You want me to lie?"

"Yes. I do."

She gives Ass Face another once-over. Then covers her eyes. "My god, he's hideous! I can't bear to look at him. Move over, Quasimodo, Jimmy Dean is in the house."

I sigh. "Sofia?"

"Yes, Stanton?" she says sweetly.

I lean in, so my lips are just a hairbreadth from her ear.

"Lie better."

As the happy couple heads our way I turn to face them, asking Sofia out of the side of my mouth, "How should I play this? Scare him with threats, or just go straight to the ass-kicking?"

Please, let her opt for the ass-kicking.

"You should be polite. Charming—show her you're the bigger man."

I nudge her with my elbow. "Bigger is better—and his fuckin' nickname was Sausage Link, so it looks like I've got the monopoly on bigger."

That gets a small chuckle out of her. "You should make friends with him, as fast as you can. Go drinking or hunting—kill something together. Keep your friends close, and your enemies closer."

Not for the first time, I congratulate myself on the wisdom of bringing Sofia with me. Having a direct line of contact with a woman's brain is the best kind of resource. Without her here, I would've just clocked the son of a bitch—which apparently would've pissed Jenny off instead of impressing her. Might've sent her racing to Vegas to fucking elope with Ass Face.

I quickly glance Sofia's way and I mean every word when I tell her, "I don't know what I'd do without you."

She gives me a funny look, brows drawn together.

But then they arrive in front of us.

I stand opposite Jenny, looking sideways at Sausage Link. He holds out his hand to me. "It's been a long time, Stanton. Good to see you."

I read his eyes, his expression, not sure if he's being for real. But all I see staring back at me is a friendly smile and unguarded dark brown eyes.

And I realize something: Jenny didn't fucking tell him. Didn't talk to him about our visit at the river yesterday, or how I found out about his existence in her life at all.

I shake his hand. Hard. "JD."

He winces, and the caveman inside me grins with rotting teeth.

Then he puts his arm around Jenn. "We're glad you could make it home for the wedding—wouldn't be the same without you."

My eyes meet Jenny's nervous gaze and I smirk; chuckle just a little. "You can fuckin' say that again—it definitely will not be the same."

I introduce Sofia, and Jenny's smile thins. They mentally circle each other, like women—and cats—do, wondering if they'll be needing their claws anytime soon.

"We're grillin' at the Monroes' this afternoon. Y'all are comin', right?" JD asks.

Jenny opens her mouth, but before she can get a word out, I answer. "We wouldn't miss it. I'll bring my special sauce. You always loved my sauce, remember Jenny? Couldn't get enough of it."

She gives me an evil look.

I wink.

"Momma." Presley skips up, taking my hand. "Can I go back to Granny and Granddad Shaw's with Daddy and Miss Sofia?"

Jenny smiles softly. "Of course you can. But don't get your dress dirty."

With a sigh, Jenny regards me. "We'll see you later, then."

"Count on it."

• • •

Back at the parents', I'm in the kitchen, trying to make the most of my time—mixing in Worcestershire, vinegar, and brown sugar—though molasses would be better. Barbecue sauce is important to a southern man—it's a pride thing. Mine has a legendary reputation and I don't want to disappoint the fans.

Outside the window, Presley leads Sofia around to where the herding dogs are penned, chattering away. "That's Bo, that one's Rose—oh, and this is Lucky. He got stepped on by a horse when he was a pup. Squashed half his little head—see the dent?"

I glance up and catch Sofia stroking her hands over the dog's tan coat, then puckering those ruby lips and peppering the dog with kisses.

Lucky certainly is that.

"Granddad thought we should put him down, but Daddy said to give him a chance—he looked like a tough one. And he pulled through."

Fifteen minutes later I have pots bubbling on the stove like a chemistry experiment. Sofia strolls in while Presley is on the swings. She watches as I mix all the ingredients into a rectangular tin. "I thought you said you couldn't cook."

I gesture to the pots and pans. "This? This isn't cooking. This is grillin'. Totally different."

She smiles. And steps closer. "Charming the panties off of jurors, saving injured puppies, and now—*grillin'*. Is there anything you can't do well?"

I smirk, looking down into those eyes. And I'm possessed with the sudden urge to kiss her. Thoroughly.

But I shake it off—kissing in the kitchen isn't what Sofia and I do. Instead, I confirm her inquiry about my limitless talents. "Not one."

"Why don't you ever grill in DC?"

"I don't know—no time, I guess. And I forgot how much fun it is." I stir the tin a few more times, then scoop some up with the spoon. Sofia stares at my mouth as I blow on it.

"Taste this."

Her soft pink tongue ventures out first, hesitantly sampling, followed by her lips that wrap around the head of the spoon. When she moans, *Christ*, it goes straight to my dick—gets me thinking of other moans and other heads.

"Mmm . . . I would happily lick that sauce off anything you put it on."

Dangerous words. I grip the counter to stop myself from laying her back on it.

Maybe kissing in the kitchen is something we *should* start doing.

"That wouldn't be a good idea," I tell her. "There's crushed hot peppers in it. Might burn the skin."

Grinning like a she-devil, she hands me back the spoon. "Guess I'll stick to chocolate sauce, then." She turns and walks out, hips swinging.

Hmm . . . a little burn could might absolutely be worth it.

15

Stanton

By the time we get to the Monroes', half the town is already there. After church everybody always lands at someone's home, bringing food and settling in for an afternoon of barbecue, drinking, and conversation. Throughout the yard, there are clusters of people talking and laughing, groups of kids running and shouting. Presley joins a herd as soon as we enter the yard. Nana eyes the whole affair from her spot on the porch like a watchful, gun-toting gargoyle. Typical Sunday.

I pass my tray of sauce to June, who brings it to her husband, stationed at the meat-laden grill, surrounded by fragrant smoke so thick he could be Alice Cooper in concert. Ruby—Jenny's sister—brings me a beer and a hug. Like her parents' home, the years go by, but Ruby stays the same. Same flaming red hair, same wild laugh, same piece-of-shit scraggily bearded boyfriend—just with a different name. This one's Duke or Dick, doesn't really matter—none of them stick around long, and that's really for the best.

I introduce her to Sofia and can tell right away Ruby doesn't like her—for the simple fact that she's here with me. Even though the whole town seems to be gung-fucking-ho about the wedding, Ruby obviously thinks there's a chance Jenn could change her mind. So she's not going to get friendly with a woman whom she views as her sister's potential competition.

I look around for Jenny but don't see her.

As we walk to get Sofia a drink, I introduce her each time we're stopped—which is often. There's the tan-skinned, blond Mrs. Mosely. I went to school with her girls, but their mother was the one all the boys were interested in. Guys used to fight over who'd offer to mow her lawn first—just for the chance to see her catching the sun in her bikini in the backyard. Then there's Gabe Swanson, the town historian and bookshop owner—one of the nicest and most fucking boring men I've ever known. After I pour Sofia a mint julep at the checkered-cloth-covered drink table, we turn and see the smiling face of Pastor Thompson approach.

"Good to see ya, Stanton."

"You too, Pastor." I sip my beer. "It was a fine service today."

"I thought you might like it." He taps my arm with a shaky hand. "How long's it been since you've been home?"

I scratch the back of my neck, trying to recall. Until a honey-toned voice I'd know anywhere recalls for me.

"Fourteen months, twelve days."

I turn to my right, and Jenny's there, wearing a white eyelet dress now, her hair pulled back with a yellow ribbon, looking like an angel . . . with the body of a devil underneath. My favorite kind.

Ass Face is there too. Unfortunately.

"That can't be right," I correct. "I spent Christmas with Presley."

Jenny's smile is calmly resentful, an "I told you so" smile.

"'Cause you bought her a plane ticket and she flew out to spend Christmas with you. You said you couldn't make it home. Again."

I'm shocked when I realize she's right—it has been that long. Talking to Jenny practically every day, seeing her when we Skype, the days blended . . . passed . . . and I didn't notice.

Sofia rests her hand on my arm. "You were working on the Kripley case in December, remember?" Then, almost like she's defending me, she explains, "It was a big case—armed robbery, with a minimum sentence of twenty years. Mr. Kripley was wrongfully ID'd as the perpetrator. Stanton was able to show the jury how unreliable witness identifications are and he was found not guilty. A few weeks later, the actual robber was apprehended trying to sell the stolen merchandise."

Sofia looks at me with proud eyes, but when she turns to Jenny, her gaze turns frosty. "He saved a man's life and still found a way to spend Christmas with his daughter—that's pretty impressive, don't you think?"

Jenny's eyes drop to the cup in her hand. "Of course. We all know how important Stanton's work is."

Pastor Thompson raises his glass. "You keep fightin' the good fight, son."

"Thank you, sir. I will."

After the preacher walks off, I see a golden opportunity—Ass Face be damned. "Jenny, there's some things we need to talk about. Let's take a walk over . . ."

And my brother pops in between us, shoving a football in my face. "Hey, Bubba—you wanna toss the ball around?"

"Good idea, Marshall." JD grins. "Mind if I join you?"

"Sure, Coach Dean."

Coach Dean—what a fucking joke. But if nothing else, it'll give me a chance to show him up. I pass my beer to Sofia.

"You boys run along and play," Jenn teases. "Sofia and I will get better acquainted." Something in her voice makes me pause, and I look to see if Sofia's okay with that. Her smile tells me she is.

I take the ball from Marshall and launch it at JD's stomach, just a few feet away. He catches it with a painful "Ooomph."

Oh yeah—this is gonna be all kinds of fun.

• • •

After a few minutes of throwing the ball, I decide to take advantage of the chance to question JD—maybe get something on him I can use. "So," I start casually, "you're coachin' at the high school. What's that like after so many years?"

Inappropriate student-teacher relationships are all the rage these days, and I'm kind of hoping JD is a trend follower.

He shrugs self-deprecatingly. "You know what they say—those who can't do, teach. Those who can't play—coach. I was always good with strategy, makin' plays—the physical stuff was tougher. I'm not real coordinated."

As if reinforcing his point, his next throw is about four feet above my head—I have to leap to catch it. But I do.

"Jenny says you used to live in California?"

Already had a background check done—came back clean.

"That's right—San Diego."

I receive Marshall's pass and hurl the ball at JD's face. He catches better than he did in high school. *Damn it.*

"Must be hard movin' back here, after being away so long. Leavin' your job, friends . . . maybe an old girlfriend?"

JD grins, and it's annoyingly genuine. "My friends come to visit every now and then—get a taste of small-town livin', you know? No serious girlfriend to speak of. And with the way things were with my daddy at the time . . . wasn't hard at all. Sunshine still felt like home."

I glance at my own father across the grass, where's he's having a beer with Wayne Monroe, his arm wrapped securely around my mother's waist.

"I'm sorry about your daddy, JD. Truly."

He holds on to the ball, his brown eyes earnest. "Thank you. I'm glad I came back and had that time with him. In the end, he could see things developing between me and Jenny, and he told me everything happens for a reason. She's my reason. She made all that sadness worth somethin'."

I want to be pissed. Jenny was *my* fucking reason, before this little shit even knew her name. But he's just so damn sincere.

Going after him would feel like kicking a little brown tail-wagging puppy, and only an asshole would do that.

He tosses the ball to Marshall, then turns to me. "Can we talk for a minute, Stanton?"

"I thought that's what we were doin'."

"I mean privately."

This should be interesting. "Sure."

Marshall goes to find someone else to play with while JD and I walk side by side across the yard.

Along the way I see Presley and a few of her cousins getting rowdy, throwing grass and screeching like banshees. I bring my fingers to my lips and whistle harshly.

"Hey—settle down."

They immediately freeze; Presley in particular looks disheartened at the reprimand. I think it's important for children to have a healthy fear of their parents. Especially their fathers. I was scared shitless of my father and he barely ever laid a hand on me. He didn't need to—just knowing he *might* was enough.

I give my daughter a wink to soften the blow. "If y'all are gonna act like animals, I'll put you in the barn."

Presley smiles and they go back to playing, but calmer.

JD and I stand near the oak tree, set away from the rest of the gathering. "You have somethin' you want to say?" I ask him.

He straightens up and looks me in the eye. "I know the wedding happenin' so fast took you off guard. I've learned the hard way that life is short—that's why I didn't want to wait. And I know that you and Jenny are close, you have a bond. I trust Jenny, and I'd never give her a hard time about her friendship with you. As for Presley . . ."

I automatically stiffen. If he says any wrong little thing, I will punt this puppy into next fucking week.

"... she's a great girl and I care about her. But you're her daddy. I don't want to undermine that, or replace you. I couldn't if I tried. All I want to be is a friend to her." He pauses, takes a breath, and goes on. "I know even after Jenny and I are married there's a part of you that'll still think of them as your girls. So I want you to know, all I plan to do for the rest of my life is make them happy."

He holds out his hand to me. "And I think it would make them happy if you and I could be friends. What do you say?"

Sonofabitch.

I can't decide if Jimmy Dean is an idiot or a maniacal fucking genius. All I know for sure is I was really looking forward to hating him. And he . . . pretty much just made that impossible.

• • •

After I shake his hand, JD and I head back over to where Sofia and Jenny seem to be getting along. Sofia's dark hair shines in the sunlight as she tips her head back and laughs, her mouth wide and uninhibited. And I grin just watching her.

We only make it halfway across when there's a disturbance from the far end of the yard. A ruckus. They're fairly common too. Give alcohol to a bunch of people who've lived among one another for practically their whole lives—something's bound to be said that someone doesn't like.

This time it's coming from Ruby and her boyfriend.

"Just get out!"

He grabs her by the biceps, his fingers digging in. "Who do you think you're talkin' to, dumb bitch?"

This isn't my first ride around this particular track. I know where it's headed. Apparently so does JD.

"Aw—"

"Hell—"

He intercepts Jenny as she stands—always ready to open up a can of whoop-ass in defense of her big sister. "Jenny, hold on!" he pleads. "You get yourself involved all the time—"

"She's my sister! I'm not gonna sit here while that piece of shit talks to her like she's trash!"

I brush past them, heading straight to the source.

People say there are two kinds of men. One who would never dream of putting his hands on a woman in anger, and one who deals with his own frustrations and shortcomings by blaming the closest woman to him with his fists. But I disagree. Because a man who would hit a woman is no man at all—just garbage impersonating a human being.

"Hey, ZZ Top!" That gets his attention. "It's time for you to go."

Ruby flinches when his hand tightens around her arm. Spit dribbles on his beard as he snarls, "Who the fuck are you?"

I smirk. "You're not from around here, are you?"

"This ain't your concern—piss off."

He turns back to Ruby, but I step closer—getting in his face. And my voice is low, lethally calm. "See, that's where you're wrong. Because my daughter is here and she's watching us right now—that makes it very much my concern. So you're gonna take your hands off her aunt right motherfucking now. Or I am gonna knock your teeth so far down your throat, you'll be shittin' molars."

We stand off for a few seconds, unblinking. And I can see the wheels turning in his ignorant head—debating whether he can take me. Dipshit must have a shred of intelligence after all, because he lets her go, then staggers out of the yard.

"And don't come back!" Ruby calls after him.

I shake my head. "For Christ's sake, Ruby."

She throws up her hands. "I know, I know, if I didn't have bad luck with men—I'd be a lesbian."

That makes me chuckle.

She nudges me with her elbow. "Let's go get a drink."

I loop my arm around her shoulders, and we do just that.

• • •

When I find Sofia, she's holding two plates of food—one for herself, one for me—filled with chicken, potato salad, and ribs. "Thanks."

We grab an empty spot at a picnic table and sit down to eat. "Well, that was interesting," she says.

"That was nothin'—it's still midday. The real interestin' comes out after dark."

"Everyone turns into sparkly vampires?"

I shake my head. "Rednecks." I take a bite of rib that melts in my mouth. "So you and Jenny get acquainted?"

"Oh, we did. Comparing notes on your sexual prowess gave us solid common ground. We both gave you two thumbs up, by the way."

"Just two?" I grin. "I gotta up my game."

"So how did your chat with JD go? Did you make friends like I suggested?"

I wipe my mouth with a napkin. "I'll tell you about it later. I was hopin' to find Jenn, get some time alone with her."

Sofia pushes her plate back—apparently finished. "Um . . . I think she went in the house."

Laughter and whoops travel from across the yard, getting our attention. "I take back what I said about after dark," I tell her. "Real interestin' is headin' our way right now."

And my big brother, Carter, comes strolling up, wearing tight, stonewashed jeans and a white T-shirt with a picture of Bob Marley. A gold chain hugs his neck with a large, strange medallion hanging at the end. Carter is very similar to me in looks, if I was taller, lankier, and had a thick, carefully groomed mustache like a blond Magnum fucking PI.

I stand and accept the strong hug that almost lifts me off the ground. "There's my little brother!"

Growing up with Carter four years older than me, he was my idol. I wanted nothing more than to follow in his perfect footsteps. He played ball in high school too—still holds the most completed passes record. He got a scholarship to Ole Miss, but dropped out after just one semester. Then he came home . . . different. Born again. But not in the Christian way. Now he's *that* guy—the thirty-two-year-old who still goes to all the high school parties. Who gets beer—and other enjoyments—for the local teens. He's the life of the party, and every one of them worships the ground he walks on.

"Good to see you, Carter," I tell him with a smile. And I mean it.

He looks me over, smacking my arm with pride. Then he turns to Sofia. She offers her hand. "Hi, I'm—"

"You're Sofia," he finishes reverently. Then he hugs her—a bit too close and a hell of a lot too long for my taste. Finally, he backs off, holds her hands out to the sides, and rakes his eyes over her. "The birds told me your name."

Her eyes flash to me, but I just shake my head. "The birds?" she asks.

"That's right. I commune with nature every morning. You'd be surprised what she tells you, if you just take the time to listen." Again, his eyes are all over her. "And you are every bit as lovely as they said you were. Look at these hips, your cheekbones, your . . ."

"Yeah, yeah, she's beautiful." I slap my hand square on his chest, pushing him back. "What are you doin' here? I thought you parted ways with the church."

He shrugs. "Even us pagans enjoy a good barbecue."

The two girls standing behind him move closer. Blond, braided hair, petite, wearing hippie peasant tops, fringed tan vests, and beaded moccasins. They might be twins—definitely sisters. "Let me introduce you to my ladies," Carter says. "This is Sal and Sadie."

The one on his left steps forward. "I'm Sal, she's Sadie." She pinches my brother's cheek familiarly. "You always get us confused."

"Heeey y'all!" Sadie greets us with a giggle.

"We're gonna go get some food," Sal says. "You want me to fix you a plate, baby?" she asks my brother.

He kisses her brow. "You're too good to me." As they turn to go, he smacks Sadie's ass. "Make sure you get some of my momma's fried chicken too." She squeaks and bats her lashes back at him.

After they head off, I ask, "Are they legal?"

He squints. "Depends on your definition of legal."

"No, see"—I raise my finger in explanation—"that's the beauty of 'legal.' You either are or you aren't—it's not subjective."

"You worry too much, Stanton."

"And you don't worry near enough."

He smacks my arm. "You sound like Daddy."

I snort. "How would you know? Or are you and Daddy speakin' to each other again?"

After Carter came back from college, he decided he could no longer live under the fascist rule of my father's household. He bought a run-down double-wide trailer on the outskirts of town, fixed it up himself, and tried his hand at . . . farming.

A specialized, unique crop that's now legal in Colorado.

During this time, Carter also developed an efficient, high-potency liquid plant food that provides weeks' worth of nutrients with just a few drops. He patented it, sold it to the federal government, and became extremely wealthy. But you'd never know it—his tastes are simple. He still lives in that same double-wide, though he bought the surrounding acres for privacy and raising . . . crops. It's a commune kind of thing—free living, free love. Like Woodstock all day, every day. The kids around town take refuge at Carter's. When last year a schoolmate of Marshall's drove drunk, smashed into another truck, and took off—he fled to Carter's. And my brother took him in, talked him down, and convinced him to turn himself in to the police. Carter even went with the boy to the police station.

My brother's alternative lifestyle is a bitter pill my daddy refuses to swallow. He hasn't banned him from the house—Carter still shows up for holidays and family gatherings at my mother's insistence—but my father just flat-out pretends he's not there.

Carter shrugs his shoulders. "Daddy just needs more time—he'll get used to things."

I take a swig of my beer and wonder if bourbon's available.

"I'm havin' a party this week," my brother announces, arms raised. "And I wanted to make sure you and your lovely Sofia will attend. My place, Tuesday night."

"You're having a party on a Tuesday?" Sofia asks.

"I believe Tuesday is the most neglected day of the week. Everybody complains about Monday, Wednesday is the hump day, Thursday's almost Friday, and Friday is the favorite. Nobody remembers Tuesday—it's the black sheep." He winks. "Like me."

I have too much to do to waste a night at my brother's, partying with high school kids, getting high off of secondhand pot smoke.

"Don't know if we'll be able to make it."

He grins knowingly. "Jenny and JD will be there." He grasps my shoulder. "Change is difficult, brother, especially for someone as goal oriented as you. I would like to volunteer my services to ease the transition." He links his fingers together. "To bond our families into one, you hear what I'm sayin'?"

I sigh over his New Age, touchy-feely, bullshit outlook on life. But . . . if Jenny will be there, it may give me the chance to talk to her. To get her alone. To romance her—bring back her feelings, memories, of all the good times we shared. This could be useful.

"Yeah, I hear you, Carter."

He nods. "Good. I'm gonna go see Momma." He kisses both Sofia's cheeks. "It was sublime meetin' you in person. I look forward to entertainin' you on Tuesday."

And then he strolls off.

"He was high, right?" Sofia asks, grinning.

"It's hard to tell with Carter . . . but I'd be shocked if he wasn't."

• • •

A few hours go by, filled with cold beers and good conversations. Sofia and I go undefeated in a horseshoe tournament. The crowd thins out; people start to head home to get ready for the week ahead. A handful of us sit in folding chairs around a fire as the sky goes pink and gray with the sunset. Jenny's there, sitting beside Ass Face. Sofia's next to me and Presley sits on my lap. I smooth her hair down, kiss the top of her head, and enjoy holding her like this. Because in the space of a moment she'll be too old for lap sitting, and instead of being her hero, I'll be her ultimate source of embarrassment.

Mary sits cross-legged on the grass with her guitar. "Sing a song, Stanton?"

I shake my head. "Nah, not now."

"Aw, come on," Mary pushes. "It's been ages. We can do 'Stealin' Cinderella'—I love that song."

Sofia's legs are curled under her, her head resting on her hand. "I didn't know you sang."

"Stanton has a lovely voice," my momma volunteers. "He used to sing in church every Sunday."

Sofia smirks. "You were a real live choirboy? How did I not know this?"

"I was seven," I tell her dryly.

But then Presley takes all the argument out of me. "Come on, Daddy. I like listenin' to you sing."

Simple as that.

I nod to Mary and she starts plucking at the guitar. It's a mellow, almost sad melody. A song about fathers and daughters, moving on while staying exactly the same.

"She was playin' Cinderella, ridin' her first bike . . ."

I run my hand through Presley's hair again, but as the song continues the lyrics take on bigger, more relevant meaning. I feel the heat of Sofia's gaze, watching me—this different part of me she's never seen—with fascination. I see JD's eyes all over Jenny, almost willing her to turn her head. But she's not looking at him. Across the campfire, through the smoke and licking flames, she's keeping her blue eyes straight on me. And while I sing about precious memories—old loves and new—I stare right back at her.

"In her eyes I'm Prince Charming, but to him I'm just some fella, ridin' in stealin' Cinderella."

•   •   •

I'm a picker—one of those guys who combs over the leftovers just before everyone's about to head home. At the food table, by the light of the fire, I see that JD is also one of those guys. I put the last chicken leg on my plate, and JD goes for the last of the beef tips. I coat the chicken with my homemade barbecue sauce and he asks, "That's your sauce?"

"Yep."

"I heard it was pretty good."

I offer him the spoon. "You heard right."

He douses his own plate, then licks his fingers and shovels the bite-size beef into his mouth. He gives me the thumbs-up while he chews.

"My brother mentioned a party on Tuesday. Think you'll be goin', or will you be too busy?"

I'm really hoping he has something else to do—then I'll get Jenny all to myself. I mentally rub my hands together—eager for the prospect.

He nods. "Yeah, I'll be there. Pretty mush cleared my schedbudle por de wheek."

My brow furrows as his words get harder and harder to understand. Then I peer closer . . . because something just doesn't look right.

"Ib my pace pubby, Thanton? It peels pubby."

"Holy mother of fuck!" I jerk back, revolted.

Because Jimmy Dean doesn't have the face of a Calvin Klein model anymore.

Now he resembles the lead role in a production of the goddamn *Elephant Man*.

"Are der pebbers in dis?" he asks.

Pebbers?

Peppers.

Uh-oh.

• • •

"You unbelievable bastard!"

"It was an accident!"

"Accident my ass!"

"I didn't know—"

"Nana said she tol' you he was allergic to peppers!" Jenny yells from the side of her truck, after a Benadryl-chugging JD is loaded into the passenger seat.

"I put pepper *flakes* in it, Jenn—I thought he was allergic to actual peppers! Not the goddamn flakes of peppers!"

And the awful irony of it? I'm telling the truth. After this I'm gonna have to seriously recalibrate my horseshit detector when listening to the outrageous claims of innocence from my clients. Apparently sometimes it's not utter horseshit—no matter how much it may sound like it.

"I hate you!"

"That's a little extreme, don't you think?"

"Extreme!" she screeches, making me flinch. "You tried to poison him!"

I kick the tire of the truck. "If I wanted him poisoned he'd be fuckin' dead!" I run a hand down my face. "But, maybe you should think about postponin' the weddin'; at least until JD doesn't look so"—I motion to the passenger window—"like that."

Her eyes flare. So do her nostrils. "That's why you did this? You think you can sabotage my weddin', you rotten sonofabitch?"

"What? No!"

Now *that* is actual horseshit.

"You listen to me and you listen good," she hisses. "I'm gettin' married on Saturday and I don't care if I have to wheel him, half-dead, down the aisle and prop him up against the goddamn organ to do it! Until then you stay away from us! I don't want to see you, I don't want to hear you—I don't want to look at you!"

"When did you turn so fuckin' stubborn?" I yell.

She stomps her way around the back of the truck, replying, "When you became so fuckin' selfish!"

"Jenny! Wait . . ."

But she doesn't. She does the opposite of waiting—climbs in the truck and drives off. To take JD home and nurse him back to health.

Sofia stands beside me on the driveway, watching the taillights fade. "Well, that didn't go as planned," I grumble.

"Was it really an accident?" she asks with a lifted brow.

"Yes! It really was." Then I pause, and rephrase. "A wonderful, serendipitous accident."

She grins and I give my smirk free rein.

Then Sofia gasps. "Holy shitballs!"

"What? What's wrong?"

She snaps her fingers and points to the sky, smiling broadly with discovery. "Allergic reaction!"

"Yeah?" I question.

"The perfect murder. Triggering an allergic reaction." She folds her arms, proud of herself.

"Really?" I ask with a straight face. "My life is fallin' apart, and you're still playin' the perfect murder game?"

She shrugs. "Well . . . it's a good one. Brent and Jake will be impressed."

16

Stanton

I've never seen one so big. It's too big."

"It's not too big."

"It's monstrous! It'll kill me."

"I promise, you're gonna love it, darlin'. Touch it."

She gasps. "I can't."

I take Sofia's hand and press it against warm flesh. Forcing her fingers to stroke.

"See? It likes you. Now you just have to ride it—then it'll really like you."

On Monday morning I finally brought Sofia to the co-op to get a decent pair of boots. She fawned over a pair of dark brown leather riding boots with pink stitching and a hat to match. And I have to hand it to her—the woman can wear a fucking hat like nobody's business.

Once we got home, it seemed like a good idea to put her equipment to good use.

And take her horseback riding.

She rests her hand on the black coat and sighs. "So this is how I die."

I roll my eyes. "Since when are you so dramatic? Or a coward for that matter? You've got a dog the size of a small bull."

We're outside the stables, saddling Blackjack, a gentle, even-tempered stallion—the first horse Presley rode by herself.

Sofia eyes him warily. "My dog isn't going to throw me off and break my neck. Or kick me. Or trample me."

I hoist the saddle onto Blackjack's back. "No—he'll just rip your throat out if you piss him off."

She takes exception to my observation. "That is a vile Rottweiler stereotype. Sherman would never do that! He's my sweet baby boy."

"I've never seen a baby with teeth like his." I tighten the cinches and secure the last buckle. Then I slap Blackjack's flank—the way I'd like to be slapping Sofia's ass.

"Now saddle up."

Sofia gazes up at the massive animal. Her eyes are round, her expression all intimidated and vulnerable. And part of me must be a sick sonofabitch, 'cause it's turning me the fuck on.

She takes one step forward, lifts her hands, bends her knee . . . and completely pusses out.

"I can't! I can't, I can't, I can't, I can't. I just can't!"

I laugh, patting her shoulder. "All right, don't have a heart attack—it'll be more fun this way anyway."

I swing up onto the back of the horse, look down, and hold my hand out to her.

Her brows furrow. "I don't know if humans were meant to mount something so large."

I smile. "Come on, Soph—trust me. I got you."

Sofia takes a breath, grasps my hand, and puts her left foot into the stirrup. Blackjack stays perfectly still as I pull and she swings her leg up and over his back, settling in front of me.

Her denim-clad ass presses right up against my dick. Her back leans against my chest, her hair brushes my face, and I smell gardenias. This ride is going to be the best kind of awful. Feeling her, holding her tight, but not being able to do anything about it—delicious fucking torment.

I wrap my arm around her waist, pulling her back, holding the reins in my hands. "Relax, Sofia," I tell her softly. "I would never let anythin' happen to you."

She sinks against me, turns her head and smiles. "Okay."

Then we start to move.

"Whoa!" she squeaks, gripping my thighs. "Easy! Remember—slow and steady wins the race."

"But hard and fast is a lot more fun."

We trot uphill, and I know just the spot I want to show her. It's the highest point of my parents' land, where you can see acres of grass—like an emerald ocean.

"You know," I tease, "the only thing better than riding a horse is being ridden on one."

Sofia laughs. "Are you speaking from experience?"

I tip my hat back. "Only from my vivid and sadly unfulfilled fantasies. It'd take a little thought—holdin' on in just the right way, balancin' your legs around my waist or over my shoulder . . ."

"Are you trying to distract me so I'm not afraid?"

I lick my lips, smiling. "Maybe . . . maybe not. Is it workin'?"

Her hands go from gripping my thigh, to rubbing. "Why, as a matter of fact, it is. Tell me more . . ."

• • •

"My God . . . it's so beautiful."

I've seen this view a thousand times, but being here with Sofia, seeing the delight on her face, the wonder—it's contagious. Makes me grateful all over again for where I'm from, the blessings we had growing up. She sighs, and together we enjoy the quiet, gazing at the green pastures and valleys dotted with brown and black cattle.

"Hmm."

She looks over her shoulder at me. "What?"

I point at the grouped livestock. "See how they're bunched together like that?"

Sofia nods.

I gaze up at the sky, looking for a sign, but there's nothing to see but blue.

"When cattle cluster, usually means a storm's comin'."

Now she's looking up at the sky too. "You mean they can sense it?"

"Yeah."

"That's amazing."

I shrug. "It is pretty cool." I offer her the reins. "You want to steer?"

She wiggles her fingers, smiling giddily. And it makes me smile back.

"You think I'm ready?"

"Definitely."

She pats Blackjack's neck and takes the reins.

"All right, Blackjack, work with me."

The next twenty minutes are spent with me explaining how to ride a horse—make him turn, stop, speed up. Then Sofia is on her own—and she does pretty damn good.

And we're talking, about nothing and everything—the ins and outs of ranching, her father's construction business, and how we think things are going at the firm without us. Sofia tells me about the first time her parents let her ride the subway alone in Chicago, and I tell her about riding these trails after school with Jenny.

I laugh as I remember. "When we were young, we'd try to find the perfect tree for climbin'. Then, when we were older, we tried to find the perfect tree for screwin' against."

Sofia chuckles, and then she turns somber. We sway with Blackjack's soft steps, and she asks me, "You really love her, don't you?"

Without pausing, I answer, "Yeah, I do."

She's quiet for a few moments, watching the ground. Then she asks,

"Have you thought about what you'll do if you can't talk her out of getting married?"

I shake my head. "Failure's not an option—I don't do plan B's."

Sofia turns to look at my face. And there's something swimming in those hazel eyes I can't read. "Stanton . . . you mean a lot to me. And I . . . lately . . . it feels . . ."

I brush her hair back. "You mean a lot to me too, Soph."

"You know . . . if you do talk Jenny out of marrying JD, there's a high probability that she'll want you two to be exclusive. And if that were the case . . . I wouldn't want things to be awkward or strained between us. I don't want to lose . . . your friendship."

I lean forward and kiss her forehead. And I promise her, "You're not going to lose me—I'd never let that happen."

• • •

Later in the afternoon, after we get back from riding, I try to call Jenny. But it goes straight to voice mail. I text her, once, twice, three times— but hours later, there's no answer. So I call again after dinner. Voice mail.

Fuck. This.

It's dark when I get out of the truck in front of Jenny's house, knock on the door, and ask for her.

"She won't come down, Stanton," Wayne tells me, stepping outside, chewing on the straw in his mouth. "Says she's still mad."

"I'm not leavin' until I see her. I'll sleep right fuckin' here on the porch steps."

"One between the eyes will get ye leavin'!" Nana shouts from inside the front parlor. "Get me the shells, Wayne!"

A few minutes after Wayne goes in to try again, Jenny comes stomping down the stairs—hair down, wrapped in a lavender terry-cloth robe, and spitting mad.

"I've been taking care of JD all day and I have work in the mornin'! I don't want to get into this with you right now, Stanton."

"Then you should've picked up the goddamn phone when I called earlier. We need to talk."

Arms crossed and scowling, she leans forward and declares, "I've done all the talkin' I'm gonna do with you."

My jaw clenches and I take a step closer to her. She takes one back. "Tell me somethin', Jenn—are you really *that* angry with me?" My eyes drift over her face, her clenched hands, her tiny waist cinched with her robe's belt. Then they settle on her eyes and I ask in a low voice, "Or are you scared to be alone with me? Afraid to listen to me? Cause you know this is a mistake. Because you still love me."

Her mouth clamps closed and her chin rises. "Go home and spend some time with your daughter. You need to have her in school by eight tomorrow morning."

Her nonanswer is all the answer I need.

"I know what time school starts."

"Then good night, Stanton." She hurries to the door, into the house, like she can't get away fast enough.

I spin the keys around my finger. "Sweet dreams, Jenny."

●　●　●

Twenty minutes later I'm climbing the stairs to the bedrooms, trying to think of something new . . . unexpected . . . that'll bring Jenn to her senses.

As I start to open the door to Carter's old room I hear voices behind the closed door of mine—giggles and girly chatter. Grinning, I open that door and there, sitting on my bed decked out in pajamas and fuzzy slippers, are my baby girl, my sister, and my . . . Sofia.

"Hey, Daddy!" Presley greets me with a toothy smile. She holds up her hands, bright blue, polka-dotted fingernails facing out. "Miss Sofia gave us mani-pedis!"

Mary shows me her fingers and toes—red with orange flowers—as she moves to the overstuffed chair in the corner, making room for me on the bed.

"Beautiful. Y'all have the prettiest nails in town."

"And we're watchin' a movie," Presley says, scooting closer toward Sofia. "*The Lion King*."

"*The Lion King*, huh? Don't think I've seen that one yet."

I climb on the bed as a montage begins on the screen—two lions having a date in the jungle.

"How'd it go?" Sofia asks quietly, passing me a bowl of popcorn.

My eyes tell her everything I can't say. "It went."

Presley leans her head against my chest and I settle in, kissing the top of her head—enjoying having her close. I glance over at Sofia as she places a piece of popcorn on her tongue, licking butter from her pretty pink fingertip. And there's something about the whole thing—her, here in my bed, with my sister, my daughter—that feels warm and right, and makes her look even more beautiful that I've always thought she was.

"I want a Simba of my own one day," my sister sighs. "Some strong, hairy man who'll roll around on the jungle floor with me."

Hairy?

I frown at Mary. "I don't even know how in the hell I'm supposed to respond to that."

"Not me," Presley says disgustedly. "All the boys I know are short. And ugly."

I pat her head. "That's right—*all* boys are short and ugly. Like trolls."

Sofia laughs at my troll face.

Presley nods. "I do like this song, though."

Sofia practically squeals when she hears that. "Oh my God, Elton John—best singer ever! If your daddy says it's okay, I'll download all of his greatest songs for you."

My daughter's big blue eyes look to me for affirmation.

"Daddy says it's okay."

And I get a hug in return.

With my arm across the pillows at our backs, my hand rests just beside Sofia's head—close enough to touch her. So I do—massaging her scalp, running my fingers through the soft, dark strands of her hair, relishing the feel of them sliding over my palm.

She leans her head into my touch with a contented sigh. And together, we all watch the rest of the movie.

17

Stanton

About ten o'clock the next night, we pull into to my brother's trailer lot, among a sea of pickup trucks. It's like spring break in the country—teenage kids everywhere. Mary and Marshall disappear into the throng of red-plastic-cup-holding, walking, talking hormones. Sofia pauses to look around as we walk up the path to the door—twinkling lights sparkle in the trees, a full moon hangs in the sky, Led Zeppelin floats out from somewhere in the back.

"It's nice here," she says. "Peaceful."

While she's checking out the compound, I check her out—again. She looks drop-dead gorgeous in tight, dark blue jeans, knee-high heeled black boots, and a V-neck sleeveless white top that clings in all the right places. Her hair is thick and bouncy, curled at the ends, and a long string of pearls hangs around her neck. My grandmother used to wear pearls—but she never wore them as well as Sofia Santos.

Before I can open the door to the trailer, it's jerked open for us, and one of my brother's blond hippie followers—Sadie or Sal—stumbles out. She spots us with happy, glassy eyes.

"Heeey!" She hugs us, smelling like marijuana. "Welcome to the jungle! We're gonna turn on the Slip 'N Slide down the hill, y'all comin'?"

Sofia smiles indulgently. "Maybe later."

After hippie girl staggers away, Sofia says, "It's like college all over again."

I snort. "Columbia wasn't anything like this, and I lived in a goddamn fraternity house."

Just then a guy who looks more my age goes streaking past us—butt-ass naked. I cover Sofia's eyes. "All right, it *is* like college all over again."

We head inside, pushing apart the strings of turquoise beads hanging down in the doorway. A stick of incense burns on a shelf, filling the room with a pungent odor. Carter smiles broadly when he sees us through the crowd of bodies that fills the room to capacity. He hugs me, bare chested except for a tan leather vest and prayer beads. "Welcome. Glad you could make it." Then he hugs Sofia—for a while. "Let's get you something to drink."

Carter gives Sofia a tour of the tricked-out trailer and I'm relieved to see adolescents aren't the only guests at the party. It's actually a lot like a high school reunion. Everyone in my graduating class who hasn't left town—which is pretty much all of them—is here. We catch up, and I proudly introduce them to Sofia. About an hour later, she says in my ear, "I'm going to go outside—get some air."

Colorful Chinese lanterns hang from strings above a line of white rosebushes, framing in the stone patio. A bonfire roars further down, lighting almost the whole yard. I search through the groups of people standing on the grass and—fucking finally—I spot Jenny. She's talking to tiny, brunette Jessica Taylor—a former member of the cheerleading squad. But most important, JD is nowhere to be seen.

Time to turn on the charm.

I pass Sofia my cup of Jack Daniel's. "Can you hold this for me?"

She follows my line of sight. "Sure."

I snap off the stem of a full white rose and show it to her. "What do you think?"

Her grip on the cups tightens. "I think she'll love it."

"If all goes as planned, I'll be gone for a while. Marshall will take you home if you want to go sooner, okay?"

Sofia stares down at her shoes. "Okay."

I wink. "You're the best, Soph. Wish me luck."

But as I walk away . . . she doesn't.

Jessica Taylor greets me with a hug. Jenn eyes me warily. I hold out the rose to her. "A peace offerin'."

Her face thaws just a bit, her pretty pink lips forming a reluctant smile. "Thank you."

Jessica laughs. "Lord, I wish I was as friendly with my ex. He can't be bothered to even give me rat poison." She shakes her head. "But you two always were the perfect couple. Remember that football game junior year, after Stanton scored the winning touchdown? And he came trottin' off the field, straight to you, Jenn? Picked you up and kissed you in front of the whole school—like somethin' straight out of a Drew Barrymore movie?"

Jenny's eyes warm and I know she remembers, the same as I do.

I'd been late picking her up, we'd argued. One word led to another, and by the time we got to the field she was swearing she'd never speak to me again. My romantic gesture dispelled her of that notion, and she spent that night after the game in the backseat of my truck, speaking all kinds of wonderful words like, *yes, more, again.*

Jessica moves on to refill her drink, and I don't stop staring into Jenny's eyes.

"JD fully recovered?"

She snorts. "Like you care, but yes, as a matter of fact. Carter brought some herbal compresses by the house for him—cleared up the rest of the swellin'. He's inside the trailer right now, gettin' more."

My smile turns tight. "I'll be sure to thank Carter for that." Then I lean closer. "Why don't we—"

I never finish the sentence.

From behind us, on the patio, there's a whistle, hollering, and rowdy catcalls. I turn and look toward the noise—to see it's being directed at Sofia. From four assholes I've never seen before, whose names I don't know, but wouldn't mind reading on a couple of headstones.

Then one of them reaches out and grabs her ass.

When they say *so mad I saw red*, I never knew that you actually see red—but that's just what happens. My vision tunnels, bordered with hot crimson. I don't remember walking away from Jenny, I don't recall crossing the yard. The next thing I'm aware of is my hand around a scumbag's throat—slamming his head up against the side of my brother's double-wide.

"Touch her again, I'll rip your fuckin' arm off and shove it up your ass."

His hands claw, trying to pry my fingers off—I just tighten my grip.

Then Carter's next to me. "Easy, Stanton, we're pacifists here. You need to settle down, brother."

When the dickhead's face turns an acceptable shade of purple, I let him go. He holds his neck, heaving and gasping. And I snarl at my brother, "Don't tell me to settle down. Tell your friend to watch where he puts his fuckin' hands."

With one hand on his chest, I pin the grabby prick to the wall of the trailer one last time, for good measure.

Then I wrap my arm around Sofia and lead her away. Her eyes glow up at me softly. "You know I could've handled that."

"I know. But you shouldn't have to."

And I don't leave her side the rest of the night.

• • •

At 1 a.m. the party is still going strong. Sofia's silly, happy drunk— sitting next to me on a lawn chair, teaching Sadie naughty words in Portuguese. After six or seven Jack and Cokes, I'm pretty shit-faced myself. Carter runs out from the side of the trailer, calling me over, telling me to hurry. I hold my hand out to Sofia and we follow him around to the front. My brother puts his finger to his lips and jerks his head toward my truck.

My truck that has windows as steamed as that car in *Titanic*.

Carter takes one side and I take the other. As I bang on the windows shouting, "Police! Open up!", he wrenches open the door.

Then he sings, "I see London, I see France, I see Marshall with no underpants!"

We laugh like hyenas as my little brother hops out in unbuttoned jeans and his hat, cursing the day we were born. A pink-faced blonde follows close behind, and much to Marshall's disappointment, disappears into a group of her friends.

"Y'all suck!" Marshall scowls.

A bit later, we're sitting around the bonfire—me, Carter, Marshall, Jenny, and JD. Carter takes a drag on a joint, then offers it to me. I shake my head. Sofia declines too. Jenny, however, readily accepts and hits it like a pro.

"I thought you said you weren't as fun as you used to be?" I tease.

She blows out a cloud of smoke. "At twenty-eight, I smoke for completely different reasons than I did at sixteen."

JD also takes a few hits.

"Alright, listen up, children—I got somethin' to say," Carter announces, and all eyes turn to him. "When Jenny and JD get married on Saturday, we'll all be one family."

Nope, not really.

I open my mouth, but he goes on. "Like the buzzin' bees of a hive, we all must live in harmony for the colony to flourish. And I am sensin' tension between Stanton and JD."

JD's shiny eyes squint. "There's no tension. Stanton and I get along great."

Sure. And as far as I'm concerned, we'd get along even better if he moved to China, tried climbing Mount Everest . . . died.

Jenny raises her hand like we're back in school. "I agree, Carter. There's tension." She pats JD's leg. "You're just too sweet to see it, baby."

"We have to purge the negativity," Carter explains. "I have a fool-proof plan to reestablish the natural order and reinforce a functioning hierarchy we can all be happy with."

JD scratches his head. "That's a lot of words, man. You wanna run that by me again?"

Natural order.

Hierarchy.

It might just be the whiskey . . . but that sounds like a damn good idea.

· · ·

It was definitely the whiskey.

"This is a terrible fuckin' idea!"

Life's funny. One day you're wearing a suit that costs more than most people bring home in a month, impressing the boss with your skill and expertise. And a week later, you're in the middle of a cattle pasture at two o'clock in the morning, too drunk to see straight, getting ready to race a tractor.

Yes, a tractor.

That was Carter's grand idea. Healthy competition, may the best man win, and all that crap. Now my father's tractors are spitting diesel smoke, rumbling like thunder—me in one, JD in the other. Carter's got the song "Holding Out for a Hero" blasting from my truck speakers and Jenny's standing in front of us. "Ready, set, go!"

She throws JD's hat in the air and we take off. It's a quarter of a mile to the tree, then we have to circle around and back. I push the pedal to the floor, shifting into high gear.

I hear Jenny scream, "Kick his ass, JD!"

And Carter, "That's the way, boys! Feel the balance comin' back—it's all about the balance!"

Sofia cups her hands around her mouth and yells, "Go Stanton! Drive that fucking tractor!"

And I laugh, loud and hard. I glance over at JD and he's laughing too. Because it's all so goddamn ridiculous . . . but in the best kind of way. As I start to turn around the tree, that's when I decide I want to win. It'd be a great way to end a good night. With a victory.

But there's a reason you're not supposed to operate heavy machinery under the influence of drugs and alcohol. That reason becomes clear when JD and I don't leave enough clearance as we both try to make tight U-turns and end up scraping the machines against one another. I move my leg just in time to not get pinned, but the tractors get hung up, caught on one another.

"Back it up!" I tell him, jerking the wheel.

"You back it up!" he retorts.

And just when I consider punching him out and backing up the fucking thing for him, a gunshot rings out, echoing across the field.

I instinctively flinch down. With my ears still ringing from the sound, I look over . . . and see my daddy, dressed in a blue robe and black boots, holding his shotgun.

The party's definitely over.

• • •

"What in holy hell were you thinkin'?"

The six of us sit at the kitchen table, heads down, mouths shut.

"The two of you with a child! You didn't act this way when you were in goddamn high school!"

It's best to just let him get it all out. The more you talk, the longer he'll yell.

"My son, the lawyer, tearin' up my winter grass like a fool, with my other son—the drug dealer—helping him along!" he hollers, his cheeks bright and rosy, like a pissed-off Santa Claus.

Carter takes this moment to interject, "It was a bondin' exercise. I'm a healer, Daddy."

"You're an idiot!"

And those are the first words my father speaks directly to my brother in two years. Makes sense.

Carter stands. "You need to relax. Stress is a silent killer. I have some herbs that can help you with that."

"You can help yourself to my boot up your ass!" my father yells louder.

But Carter is not deterred. He throws his arms around my father's neck. "I love you, Daddy. I'm so glad we're talkin' again."

For just a moment, my father pats Carter's back and his eyes go gentle. And I know he's happy to be talking to my brother again too. Even if it's just to yell at him.

Then he pushes him away and he's back to glaring at us. "Every one of you are gonna get up at dawn to reseed my goddamn field, or I'm gonna break some asses!"

"Yes, sir," JD answers.

"Yes, sir," Jenny replies.

"Definitely don't want any asses getting broke," I agree.

And because she's a smartass, Sofia adds, "Or cracked."

I cover my mouth so my father doesn't start up again. Marshall giggles behind me.

Just as he turns toward the stairs, Mary comes strolling in the back door wearing the same outfit she had on earlier—denim shorts, red top, white denim jacket, blue sneakers. Of course it's the same outfit—because she hasn't been home yet to change into anything else.

She screeches to a halt just inside the door, looking at the group of us like a deer in the light of an oncoming tractor trailer. "What's goin' on? Did somebody die?"

No. But the night is still young.

"Are you just gettin' home?" my father asks, his tone turning more threatening with every syllable.

Her face goes blank. A liar's face—the kind who's trying to not show any tells that they're bluffing. "Of course not!" she claims. "My curfew is at midnight, and it's after midnight. If I was just gettin' in now . . . that would be wrong."

My sister is not a good poker player, and she'd make a terrible witness in a court of law. But my father, like so many others when it comes to his youngest, his only girl—is blind. Or he's just getting too goddamn old to keep up.

"Then where the hell were you?" I ask, tilting my chair back.

She gives me the evil eye for a split second. Then more smoothly she says, "Couldn't sleep. I . . . got dressed and went for a walk."

She kisses my father sweetly on his cheek. "You should head up to bed, Daddy. You're lookin' kinda flushed."

He pats her on the top of the head, then goes up the stairs mumbling that we kids will be the death of him yet.

I'm prepared to let it go—shit, I blew through my curfew ten times more often than I made it. But then my baby sister pulls a pitcher of juice out of the refrigerator, and takes off her jacket—revealing half a dozen red clusters of broken blood vessels on her lower neck and chest.

Marshall takes the words out of my mouth. "What in the actual fuck is that?"

Mary almost drops her glass of juice. "What? What's what?"

Carter, Marshall, and I surround her. "That!" I point to the marks. "Did you get into an altercation with a vacuum cleaner hose?"

She looks down. "Oh." And lies again—badly. "I scratched myself on a bush."

Carter inspects her neck more closely. "Those are hickeys, little girl. Fresh ones. Who's been suckin' on my baby sister's neck?"

"I'd rather not say," she replies, clapping her lips together.

"I don't give a rat's ass what you'd rather," I tell her. "You're gonna say, and you're gonna say now."

Sofia stands up. "Hold on a second."

I lift my hand. "Just sit back down, Sofia. This is a man thing—you wouldn't understand."

As soon as the words are past my lips, I know they were the wrong ones to say.

Her eyes go wide, then narrow. She folds her arms and takes deliberate steps toward us. It's her court stance, defense attorney mode—and it's sexy as fuck.

"I'm sorry," she says, not sounding sorry at all. "Did you just say, 'It's a *maaan thang*'?"

"I don't talk like that."

"Well, that's how Neanderthal sounds in *my* head. I'm just waiting for you to grunt, pound your chest, and rub some sticks together. Or have you not discovered fire yet?"

"Soph . . ."

Now she raises her hand. "Don't *Soph* me. I didn't see either of you putting the screws to Marshall about the name of the girl he was spending time with in your truck—with his pants down at his ankles!"

Mary gasps. "Who were you with, Marshall?"

He backs up a step. "I'd rather not say."

Mary looks to Jenny, who supplies the information. "Norma-Jean Forrester."

"I knew it!" Mary squeals, then smacks Marshall's arm. "She is so skanky!"

"She *is* skanky!" Jenny agrees. "Her whole family's skanky."

I raise my arms. "Can we focus here, please?" I pin Sofia with my gaze. "The reason we're not interrogating Marshall is because Norma-Jean Skanky didn't leave a horde of hickeys behind her."

Sofia nods. "So it's the hickeys you have a problem with?"

Not really—but it sounds better than being enraged at the thought of my sister doing the same things I could care less if my brother does.

"Yes."

Unfortunately, there's a reason Sofia is a top-notch attorney—because she can see straight through bullshit.

"You're sure?" she smirks.

"Yes, Regis, that's my final answer."

"I see." She grasps the collar of her shirt and pulls it down. "So then I guess you have a major problem with all of *these* hickeys too?"

Four—no five—fading hickeys and two bite marks mar Sofia's otherwise flawless skin. Looking at them makes the blood rush straight to my crotch.

"My word!" my sister exclaims. "Did you turn vampire while you've been in DC?"

Jenny adds her two cents, laughing. "For Christ's sake, Stanton!"

It should bother me that Jenny's not more upset by visual evidence of my dalliances with another woman. But . . . it doesn't.

I point to the hickeys at hand. "That is totally different!"

"Why?" Sofia asks, her gorgeous eyes burning with challenge.

"Because you are not my sister."

"Well, she's *someone's* sister," Mary counters.

Keeping her eyes on me, Sofia holds up three fingers.

"Three!" Mary catches on. "She's three someones' sister!"

"And my oldest brother could kick your ass without breaking a sweat." Then she folds her arms, pacing like she's giving a closing argument. "So, Mr. Shaw, it would seem we are at an impasse. You can let your sister go to her room without further pressure to produce a name. Or . . . the *womenfolk* and I will go into the other room and take photographs of my hickeys—and send them to my brother. To see if he agrees with your allegation that it's *a man thing*."

For a minute, I forget that Sofia and I are not the only ones in the room. "I love it when you get all defense counsel on me."

She just smiles back.

I sigh. And roll my eyes. "Go to bed, Mary."

"Yes!" She gives Sofia a high five as she passes. "You go, girl!"

Marshall announces that he's going to bed too, and follows Mary up the stairs.

Carter yawns. "I'm beat. The couch is calling my name." He crosses the kitchen, peeling off his clothes as he goes. By the time he exits the room, the last view I have of him is his lily-white ass.

I rub my eyes, to erase the image and because I'm exhausted myself.

"Hey, Stanton?" JD asks. "Since we all have to get up in"— he checks his watch—"two hours to reseed the field, would it be all right if Jenny and I crash here?"

Without thinking, I shrug. "Sure."

And the four of us head out to the barn. After Jenny and JD are settled in Carter's old room and Sofia and I are under the covers in my bed, she whispers to me.

"Is this weird? This is weird, right? Does it bother you that they're . . . there?" She points to the open door to the bathroom that connects the two rooms.

Again—it probably should. I should want to rip Sausage Link's head off. Smother him with a pillow. Throw him out the window and watch him fall the two stories, praying he'll land on his head.

But I just pull Sofia closer. "I'm too tired to give a shit."

18

Stanton

Marshall gets out of seeding the field because he has school. The rest of us—Sofia, me, Carter, Jenny, and JD—aren't so lucky. We have breakfast together and spend the morning raking seed and fertilizer into the dirt so my father isn't tempted to come out and break our asses. But later, after a long shower, the pressure starts to build. And by the evening it feels like a renewed weight is pushing on me—the little time that's left before Saturday.

So I take matters into my own hands.

"Ow!" A branch rakes across my forearm as I climb, drawing blood.

"Shit!" A thin, leaf-covered limb boomerangs into my face.

"Fuckin' hell almighty!" I smack my head on the underside of a particularly solid bough.

Why was this easier when I was seventeen? Maybe the horniness made me immune to pain. Eventually, I make it to the top—to my golden, glowing goal.

Jenny's bedroom window.

It's unlocked, like I knew it would be. I open it and brace my hands on the ledge to pull myself through.

"Christ on a fuckin' cracker!" Jenny screeches from her vanity chair—where she sits, clad only in a tiny pink nightgown with thin straps. "Just scare the everlovin' shit out of me, why don't you?"

"Kiss your nana with that mouth?" I grunt. "Explains a lot." When she just continues to sit, arms folded, I frown. "You're not even gonna give me a hand? That's pretty cold, Jenn."

She rolls her eyes and exhales loudly—but then she gets up and helps pull me in.

I stumble forward, gripping onto her hips to keep us from falling—and we both freeze when we realize our faces are just millimeters apart—sharing the same breaths.

Then Jenny blinks and backs away. "You can't be here, Stanton."

I ignore her and glance at the bed. "Where's Presley?"

"She fell asleep on the couch downstairs. I'll carry her up in a bit."

And then my gaze falls behind Jenny—to the flowing white dress hanging on the wall. And every bone in my body turns to Jell-O, held together by loose, shredded straps of tendon.

"Is that it?" I whisper.

"Yeah," Jenny says—so softly. "That's my weddin' dress. Isn't it pretty?"

I see her wearing it in my mind. Delicate lace, embroidered flowers wrapped around the body I know so well. Pretty doesn't even come close.

"It's beautiful."

Then I remember she'll be wearing it for someone else—and my heart squeezes so hard, it feels like it'll evaporate in my chest.

"I don't want to hurt you, Stanton."

I turn to her—desperate now. "Then don't do this. Talk to me— *listen* to me."

"I *have* talked to you! It's you who hasn't been listening!" she claims, wearing a fallen face. "You're so stubborn—you're so stuck on what you think is *supposed* to be, that you're missin' what's right in front of you."

I sit down on the edge of her bed, pushing a frustrated hand through my hair. "You sound like Carter."

I notice a pile of boxes near my feet, opened with ribbons hanging off. "What's this?"

"The girls from my club threw me a little weddin' shower."

I notice a scrap of material peeking out from the closest box. Black and . . . *leather*?

I pull it out and hold up a set of black binding cuffs with shiny silver locks. Attached to the cuffs is a matching black flogger.

What the hell?

"Stanton, don't—"

But I'm already looking. Blindfold, ball gag, riding crop that's definitely not meant for a horse, cock ring, and a wide array of dildos—purple, blue, glass, and a particularly huge battery-operated sucker.

My near-speechlessness is clear in my tone. "What the fuck kind of club are you in?"

With a scarlet blush, she takes the giant dildo from my hand and sighs. "I told you there were ways JD knew me better than you."

"He's into this kind of stuff too?"

She nods.

"Why didn't you ever tell me?"

She doesn't meet my eyes. "I don't know—do you tell me everything *you* like to do these days?"

Jenn and I have always had terrific sex—but it's a familiar, practiced kind of awesome. Asking her if she wants to be fucked hard, making her beg to come, bending her over a desk and nailing her without bothering to take off our clothes just because it's dirtier that way—has never, ever crossed my mind.

"No, I guess not. Thought you'd slap me if I did."

"What would you have said if I told you?"

I take the dildo from her, turn it around in my hand appreciatively. "I'd have said . . . make sure you have extra batteries."

She giggles, drops the dildo back into the box, and rests her head against my shoulder. "I love you."

That brings me back to serious. "So don't do this."

She just smiles sadly. "There's all kinds of love, Stanton. Ours is what makes the best kind of bond, one that will last our whole life. But it's not the marryin' kind."

"That's not true." I take her face in my hands. "I'm in love with you, Jenny."

Her eyes are dry, but there are tears in her voice. "No, you're not. It's an echo. Of who we were, the promises we made, the passion we had. But an echo's not real—you can't build a life on it. It's just a memory of a sound."

I stroke her cheek with my thumb, hearing her words but not really listening. "I just wish . . . I wish I had known that the last time I kissed you was gonna be the last." I trace her lips with the tip of my finger. "I would've taken more care to remember. Let me kiss you now, Jenn. Give us that. And after, if you still want to marry him, I swear I'll stand aside."

I see it in her eyes. Desire. Maybe she regrets not cherishing that last kiss more, too. She stares at my mouth and her hands cradle my jaw. I lean in closer—giving her time to say no.

But she doesn't.

And then our lips touch, brush, mold together. She sinks into the kiss with the barest of moans, and I pull her nearer. I move my mouth over hers, and she tastes just the same—just like I remember—sweet summer cherries.

And I wait for that feeling that always comes—that undeniable pull that makes me want to touch her everywhere, all at once. I wait for that sensation of certainty, flawless perfection—that I'm exactly where I'm supposed to be, and the woman in my arms is all I could ever ask for.

The problem is . . . those feelings never come.

My heart doesn't hammer in my chest, my hands don't shake with the need to caress. There's just . . . nothing. I mean, I'm in a dark room with my mouth pressed against a beautiful woman—so there's *some-*

thing. But it's not what it's supposed to be—not powerful or mind-blowing, not tender or exciting.

It's nothing like when I kiss . . .

Oh shit.

I'm reminded of the fairy tales I read to Presley when she was smaller. The ones where the kiss always broke the spell. Lifted the curse.

Opened the eyes.

We slowly pull away, and Jenny and I stare at one another.

"You feel it too, don't you?" she asks.

"What?"

"Like tryin' to squeeze a puzzle piece into the wrong slot . . . like there's somethin' missin'. You feel that now, don't you?"

In a shocked whisper, I finally admit to myself—and her, "Yeah. That's it—exactly."

I put my hand on her shoulder. "Jenny, I—"

Suddenly she covers her mouth with her hand, her face morphing into a mask of regret and guilt. "Oh my God! What have I *done*?"

"Jenn—"

She stands up and paces, talking with quick, horrified words. "Oh my *god*! I kissed you! Three days before my weddin'! Three days before I'm about to stand up in front of God and my family and promise myself to another man! A man who's done nothin' but love me, trust me, respect me! Oh my fuckin' God!"

"Calm down! It's all right. We don't—"

She turns on me like a viper. "Don't you tell me to calm down! JD's always been intimidated by you. You were like—a legend to him. He always worried that I couldn't love him like I loved you. He never thought he could measure up . . ."

I can't stop the satisfied smirk from tugging at my lips. "Really?"

She points her finger and grits out, "Wipe that smile off your face or I'll slap it off!"

My smile flees in terror.

"How am I gonna tell him? How am I supposed to explain without him feelin'—"

I stand up, blocking her way. "We'll keep it between us. You don't have to tell him shit."

"Yes, I do!" she wails. "Secrets are poison. They eat away the soul of a relationship."

"Oh, for fuck's sake, Jenn—you *really* need to stop hangin' out with my brother."

She points in my face again, backing me up toward the window. "This is all your fault! You tricked me!"

"I didn't trick you!"

"My nana was right about you—you're a Satan." She picks up the first thing she can grab—the ball gag—and throws it at me. "Get thee back, Satan!" The blue dildo follows next. Then the handcuffs.

I put my arms up as sex toy projectiles hurtle toward me. The giant dildo bounces off my forehead.

Probably gonna leave a mark.

"You're supposed to fling holy water!"

I turn and scramble out the window. Descending quickly, I make it about halfway down before my foot catches—and I fall the other half.

"Oooof!"

I land on my back—possibly rupturing a kidney.

As I breathe through the pain, I hear Jenny slam the window shut above me and I stare at the sky. It's black as ink and white stars blink down on me—like a million mocking eyes.

I cover my face with my arm. Tonight did not go as planned. That's been happening a lot lately.

But I realized something crucial. Absolutely life changing.

I am a man in love. Just not a man in love with Jenny Monroe.

My first thought after this realization is: *fuck me.*

The second is: *Drew Evans is going to laugh his ass off.*

• • •

I take my time getting back to my parents' house, trying to process it all. My brother would tell me I should meditate, and for the first time since he went off the deep end, I consider that he could be onto something. Feelings rush through me, too quick to hold on to, like a twig going down a raging river.

I push the door to Sofia's room open gently, making out her form in the dim moonlight streaming in from the open window. She's on her side, the luminous skin of her bare back facing me.

Tenderness floods my chest, and a sweet, relieved feeling—like coming home. I force my mind to silence, push out the crazy confusion that's swirling, stripping down to bare skin. Then I slide into bed, determined to focus on this moment. The simple here and now. Just her.

But before I touch her she turns over, surprising me.

"How'd it go with Jenny?" she asks.

I push damp hair back off her face. "It was . . . enlightening."

"What do you mean?"

Truthfully? I have no idea. For so long, I thought Jenny Monroe was my endgame. It was a certainty, like the sun rising in the east. To realize that nothing about it is certain, and that I'm actually okay with that, is throwing me for a major goddamn loop.

I wonder if this is how people felt when they discovered the earth wasn't flat? It's a shift in perception—in how I view the world—and what my place is supposed to be in it.

My thoughts about Sofia are a whole other level of fucked up. What I feel for her extends further than admiration for her stupendous tits and magnificent intelligence. Deeper. I know that now—I just don't know what I'm supposed to do about it. *Would she believe me if I told her? Is there any chance she feels the same way?*

So I'm not going to do anything. Because when you're driving a car, if you try and change gears too quick? They'll grind, screech, possibly cause the transmission to drop out of the bottom of your car.

When in doubt—it's better to wait it out.

"I don't want to talk about it."

Her face tightens, like she's going to push the issue, but then she turns onto her back and complains, "It's so fucking hot—I'm literally melting." She wipes sweat from her forehead.

I smile. "My grandma used to say Mississippi was closer to God. The downside is when you're closer to the heavens, you're nearer the sun—and that's why it's always so goddamn hot."

Sofia chuckles. Then she arches her back and rolls her neck uncomfortably. "I'm never going to be able to sleep."

That's when I have the best fucking idea.

"I want to take you somewhere."

•   •   •

"Are you sure it's safe?"

"Completely." I pull on the handlebars, testing the weight the rope will handle. It creaks like an old house in a storm, but holds. "See?"

We're at Sunshine Falls, a few miles down from Jenny's and my spot—where everybody goes swimming. They're not really waterfalls—more like a three-foot ridge of rock that the water cascades over, cool and clear. But . . . that's the name. The best part is the line of deep-rooted old trees on the bank, whose branches hang out over the water—making the perfect, most epic swing. This one has old bicycle handlebars tied to the end, instead of just knotted rope, which helps with the grip.

"The only thing you have to remember is to let go."

She nods with rapt attention. "Let go. Got it."

"Don't freeze up and hang on. You'll swing back and smash into the trunk . . . which will be fucking hilarious, and I'll never let you live it down. But it will also hurt like a mother. Don't get nervous."

"I wasn't nervous, but now you're making me nervous." Sofia shifts from foot to foot, and her awesome breasts shake beneath the triangles of her tiny red bikini.

I lick my lips. It would be so easy to just bend down, suckle on her tasty, peaked nipples through the fabric of her suit. And the things I could do to her with this rope and handlebar . . .

I close my eyes with a groan, a full-out hard-on now aching against the fabric of my trunks. But I ignore it—'cause it's time to swim. Sofia is hot. *So hot.*

Swim, swim, fucking swim.

"I'll go first." I grip the bars, lift my legs, and swing out over the water in a seamless arch. When I reach the threshold—a second before the rope starts to swing back—I let go, landing feet first in the water after a perfect backflip. I break the surface and sigh with pleasure; the cool water feels amazing against my overheated skin.

Squinting through the darkness, I spot Sofia on the bank. "Come on! It's beautiful."

Then, with an earsplitting shriek, she's swinging out toward me. Just as I shout, "Let go!" she does, and cannonballs into the river.

She comes up laughing, choking just a bit. Her skin is slick and shiny, her wet hair heavy and long.

"Is my top still on?" She checks the strings tied around her neck.

"Unfortunately, yes."

Her face is ecstatic, like a little girl seeing the vast ocean for the very first time. "I'm doing that again!"

• • •

Later, Sofia lies on her back on the bank, her foot stirring through the water. "This is the best idea you've ever had," she sighs.

I watch her from the shallows, ripples lapping around my hips. My voice is hoarse—almost unrecognizable. "I'm thinkin' of a few better ones right now."

She lifts her head and meets my eyes. And just like that, her breathing picks up. Her chest rises and falls a little faster. Her pulse throbs in her neck just a little bit harder.

"Come here, Sofia."

Her gaze doesn't leave my face as she slides into the water, moving closer. When she's just an arm's length away, I take a deep breath. "You said no sex when we got to my home—but I want you so badly, I can taste you."

She stares at my mouth, debating. And I can't help but smirk.

It's the smirk that does her in. Because a second later, she's pulling me to her, murmuring, "Fuck it."

"Oh, darlin', I plan to."

The moment my lips touch hers, the second my tongue invades the wet heat of her mouth, I'm moaning. It feels like it's been fucking forever. She grips my bicep, nails digging in, her tongue as eager as my own.

I pull the string on her bikini, releasing soft, lush flesh. In one motion, I wrap her legs around my waist, hoist her higher and lower my head. And my mouth is on her, sucking her already pointed nipple into my mouth, laving with my tongue, lapping at the water on her skin and the taste of her. Christ, I could do just this for *hours*.

And sensations hit me, blinding and contradictory.

Everything that wasn't there when I was kissing Jenny. The insane desire, the unexplainable need, wanting to spend hours and days with the woman in my arms, yet never wanting this moment to end. Needing to come so badly my dick throbs painfully, yet wanting to stay buried inside her all night.

I'm totally screwed. But in this second, there's not a goddamn thing I would change.

Sofia writhes and whimpers in my arms. Her hips rub, gyrate against the planes of my stomach, her hands clasp at my head, pull at my hair.

And I take my time worshipping her gorgeous tits. Keeping one arm around her back, my free hand massages her breast, pinching the nipple until she gasps.

Sofia doesn't seem to have the same patience as I do.

"Stanton, please," she begs, her chin rubbing against my hair. "Oh God, I need you to fuck me."

I trace over the hickeys on her chest with my tongue, then suck, re-marking her. "Not yet."

She uncurls her legs and slides down my front. My cock aches from the friction and my hips grind forward, searching for more. Then Sofia takes matters into her own hands.

Literally.

I kiss her mouth, nipping her lip with my teeth, when I see her hand dip below the water, into her bathing suit.

Oh, fuck.

Her groan grows deeper, more feral, and her free hand slides around my back, into my trunks, grabbing my ass. Pulling me closer where she needs me most.

I lift her against me and drag us to the bank. I lower her down and press on top of her, bare chests rubbing. She pushes down her bikini bottoms and I yank them the rest of the way, then free myself from the stifling constraints of my trunks. Her thighs spread wide when I push against them with my hips. Gripping my cock, I drag the head through her folds, feeling her heat, wanting to thrust and grind and ride her until we both lose our minds.

Jesus, it's never felt like this. So fucking urgent. So desperate.

I push inside her—just the tip—and her muscles clench around me greedily. She's so fucking warm . . . slick and snug. Too warm.

I look into her eyes. "I don't have anything, Sofia."

A whole box of wonderful condoms is back at the house, in my room. Shit.

She shakes her head, her voice high and breathless. "I don't care."

I grow stiffer with the thought of screwing her raw. Illicit, decadent images flash behind my eyes, telling me it doesn't matter. Urging me to just *push, thrust, fuck.*

I drag my nails up her thigh gently. "I'll pull out," I rasp. Promise. "I want to see my come on you." I slide my hand up her stomach, across her breasts. "Here. Glistening on this perfect fucking skin."

She nods with a whimper, pulling me down to her. Lifting her legs, making me slip further inside.

I thrust hard—and stop. Sinking into the sensation of her wrapped so tight around me, filling her completely without anything between us. I don't remember the last time I was inside a woman bare—but that's not what makes it different.

It's beautiful. Intense.

But only because it's her.

I drag out slowly. She arches her back, rubbing against me. And I push back inside her, groaning and grasping. I let go, fucking her without an ounce of restraint, inching us up the bank, rocking her breasts with every thrust of my hips.

I pull on her shoulders and she clasps my head, holding me as her tongue plunders my mouth. Her lips slant across my jaw, biting, and she comes with a muffled scream against my skin. I feel her contract, squeezing so tight it borders on painful. The best kind of pain.

When her muscles relax I push into her again, feeling the tension coiling in my stomach. Electric tendrils spark up my thighs, and at the last possible moment I pull out and rise to my knees. I move my fist up my length, and Sofia watches with rapt eyes. She covers my hands with her own, helping me get there.

The sound of my rushing blood crests in my eardrums and I come in hot, forceful spurts. She moans with me as my orgasm paints her breasts in gleaming splashes that go on and on.

With a final groan I collapse on top of her, both of us panting, chasing our breath. She cradles me against her neck and my arms come around, pressing her close. And we stay just like that until the sun peeks over the horizon in the east.

And a whole new day is born.

19

Stanton

On Thursday afternoon, Jenny's sister throws a big party for her and JD at her parents' house. It's fancier than a Sunday barbecue, but not as extravagant as a catered affair. The bride- and groom-to-be have foregone bachelor or bachelorette parties—much to Ruby's displeasure. It seems she was looking forward to giving her little sister the kind of send-off into married life that included fireman strippers and mechanical-bull riding. Obviously, Ruby is unaware of her sister's kinkier proclivities—and the fact that she already has her very own collection of handcuffs, so the stripper probably would've been a letdown.

Being close as they are, my whole family is invited. Walking into their house decorated with bridal-themed streamers and balloons does little to sort out the fuckery in my head right now. I'm still not thrilled about Jenny getting married, but the idea doesn't make my insides burn with jealousy or panic anymore. I get it now—after last night, after the nothing kiss, I see that Jenny was right. About everything.

Which is exactly why there's no good reason for her to go confessing things to JD. It'll just cause problems for nothing. That's the advice I want to give Jenn—if she'd sit still long enough for me to say it.

"Not now, Stanton." She walks out of the kitchen with me right behind her. Her mouth is grim, her eyes are weary and dull with remorse. She looks stressed, but what's worse—she looks guilty.

"Jenny, just give me a second." But she's already in the living room, moving among a sea of people—each one nodding and smiling and making conversation. The sky outside is the color of gray smoke, quickly turning to charcoal, so everyone's inside. In the living room, JD's eyes light up when Jenny walks into the room. She stops short, gazing at him with an expression I can't read.

"Don't say anything, Jenn. Not yet," I say against her hair.

Ruby walks around the house with a microphone, playing bridal bingo. "Okay y'all, who knows the month and day when JD and Jenny went on their first date? Mark it down on your card." She leans down toward the tiny, gray-haired Mrs. Fletcher, who's deaf as a post and yells into the microphone. "The first *date,* Mrs. Fletcher!"

Mrs. Fletcher nods, then writes down today's date.

"I'm just gonna be honest," Jenny says to herself. "The truth will set you free."

No, I know from professional experience that the truth can land your ass in a jail cell. It's *how* the truth is presented that makes all the difference.

She's moving forward before I can grasp her arm.

"There's my girl," JD says from his seat.

I watch her swallow hard as she sits in the empty seat beside him. And she looks like she might actually puke when she says, "There's somethin' I need to tell you."

"Hey, JD," I try. "You want to go outside and throw the ball around?"

He holds up a finger at me and his dark eyes squint as he looks at Jenny with a mixture of concern and curiosity. "What's the matter, beautiful?"

"Alright, get ready for the next one, everybody!" Ruby announces into the microphone. She stands between JD's and Jenny's chairs. "Jenny's gonna give it to y'all!"

And it's like a train wreck. A slow-moving, unstoppable crash.

Ruby lowers the microphone to Jenny's mouth just as she confesses, "I kissed Stanton last night."

Smash.

Everyone stops—stares—no one moves. Even old Mrs. Fletcher heard it clearly. "Ha!" She whispers with delight to her aged bingo companion, "I knew that boy wasn't lettin' go that easy."

But's it's another voice that captures me—that clutches something deep inside me—and twists.

"You *kissed* her last night?"

The words are whispered with condemnation . . . and disbelief. But it's the look in Sofia's eyes that almost brings me to my knees. Anguish. Pure undiluted pain that she doesn't even try to hide.

And it's like I can read her mind, see her thoughts. She's thinking about our time at the river—connecting the dots. And she's assuming that I used her. Turned to her to finish what Jenn started. It's all right fucking there on her face.

"Soph . . ." I step toward her to explain, to take that look away—but she turns her back on me, walking out of the room.

With the audience still silent, Ruby clears her throat and speaks into the microphone. "Cake . . . and liquor . . . will be served on the porch, if y'all will follow me." She motions with her hand.

The room quickly clears out, leaving only me, Jenny, JD, our parents, and my older brother. JD's brown eyes watch her like he's waiting for her to continue, but can't decide if he actually wants her to. He doesn't seem angry. He's shocked. Wrecked.

Like . . . like a puppy that just got kicked.

He takes a deep breath and says, "Jenny . . . I know I'm not excitin'. I don't have a flashy job, I'm not the star quarterback, I'm a simple guy. I like . . . simple things. Quiet things—like holdin' your hand, and watchin' TV with my arms around you. I'm just a man who loves you more than I'll ever love anythin'." He straightens up. "But I'm not gonna fight for you. This isn't high school or some movie—we're adults. You need to decide what you want. *Who* you want. And it needs to be now."

Jenny's fingers wrap around one another beseechingly. "I already have decided. I want to be with *you*, JD—I love you."

Her words only seem to upset him more. He pushes at his dark hair, arms tight, hands curling into fists. "You sure about that? 'Cause it don't seem like love from where I'm standin'."

I figure it's time I step in. "Listen, JD—"

"Oh, shut up," he growls.

"Excuse me?"

"I've had it up to here with you!" He motions to the top of his head. "Everythin' was fine until you came back. You were an asshole in high school, and you're an asshole now!"

I press a hand to my chest. "Jenny said you thought I was a legend."

"A legendary asshole! Always walkin' around like you were better than us—too fuckin' good for this town. Screw you!"

I'm insulted.

"Well I sure as shit was better than you—goddamn water boy."

Suddenly JD changes from a puppy into a Rottweiler. One that snaps.

"I was the *manager*!" he bellows. Then he lunges over the table, tackling me around the waist, taking us both down to the ground.

June screams.

Jenny groans, "Aw, hell."

My leg catches the leg of the side table, bringing the lamp on top of it crashing to the floor.

And Carter says, "Finally! That's what I'm talkin' about. Purge the negativity! Get it all out there in the open, boys."

I straighten my arm against JD's chest, trying to get the upper hand.

"I thought you weren't gonna fight," I grit out.

"I changed my mind!" he snarls. Then he punches me in the eye.

My head snaps to the side, but I come right back, landing a solid right hook to his jaw, making my knuckles throb. We grapple and grunt, kick and punch. But within just a few minutes, Wayne and my father decide that's enough. They snatch each of us by our collars, dragging us up, pulling us apart.

Panting, JD shakes off Wayne's grip, but he doesn't come at me again.

He looks at Jenny and bites out, "I'm done here."

And the front door slams closed behind him.

• • •

After JD's exit, Ruby announced the party was over and sent everyone home. Then she swore she was gonna put us all on Jerry Springer. Twenty minutes later I'm at the kitchen table, holding a bag of frozen peas on my swelling eye. Jenny sits on a chair next to me, while our daughter paces before us.

Presley stops in front of me. "We use our *words* to solve problems around here, not our *fists*." She paces some more. Then she looks hard at Jenny. "And you've hurt JD's feelin's. You need to say sorry."

We nod in sad unison.

Getting your ass chewed out by an eleven-year-old is no fun at all.

Presley shakes her head and wags her finger. "I'm very disappointed in both of you. I want you to sit here and think about your behavior. And next time, I expect you to make better choices." With a final reproachful *humph*, she flounces away—leaving us to stew.

Silently, Jenny picks at her nails. It's what she does when she's worried, and it doesn't take a genius to guess just what she's worrying over.

"I'm sorry, Jenn. I didn't mean—" I break off, because busting up Jenny and JD's wedding was exactly what I meant to do. I thought I'd feel victorious—another check in the win column.

But I just feel shitty.

She rests her hand on my leg. "It's all right, Stanton. It's not all your fault."

I stare at her. Waiting.

"All right, it *is* your fault. But I did my part too. If I had just told you from the beginnin', let you get used to the idea, we wouldn't—"

The front door slams open and a burst of wind surges into the house, blowing in leaves, little chunks of dirt, and . . . Jimmy Ass Face Dean.

Jenny stands as he walks into the room, hard faced and frowning. But there's something else in his eyes.

Fear.

"You came back," she breathes.

"I had to come back. To make sure you and Presley were all right." He pulls her into his arms, and the Rottweiler is back in his cage. "There's a storm comin' in." He looks up at me. "The tornado warnin' is goin' off—heard it when I got close to town. The radio cut out on the way back, but it sounded like it's on track to hit here."

Shit.

Tornado watches are pretty common in this part of Mississippi. We deal with them the way the East Coast handles a blizzard—with healthy caution and preparation—but no one really expects the Armageddon they show in the movies.

But a warning means a tornado has actually touched down. And if you're in its path, that's a horse of a fucked-up color.

At once, everybody moves—bringing in the lawn furniture, locking down windows. Not every farm has a storm cellar, but this one does. Jenny's father grabs the first-aid pack from under the sink and we all gather in the kitchen, to head out the back door. But when I look around, my heart lodges in my throat, blocking the air.

"Where's Sofia?"

I walk back through the living room, searching. I open the front door to check the yard—and have to brace my legs against a wave of wind that feels like God himself is trying to knock me on my ass.

"She went for a walk," Ruby volunteers, her face pale and tight.

"When?" I yell.

"Awhile ago—before the fight. She walked out the back door and just kept on goin'."

Pure, cold panic rises up my legs—like I'm sinking into quicksand. And a thousand horrific scenes go through my head. Sofia getting knocked down by flying debris, bleeding and calling my name. Sofia trapped under a fallen tree, her eyes lifeless. Sofia running, almost making it to the house . . . before she's swept up in the monstrous gray mass. Gone, like she was never here at all.

Her name bubbles up in my chest and I clench my teeth to keep from shouting it.

I have to find her.

In the kitchen, I tell them, "Y'all go on—I'm gonna go get Sofia."

"Daddy!" Presley throws her arms around my waist and I can feel her shaking. "Daddy, please come with us. Don't go!"

Her terror, her need for me slices through my chest like a machete, cutting me in two. I kneel, looking into her eyes, touching her little face. And I put everything I have into my words to comfort her. "I'll come back. I swear, Presley, I'll come back."

Her lip trembles.

I caress her hair and try to give her my smile. "We can't leave Miss Sofia out there, baby girl. I'm goin' to get her and then we'll come straight back to you." I look behind Presley to Jenny, who's holding JD's hand. And I know what I have to do.

I scoop Presley up into my arms, kissing her cheek. "You're gonna be with your momma and JD. They're gonna keep you safe."

She hugs me one last time—and then I hand her over.

To JD.

I never saw myself giving my daughter into the care of another man. Never imagined a scenario where that would ever be okay. But there's no jealousy, no urge to lay him out and snatch her back. I'm just . . . grateful that it's not all on Jenny alone.

She murmurs to our daughter and nods at me, gratitude in her eyes. Like an omen, there's a crash outside, snapping us out of the moment. My mother rushes everyone to the door. As JD goes to follow, I grab his shoulder, talking more with my eyes so as not to frighten the precious bundle he holds in his arms.

"Make sure you lock that door behind you. You understand what I'm sayin'?"

Don't wait for me, is what I'm telling him. *Lock the damn door and keep it locked, even if I'm still on the outside—nothing touches them.*

He nods, his face solemn. "Yeah, I get you, Stanton."

I turn and cross into the living room.

"Hey, wait!" he calls. I glance back and JD tosses me a set of keys. "Your brother put shit tires on your truck—it'll get caught in the mud. Take mine."

I look at the keys in my hand, then back up at him. He nods. I nod. And that's all there is to it.

Sofia was right when she said men are simple creatures. With this easy exchange, I've agreed not to stand in his and Jenny's way, and he's agreed to never give me a reason to kill him. *Over and out.*

I rush out the door and sprint to the truck. The stark reality that I have no idea where she is consumes me—pushes on my brain, threatening to crack it. I know the Monroe property as well as my own. If she went out the back door, there's a good chance she'd be headed toward the cornfield.

Unless she turned around.

"Goddamn it!" I yell, hitting the steering wheel, trying to drive quickly enough to cover more ground, but still scan the fields for a sign of where she could be. The truck vibrates with the force of wind, and pea-size hail pelts the windshield. I think of her out in this weather, alone—unprotected. Is she cold? Is she scared? Every muscle in my body seizes up at the thought.

"Come on, baby," I utter through clenched teeth. "Where are you?"

They say when you die, your life flashes before your eyes. I don't know if that's true. But I know for certain there's a point when your fear for someone you care about . . . someone you love . . . becomes so intense, so paralyzing, that everything else fades away. And you're consumed with thoughts of them: the way they laugh, their scent, the sound of their voice. Every moment I've shared with Sofia flickers through my mind, like a silent film. Sofia beside me in a courtroom, beneath me in bed, the days we teased and talked, the nights we moaned and sighed. And every image makes me crave more. More time. More memories. All the moments we haven't shared yet, all the experiences we haven't had, all the words I never said. I need them. I need her.

More than I've ever needed anyone. *Anyone.*

I close my eyes and pray a silent prayer, beseeching and begging. For another chance to do it right. To relive every second with her, to treat her with the reverence she always deserved.

To cherish her.

Please, God.

And when I open my eyes, I have to believe that God heard me. Because I see her in the distance—hair whipping, stumbling in the wind and on those four-inch goddamn heels. My first thought is: *thank fuck she's safe.* My second thought is: *I'm going to strangle her.*

I drive up quick and the truck screeches as I hit the brakes a few feet from where she stands. The wind pushes and the hail pours down as I climb out of the truck, tearing my way to her. It bounces off the truck, pelts my face and shoulders in icy shards.

My voice booms louder than the wind. "Which part of the *cattle are clusterin'* did you not fuckin' hear me say?"

"What?"

And then I've got her. She's in my arms, against my chest, warm and alive, being squeezed so hard she might not be able to breathe. But I can't let go.

"Don't ever do that again," I pant harshly against her ear.

She looks up at me, wide eyed and so goddamn beautiful it makes me tremble.

"Don't do what again?"

I push her hair back, holding her face. And my voice cracks. "Leave."

I press her against me, clasping her to me, sheltering her with my own flesh and blood. My body sighs, my bones slacken with relief that she's here and whole and safe.

But safety, like so many other things we think we can control, is an illusion. Because when I turn around to open the truck door and get her inside, keeping Sofia shielded behind me, a sharp, piercing pain explodes against my temple . . .

And the world goes dark and silent.

20

Sofia

It's funny, the things you remember. The moments that are branded in our minds, the minutes you wish you could forget. I don't remember being afraid during that childhood plane crash, though I'm sure I was. I don't recall the pain when my side was sliced open. The shock, the adrenaline probably left me numb.

What I can still hear though, even after all these years . . . is the sound. The crash of the impact. The roar as we slid across the runway. It was thunderous and inescapable. I remember reaching up to cover my ears, when I should have been holding on for dear life.

And this sound—right now—is almost the same. The shrill screech of wind.

The rushing.

So loud. Deafening.

But that's not what stands out the most this time. The image that will haunt me from this moment on is Stanton, unmoving, on the ground. Eyes closed, his body slack and terribly still.

"No! Stanton!"

It's funny, how quickly clarity comes when life or death is at stake. When whipping, dirty, cold hell swirls all around you, bending the trees,

flinging scraps of wood and metal through the air. And you realize—
suddenly so absolutely sure—how deeply you feel for someone, how
much they mean to you, when you're faced with the possibility of having already lost them.

"Stanton, wake up!"

I was so angry when I walked out of the house, just a short while ago.

"Can you hear me? Baby, please wake up!"

No, that's bullshit. Time to put on the big girl panties.

I wasn't angry—I was hurt.

"Oh God, stay with me, Stanton. Don't you *dare* leave me!"

When I heard Jenny's admission, it felt like a steel poker had been
plunged into my stomach. Because what had happened between us at the
river last night—the way he looked at me, touched me, held me—seemed
like more, felt like it *meant* more, than all the other moments we'd shared.
And deep inside me, I'd hoped that it was the same for Stanton.

Apparently I'm a dummy after all.

And all the mental excuses I've made over the last days—the expla-
nations, justifications, defenses—were just lies I told myself, feelings I
pushed away and ignored.

Because I didn't want to admit it. Didn't want to face the complicated truth.

"I love you," I whisper.

It's horrifying. A mess. And the most true, pure thing I've ever felt
in my life.

"I *love* you, you big, stupid idiot!"

If I was thinking clearly, I'd recall all the reasons I shouldn't: his
story about Rebecca, the pedestal he has Jenny on, and how to him
we're nothing more than "friends who fuck." These feelings are the last
thing a guy like him would want to deal with.

But none of that matters. 'Cause I'm pretty sure we're both about
to die.

I've seen *The Wizard of Oz. Twister. Sharknado 1* and *2*.

Any minute now a house or a cow is going to fly by and do us in.

"*Please,* Stanton, I love you!"

I don't realize I'm crying until I see the drops on his perfect face. His head rests on my thighs, my back is curved, leaning over him, sheltering us both beneath my wildly blowing hair. I kiss his forehead, his nose, and finally linger at his warm lips.

Then I feel Stanton's fingers flex against my waist, clutching the material of my shirt. And I lean back just enough to look at his eyes as they finally open.

His pupils are wide, confused and searching. But within seconds they contract in understanding, realizing where we are.

In one fluid motion he rolls me underneath him, his weight pressing down on top of me, protecting me from the cutting wind and debris that churns around us.

I grip his shoulders, my voice still clogged with tears. And fear.

"You're all right? Thank God you're all right! I thought—"

Stanton smooths my hair with his hand and murmurs soft, calming words against my ear. "Shhh . . . I've got you, Sofia. I'm right here. We're okay now. I'm right here."

Though I know we're still in danger, I feel warm from the inside. Safe. I'm perfectly content, because he's in my arms and I am in his.

"You're lucky you woke up—you would've been on my eternal shit list if you hadn't."

His chest vibrates as he chuckles and lifts up to gaze down at me. His eyes caress my face, and his tender smile makes my chest squeeze tight. "Couldn't have that."

He sighs, then tucks my head under his chin.

"I think this clinches it," I tell him, snuggling even closer. "I'm not cut out for prairie living."

He chuckles again. My fingers stroke up and down his back. We cling to each other, holding on tight, making it through the storm. Together.

• • •

As we drive back down to the Monroes', I look around. The damage isn't as bad as I'd imagined. Some downed trees, a lot of broken fences, but no real destruction to the house or the barn. In the back, the left-over signs from the party—overturned tables, bent chairs—are scattered around the yard. A tablecloth flaps in a tree, caught by its branches. Stanton drives around to the front of the house, just as Mr. Monroe, Jenny's father, is hustling into his own truck, his wife in the passenger seat beside him. Then he pulls out, tires screeching, driving like a bat out of hell. I catch his face as they pass—drawn, tight, terrified. Then Jenny hurries into her own truck, JD beside her, Presley and her red-headed sister in the back—and she's driving off too.

"What's wrong?" I wonder aloud. "Did someone get hurt?"

Stanton parks and jumps out of the truck quickly. I'm right beside him as he jogs over to his mother, her face every bit as dazed and worried as the rest of his family's.

"Is everyone all right, Momma?"

She puts her hand on his arm. "It's Nana."

21

Stanton

When I was young, the preacher would give sermons about hell. He made it sound like the inside of an erupting volcano with its burning lakes, molten lava, and painful depths. But I don't think hell is fire and brimstone.

I think hell is a hospital waiting room.

Interminably slow, every second ticking by like a clock with dying batteries. Frustration, fear—even boredom—so potent your head throbs.

"Is Nana gonna die, Daddy?"

Presley sits beside me on the bench, leaning against me, my arm around her. Sofia's on the other side, holding my hand. Jenny's been chasing down information, but even working here, the only answer she's able to get is "waiting on tests." JD gets her coffee, tells her to try and sit down. Jenny's parents and mine are scattered through the waiting room, along with a handful of neighbors who had family injured in the storm.

"I don't know, baby girl." I stroke her hair. "Nana's a strong woman. You should think good thoughts, say a prayer."

Just then Dr. Brown comes out and June, Wayne, Jenny, JD, and

Ruby converge. "It was a heart attack," he says, looking at Jenny's mother. "A big one. But she's stable. She'll be here a few days. We have to run several more tests, but there doesn't appear to be any lasting damage."

There's a collective sigh, heavy with relief. June asks, "Can we see her?"

The doctor replies, "Yes, she can have visitors, one at a time. But she's asking for Stanton."

And the sighs turn into a wave of *what the hells*.

I stand. "Me? Are you sure?"

The look on his face says Nana's been quite the pain in the ass about it. "She was very insistent."

My eyes meet Jenny's—both of us puzzled. Then I shrug and follow Dr. Brown down the hall, leaving June Monroe clucking in the waiting room like a hen whose egg's just been taken away.

He leaves me outside the closed door of Nana's room. I open it slowly and step in cautiously—aware that I'm entering the room of a crone who's threatened to shoot me on more than one occasion—and it's possible she's pocketed a needle or a scalpel that she has every intention of launching at my head.

Or somewhere lower.

But when I get inside, it's just Nana, in a hospital bed with covers pulled up to her chin. And for the first time in my life, she seems . . . frail. Old.

Weak.

When I swallow, I taste tears in the back of my throat. I don't think it makes me any less of a man to admit it. It's been one hell of a day.

And a hero needs his foe. It's only in this split second that I realize what a wonderfully formidable foe Nana has always been to me. How wrong it would be—how much I would miss her—if she couldn't fill that role anymore.

Her next words, wheezy and feeble, bring those tears straight to my eyes.

"Hello, boy."

I smile, my voice a bit strangled. "Ma'am."

Her brittle hand pats the space beside her and I sit in the chair next to the bed.

She regards me with a tired but determined expression—bent on having her say.

"You know why I never liked you, boy?"

I clear the knot from my throat and reply, "Because I knocked up your granddaughter?"

"Ha!" She waves her hand. "No. My Juney was bakin' in my oven for two months before I got around to sayin' my own vows."

That's more information than I ever needed to know.

"Is it because I didn't marry her?" I try again.

She shakes her head. "No." And pulls in a ragged breath. "It's 'cause, even when you first came sniffin' around my grandbaby, a twelve-year-old nothin' carryin' a football . . . even then, I could see you were goin'. Had that look in your eyes, a hankering for somewhere else—the way a colt looks at a closed gate, just waitin' for someone to leave the latch off. Rarin' to go."

I nod slowly, because she's not wrong.

"And I knew . . . if you had the chance . . . you'd take her with you." Her cloudy eyes look into mine, seeing straight through me.

"But you're not takin' her with you anymore, are you, boy?"

I blow out a breath and sit back in the chair. All the things that have been twisting me up, swirling in my head the last few days, have suddenly straightened out. So clear. Such a simple answer.

"No, ma'am, I'm not."

Nana's face relaxes a bit and she seems relieved to have the confirmation. "Some horses like bein' penned. Belongin' to someone, grazin' on the land they know—don't have the desire to venture out."

And I think back to every late-night riverbank talk Jenny and I shared, filled with fire and dreams. Of *different*. And my mind's eye sees what that seventeen-year-old boy didn't—Jenny's enthusiasm was always for *me*, but never for *us*. Because her heart was here, in this small town with its warm people. She didn't have any need for more . . . and I was already gone.

"It's important," Nana says, patting my hand, "that a woman doesn't feel like the ugly sister. The second, lesser choice. That's a bitterness that won't sweeten."

I blink down at her. "How did you . . ."

"Jus' 'cause I'm goin' blind, doesn't mean I don't see."

I close my eyes and it's Sofia's face that comes alive. Her smile, her laugh, that sharp mouth, those arms that can hold so tight and tender, I would gladly stay within them for every moment of a lifetime.

I cover my face with my hands.

Fuck me.

"I have screwed up, ma'am. Everything. Badly."

"Well then, fix it," she gibes. "That's what men do—they fix things."

"I don't know where I'm supposed to start." My hand rises. "And before you say 'at the beginning,' we've already begun. How am I supposed to show her that it's always been her—when everything I said, everything I did, told her it wasn't?"

A grin blooms on Nana's lips. "My Henry, God rest his soul, was not a handy man. Bought me a gardenin' shed once, to keep my tools. Came with directions in ten languages. Henry put it together—and it was the most pitiful thing I ever saw. Crooked walls, upside-down door. So . . . he took it apart piece by piece and started all over again. Took a bit of time, but it was worth it, 'cause in the end, that little shed . . . turned out perfect. You have to start all over again, too—from the beginnin'."

I think about being back in DC. All the things I want to do for her, all the words I want to say . . . to start over. To show her. But it'll have to be after the wedding. After things are settled here with Jenn. That way, Sofia will see with her own eyes that I'm past it. That what I share with Jenny doesn't diminish what I feel for her. So she won't have any doubts—and she'll believe me.

Nana scowls. "Now, don't you go tellin' anyone what we discussed. It's private. I have a reputation to uphold."

I laugh. Both from Nana's warning and because now I have a plan.

She points at the door. "Go on, then. Bring my daughter in here before she busts the door down."

I lean over, take my life in my hands—and kiss Nana on the cheek. "Thank you, ma'am."

"You're welcome, boy."

• • •

Back in the waiting room, I give June the go-ahead. Then I answer Jenny's inquisitional stare. "She's all right." I squeeze her shoulder. "Don't worry—that woman's too goddamn mean to die."

Jenny laughs, hugging me with relief. When we step back, I tell her I'm taking Presley back to my parents' for the night. Then I put my arm around Sofia, and the three of us walk out the door.

21

Sofia

On Friday morning, I'm pulled from the deep sleep of the emotionally spent by sunlight on my face . . . and a tickling on my nose. My eyes crack open . . . and Brent Mason's face, smiling as big as Pennywise the evil clown, is the first thing I see.

"Rise and shine, cupcake!"

"Ahh!" I yell, snapping back—hitting the back of my skull against Stanton's forehead. Presley came back with us last night—and he tucked her into bed in Carter's room across the way. Then the two of us came in here together, and promptly fell right to sleep.

What in God's name is Brent doing here? In Stanton's bedroom? In Missi-freaking-ssippi?

Stanton's arm pulls me against him and his hand pushes my head back down on the pillow. "It's a nightmare," he murmurs. "Go back to sleep and they'll go away."

They?

I sit up. Jake Becker waves at me from the corner chair. "What are you two doing here? And more important—where the hell is my dog?"

Brent peers at Stanton's football trophies. "Sherman's fine—he's with Harrison, they're best buddies."

Harrison is Brent's butler. He's an endearingly young, rigidly proper, twenty-one-year-old butler who comes from a long line of butlers. Harrison's father is Brent's parents' butler—like a happy indentured servant family. Part of Brent's life mission is to get Harrison to act like a normal twenty-one-year-old—just once.

"But why are you *here*?" I ask, my voice still scratchy with sleep.

Brent shrugs. "I've been to Milan, Paris, Rome—but never to the Gulf Coast. I thought it'd be interesting to see Shaw's hometown for the weekend. Broaden my horizons. Jake's visited before; he knew the way. And we missed you guys—the office has been lonely without you. You made it sound so great on the phone, I knew I had to come experience it for myself."

Then Jake tells us the real reason.

"Brent's parents are flying into DC for the weekend. He hauled ass like the running of the bulls was behind him."

Brent turns to Jake with a scowl. "Don't judge me. My mother is a frightening woman."

"She's a four-ten, ninety-pound socialite who doesn't speak above a whisper," Jake scoffs. "Terrifying."

"Two of my cousins just announced their engagement, and a third sent out birth announcements for their first child. My mother was going to show up with a list of debutantes and refuse to leave until I chose one. It would've been brutal."

Jake stands. "Speaking of mothers, Momma Shaw sent us up here to grab you two for breakfast." He throws a pair of jeans at Stanton's head. "You might want to put pants on."

With this wake-up call, I'm grateful to be wearing my more conservative pajamas.

"How's Operation Wedding Destruction going?" Brent asks as Stanton and I climb out of bed.

I make my tone lighter than I feel. "Well, there was a tornado yesterday. That should throw a wrench into things."

Stanton rubs a tired hand down his face. "No, it won't."

I turn my head—genuinely surprised. "Really? You don't think so?"

He pulls a T-shirt over his head. "If there's one thing citizens of Sunshine know how to do well, it's make the best with what you've got."

• • •

We fill Brent and Jake in on the tornado on the way into the house. In the kitchen, Stanton's mother is setting down plates of food on the table and Marshall shovels oatmeal into his mouth, yelling up the stairs for his sister to hurry. Mr. Shaw had left hours earlier to tend to an outbuilding damaged in the storm. I close my eyes as I sip from a cup of much-needed hot coffee. Brent comments on the beauty of the ranch, and thanks Mrs. Shaw for her hospitality. Conversation turns to the summer weeks when Stanton was in law school and would come home to visit, and bring Jake with him.

Then, much to her brother's relief, Mary comes skipping down the stairs, dressed for school in a beige skirt and pink tank top. She greets me, Stanton, and Jake—then her eyes light up like a jack-o'-lantern when they land on Brent.

"Why have I not been introduced to this piece of deliciousness?" she teases. She holds out her hand. "I'm Mary Louise . . . and you are?"

Brent swallows a bit of biscuit and shakes her hand. "Brent Mason; it's a pleasure."

As Mary sits in the empty chair beside him, she hums under her breath. "I'm bettin' it will be."

He looks at me questioningly, and all I can do is shrug back.

"You work with my brother?" Mary asks, leaning over.

"That's right," Brent says.

"That's so interestin'." She sighs, resting her chin on her hand. "Are you a college intern?"

Brent clear his throat. "No . . . I'm a lawyer. An old, boring lawyer." When she just continues to stare adoringly, he adds, "Very old."

"I really wish you boys would stay with us," Mrs. Shaw laments as she finally sits down to eat her own breakfast. "Doesn't seem right to have y'all stayin' at the hotel."

The hotel—'cause like the stoplight, there's only one.

"Brent can stay in my room," Mary announces. Before her mother can respond with more than a frown, she giggles. "I'm jus' jokin'."

Then she turns to Brent and mouths *No I'm not* with a Lolita-like wink.

I cover my mouth at Brent's horrified expression and look around to see if anyone else noticed. Jake's intent on finishing his food, and Stanton . . . Stanton stares dejectedly into his coffee cup.

"Thank you, Mrs. Shaw, but really, the hotel is great."

Mary leans back, her hands disappear under the table—and ten seconds later Brent jumps up like he's been electrified.

"Whoa!"

All eyes turn to him. Mary bats her lashes innocently.

"What's your problem, nervous and jerky?" Jake asks.

Brent opens his mouth like a fish searching for water. "I . . . just can't wait to see the rest of the place! No time like the present. Let's go!"

I bring my dishes to the sink and the four of us head toward the door.

"Bye, Brent," Mary sings.

Brent waves uncomfortably, then whispers to me, "That's it—I'm growing a fucking beard."

• • •

We spend the rest of the morning showing Jake and Brent around the ranch. Stanton is quiet—distracted.

Later in the afternoon, Stanton takes Brent and Jake out to the pastures to help his father with the clean-up. While they're gone, Mrs. Shaw tells me we'll be heading to the one local tavern for the evening and that I should get ready. The sun is setting when I step out of the bathroom, wearing my favorite red slip dress, to find that Stanton's back. Waiting in my room.

And he's alone.

He stares at me like it's the first time he's seeing me—long enough for a whole host of butterflies to dance in my stomach.

"You are beautiful," he says in a low, awed voice with just a touch of southern.

Three words.

Such a simple compliment. But because it's him—it feels like the most wonderful thing anyone could ever say to me.

The tavern is a small place, with wooden floors, a worn oak bar, a few scattered square tables, and two pool tables in the back room. Five of us sit together at a table—Jake is having a loud, raucous time with Ruby Monroe, Jenny's sister, and Brent seems more relaxed without having to dodge the wandering, underage hands of Mary Shaw.

I excuse myself from the table and head to the ladies' room. When I walk back out, I stop in my tracks. Because through the crowd I see Stanton rise from his chair and walk to the jukebox. He fills it with quarters from his pocket, and the twinkling sounds of piano keys override the noise of conversation in the crowded bar. He strides to where Jenny and JD are sitting side by side, and his lips move—asking a question I can't decipher. JD nods his head and after a moment, shakes Stanton's outstretched hand. Then Jenny stands and together they walk to the dance floor. Willie Nelson's mournful voice fills the air singing "Always on My Mind."

I watch as he takes Jenny in his arms—the strong, beautiful arms that have held me, made me feel cherished with their warmth. The arms I've gripped in pleasure and passion more times that I can remember.

He gathers her close to his chest, the chest I laid my cheek on just last night, lulled to sleep by the sound of his steadfast heartbeat.

And together, they sway.

I don't feel the tears rise until they're blurring my vision and streaming down my face. My throat constricts, and the purest of pain squeezes my chest like a cruel vise.

I can't do this anymore.

I know it now. I can't stand by and pretend to help him fight for her.

Because I want him to fight for me.

More than anything.

For him to want me—not just as a friend or a lover. But as his forever.

Like she is.

Jenny looks up into his eyes. Their expressions are tender as they speak, and I thank God I can't hear the words. Then Stanton raises his hand to touch her face . . . and I squeeze my eyes closed, blocking the intimate gesture.

A moment later I'm heading for the door. Self-preservation compels me, Willie's lyrics of love and regret chase me, but I don't look back.

Outside, the air is moist, thick—I gulp it in with pathetic hiccups and seek the comfort of my own arms, wrapped around my waist.

"Sofia?"

Brent's voice approaches from my left, coming closer as he calls my name again. I don't try to hide my . . . sadness? That's not a strong enough word. Devastation hits the nail on the head. I feel like a building that's about to collapse, the foundation I built, the structure and support that I thought would keep me standing falling away beneath my feet. And Brent sees it all.

His head angles in sympathetic reflection, but what strikes me most is—he's not surprised. Not even a little.

He sits on the sidewalk bench and pats his lap. "Looks like somebody needs a ride on the therapy train. Hop on. Tell Dr. Brent all about it."

There's no shame as I perch myself on his thighs.

"He doesn't dance," I whisper.

Brent nods slowly. Waiting for me to continue.

"But he's dancing with her."

The words sound completely ridiculous said out loud, but I don't care. The dam breaks, and my face crumbles. "I thought I had a wall, you know? I didn't think I'd be the woman who wanted more. I'm an idiot, Brent."

A low chuckle reverberates through his chest. "You're not an idiot, sweetheart—that designation belongs to the blind southerner you're crying over."

I raise my head and look into Brent's forever kind blue eyes. He's always reminded me of my brother Tomás. They share that same comforting attitude that makes you feel that anything coming their way, no matter how devastating, will be handled.

"How can he not know?" I ask. "Why can't he see how hard this is for me?"

Brent brushes my long hair off my shoulders. "In fairness to Stanton, you're a good actress. And . . . sometimes it's hard for guys to read between the lines. To pick up on all the things that aren't said. Some of us need it spelled out."

Brent holds me for a few minutes more as I soak up his calm, making it my own. Then I drag my fingers under my eyes, wiping away the melting mascara that probably makes me look like a raccoon.

"Soph?" That voice comes from the shadows behind us, deep with worry. I feel him move closer, without turning to look. "What's wrong? What happened?"

Having all of Stanton's attention, sensing his concern and knowing in my heart that he'd rain down hell in my defense—I admit it feels good. For a moment. But it's only an emotional crumb. One that used to satisfy me, but now will only end up magnifying the emptiness. Leave me starving for all the things he doesn't feel for me.

Clawing myself together, I stand from Brent's lap and face him head-on. Stanton reaches out to touch me, but I step back. "I'm fine."

"You're obviously not. What the hell happened?"

I shake my head. "I don't feel well." That's true, at least. "I want to go back to the house."

"All right, I'll—"

I step further back, bumping against the bench. "No. Not you."

The thought of being in the closed space of a vehicle with him is horrifying. I need more time to collect myself, so I'm not reduced to a quivering mass clinging to his leg, begging him to love me.

Wouldn't that be attractive?

Confusion displaces the concern clouding his eyes. "But . . ."

"I'll drive her."

We all turn to the door of the bar, where tiny, blond, and perfect Jenny Monroe stands beside her fiancé. I didn't realize we'd drawn an audience. And although she's not exactly my favorite person at the moment, I'll take her.

"Thank you."

Brushing past Stanton, I follow Jenny as she fishes keys from the purse slung across her shoulder, walking briskly to the parking lot.

Stanton doggedly trails us. "Hey! Just wait one damn—"

"Go back to the bar, Stanton," Jenny calls. "Have a beer with JD and talk about how y'all are gonna keep your brother from takin' his clothes off."

In a conspiratorial tone, she tells me, "Carter tends to get over-heated when he's drunk, and his nudist tendencies come out. The idiot'll be bare ass by midnight."

With a touch to her key ring she unlocks the doors on the shiny black Ford pickup, and I scramble into the passenger seat like a teenager fleeing a machete-wielding maniac. The engine roars to life, she shifts into drive—and the headlights illuminate Stanton Shaw, stubbornly bracing his hands on the hood of the truck, blocking our way.

Jenny opens the window. "Boy, if you don't move, I'll run you down. Won't kill you, but you won't be nearly as persuasive hobblin' around a courtroom on crutches."

Keeping distrustful hands on the truck, he moves around to Jenny's open window. I keep my eyes trained straight ahead, but I feel his gaze on me.

"Sofia." His voice is harsh but pleading at the same time. "Sofia, look at me, damn it!"

Jenny leans forward, obscuring his view. "Let her be, Stanton. Sometimes a woman just needs another woman. Give her space."

From the corner of my eye, she pats his forearm, and after a moment his hands fall away from the truck. She doesn't give him a chance to change his mind; the spinning tires spit gravel and dust as we pull out of the parking lot.

• • •

Except for my occasional sniffle, it's quiet inside the cab of the truck as we drive down the dark, empty roads. I don't quite know how I'm supposed to feel about the woman beside me. In basic terms, she's my competition. I'm well acquainted with rivalry; I live it and breathe it in my career—outperforming the prosecutors at trial, outshining my fellow attorneys as we all vie for a coveted partnership. There are moments when I know I'm better than my opposition, and times when I have to dig deep to surpass those who are my equal, if not more talented.

The difference here is I actually like Jenny. If circumstances were different, she and I could've been friends. She's smart and fun to be around. I understand why Stanton loves her. And the part of me that's his friend—that wants his happiness more than my own—doesn't want her to marry JD.

But then there's the other part—the one who loves Stanton—who wants to scratch Jenny's eyes out. Who wants her to disappear, or even better, to have never existed in the first place.

"How long have you loved him?"

The question is gently posed, like a pediatrician would ask the parent of a sick child how long they've been like this.

"From the beginning, I think. I didn't . . . admit it. I thought it was just physical attraction . . . friendship . . . convenience. But now . . . I realize it was always more."

She nods. "There's just somethin' about a man from Mississippi. Damn southern charm is in the DNA—they don't even have to work at it." She pauses as she turns the truck onto an equally desolate road. "And Stanton . . . he's even more overwhelming. Brilliant, hardworkin', handsome, and he fucks like a beast."

I bark out a shocked laugh.

Jenny laughs too. "My momma would smack the teeth out of my head if she heard me say that, but god help me, it's true."

Our giggles quiet and Jenny sighs. "A woman would have to be ten times a fool not to fall in love with that man." She glances at me knowingly. "And you don't look like a fool to me."

After she turns away, I continue to stare. "How did you do it? How did you stop loving him?"

The last few days have been like torture. Every profession of his affection for her stung like the lash of a barbed whip. The yearning I've seen in those stunning green eyes, the tenderness they hold for her, burned like an electric shock, stealing my breath.

Sex with Stanton is exhilarating; working beside him is a privilege. But loving him . . . that just hurts.

Her mouth twitches. "I don't think I ever *did* stop. It just . . .

changed into somethin' else. Somethin' quieter, less crazed. When you're young, you love fireworks 'cause they're loud and bright and thrillin'. But then you grow up. And you see that candlelight isn't so thrillin', but it still makes everything better. You realize that the glow of a fireplace can be just as excitin' as fireworks—the way it burns low, but lights your home and keeps you warm all night long. Stanton was my fireworks . . . JD's my fireplace."

"But Stanton's in love with you."

She glances at me sideways. "You really believe that?"

"It doesn't matter what I believe. Only what he does."

She shakes her head. "You should talk to him—tell him how you feel."

It's easy for her to say—she lives across the country from him. I'll have to see him and work with him every day after this weekend. Right now, I have his friendship, his admiration. His respect.

I'm not sure I could live with his pity.

Jenny drives the truck behind Stanton's parents' house, up to the entrance of the barn. Before I get out, I turn to her. "It was really nice meeting you, Jenny. You have a beautiful daughter, and I hope . . . I really hope your wedding day is perfect."

Her head tilts. "You won't be around for the weddin' tomorrow, will you?"

I confirm her suspicions with the shake of my head.

She nods, understanding. "I hope . . . well, I hope you come back here one day, Sofia, and when you do, I hope you're smilin'."

Then she wraps her arms around me and gives me a hug. It's warm and kind, and above all—genuine.

• • •

Packing takes longer than I'd thought. Why, *why* did I bring so much? Three bags down, two to go. I grab the last of my T-shirts from the drawer and turn to place them in the open suitcase on the bed. But I freeze when I hear the hoarse, fraught voice from the doorway.

"You're leavin'?"

Did I actually think I'd be able to pack and leave town without facing him? Without having this conversation? *Stupid Sofia.*

I don't look at him—if I do, I'll disintegrate into a blubbery mass. I need time—distance.

"I have to go home. I'm so behind, a lot of work to catch up on . . ."

He moves in front of me. I stare at his chest, as it rises and falls beneath the soft cotton T-shirt. He takes the clothes from my hands. "You're not goin' anywhere, until you talk to me."

I close my eyes, feeling my pulse throb frantically in my neck.

"What happened, Sofia?"

Against my will, my gaze rises, meeting his. It swims with concern, overflows with confusion . . . with affection and caring.

But it's not enough.

"What happened? I fell in love with you." The words come out in a whisper—everything I feel for him a sharp, rigid thorn lodged in my throat. And the pain that he doesn't feel the same is a noose cinching tighter and tighter. "I love everything about you. I love watching you in court—the way you speak, the way you move. I love how you scrape your lip when you're trying to think of what to say. I love your voice, I love your hands and the way they touch me. I love . . . the way you look at your daughter, I love how you say my name." My voice shatters at the end, and my eyes close, releasing a flood.

"No, baby, don't cry," he begs.

His hands rise to my face, but I step back, afraid the contact will completely break me. The words rush out. "I know that isn't what this is for you. And I tried to ignore it, to push it away. But it just hurt so much to see you with. . ."

His head is bowed from my pain. "Sofia, I'm sorry . . . just let me . . ."

I shake my head and squeeze my eyes closed again. "Don't be sorry—it's not your fault. I have to just . . . get over it. I will. I can't . . . I can't be with you anymore that way, Stanton. I know you'll be hurting from Jenny . . . But—"

"That's not what I meant! Slow down, please. *Listen* to me."

But if I stop to listen, I'll never get it all out. He'll never understand. And I meant what I said—I don't want to lose him.

"We'll be friends again. This won't come between us. We can go back—"

I never finish the words. His mouth covers mine, cutting them off, swallowing them whole. He grasps my face, pulling me to him—touching me like he never has before. With desperation, like he'll die if he has to let me go.

His desire for me is a palpable, throbbing ache between us—and I submerge myself in it, willing to drown. His fingertips are hot on my skin, scorching enough to scar. And I hope they do. I yearn for remembrance. Proof that I was here, that this is what we felt. That even for a moment . . . we were real.

He turns us and we fall to the bed, the feel of his strength, his rigid length pressing down on me, a welcome weight. I writhe beneath him and Stanton tears at my clothes like they're the enemy.

It's not a smart thing to do; it'll hurt in the morning. But I won't say no. This . . . this I get to have.

The pant of his breath, the scrape of his teeth, the sound of his moans, the pressure of his wet, perfect kisses. These are the moments— the memories—I'll hold on to and cherish.

Because they'll be the last.

22

Stanton

Everyone always talks about how quiet and peaceful the country is. But that's not totally accurate. The cacophony begins at dusk—grasshoppers, mosquitoes, crickets, and scurrying vermin, louder than you'd ever think possible. And at dawn, there's the baying of animals, the machine-gun clicking of cicadas, the thumping of hooves, and the deafening sonata of chirping birds.

It's the birds that pull me from sleep—the deep slumber of a man who's at peace with a choice he's made.

Even before my eyes crack open, I know she's gone.

I feel it in the empty space beside me, the missing scent of shampoo and gardenia and Sofia. I bolt upright, squinting, and look around.

Luggage? Gone.

Jeans on the desk? Nowhere in sight.

Red dress from the floor? Vanished.

Fuck.

How the hell could I fall asleep without talking to her first? Without telling her—

"Sonofabitch!"

I jump into a pair of jeans and run shirtless and barefoot down the stairs. I jog into the house—hoping.

But when I get there, the only person in the kitchen is Brent, sipping a cup of coffee and eating one of my mother's blueberry muffins.

"Where is she?" I growl—pissed at myself, but all too willing to take it out on him.

He swallows the mouthful of muffin, regarding me with distant, assessing eyes. "She called the hotel about four this morning. Asked for a ride to the airport. Jake wouldn't let her go alone and changed his ticket to fly back with her."

My chest goes hollow. I've fucked up so badly.

But then I remember— "Sofia doesn't fly."

Brent's gaze warms just a little—with pity. "Then I guess she really wanted to get out of Dodge—because she flew today."

I collapse in the chair, wheels already turning, figuring out ways to track her down—*tie* her down if necessary. "Why didn't you wake me up?"

"She asked us not to. Said she needed to pull herself together. She promised that by the time we get back, everything will be back to normal." He pauses, then adds, "I'm sorry, Stanton."

I bang the table. "I don't *want* things back to goddamn normal! I love her, Brent!"

He scratches the new growth of brown stubble on his chin. "I'm not Dr. Phil or anything—but you probably should've mentioned that to her."

There comes a time in every man's life when he takes a good, long look at himself and admits he's been an asshole. A self-centered prick.

I don't know if it's the same for women, but if you've got a dick, it's inevitable. Because even good men, brave men, world leaders, renowned scientists, theologians, and Rhodes scholars have a greedy, selfish space inside them. A childish, needy black hole that will never be satiated.

Look at me, listen to me, it says. It wants what it can't have, as well as all the things it can. It wants to eat *all* the fucking cakes. It knows the world doesn't revolve around us, but that doesn't stop it from trying to defy the laws of physics and make it that way.

This is my asshole moment. Forsaken by the woman I love. The infuriatingly beautiful girl I have no intention of living without.

The worst part is, I see how it all went wrong. Every mistake. Every terrible choice.

If I'd had the awareness to step back and evaluate the situation from the outside, none of this would've happened. But I was deep in the black hole—with only me, myself, and I for company.

My momma would say my chickens have come home to roost. It's a fitting metaphor. Fowl possess a never-ending supply of shit that they proudly leave in their wake. So when they roost?

It just plain stinks.

Brent wipes his mouth with a napkin and stands. "In any case, it's nine thirty—the wedding starts in two hours. I need a lift back to the hotel to get dressed. JD invited me last night—hell of a guy."

I snort. "Yeah—Saint fucking JD."

He smacks my arm. "Don't worry, you're still the coolest southerner I know."

It's only then that I notice how still the house is. This house is never still. "Where is everyone?"

Brent heads toward the back door, ticking off his fingers. "Your mother's getting her hair done, your father's taking a nap—which apparently he rarely gets to do. Carter is passed out on the living room couch, naked. And your little brother hasn't come home yet." Then he points at me. "Oh, and your sister, Mary? Scares the fuck out of me. If I go missing tonight, promise me her closet is the first place you'll look."

I laugh. And force myself to bury my feelings—the panic, the yearning—for Sofia. Swallow it down, suck it up. Because today . . . my girl's getting married.

. . .

The church is filled to the brim. Miss Bea plays the "Bridal Chorus" on that old organ. Presley scatters rose petals down the aisle. And Jenny . . . Jenny is gorgeous, as I knew she would be. I watch JD's face when she steps into the church—it's filled with wonder and gratitude and so much love.

And it doesn't make me want to punch him—not even a little. It doesn't make me sad.

It just feels . . . like it's something that's supposed to be.

The reception is held outside, behind the church, in white tents with elegantly decorated picnic tables and padded folding chairs. The grass is as green as my daddy's pastures, the sky almost as blue as my daughter's eyes. The whole town is here—the people who've known me even before I was born. Brent chats with Pastor Thompson. Marshall leans against a tree, trying to look cool talking to a girl. Mary's surrounded by a group of giggling females, all whispers and wide eyes. Carter holds court on the grass, preaching to a gaggle of worshipful-faced kids, who gaze at him like he's Jesus Christ on the mount. My parents dance to the band's music.

The only thing missing . . . is her.

I've tried calling a few times, but it goes to voice mail. I tell myself that she just forgot to turn it back on after the flight, but my powers of persuasion appear to be stronger with a jury than with my own fucking head.

"I saved a dance for you. Feel like cashin' it in?"

Jenny stands next to me, hands folded, smiling. We head out onto the wooden makeshift dance floor. As we slowly rock I tell her, "You look stunning."

She bats her lashes. "I know."

We chuckle and then, cautiously, she asks, "Sofia went back to DC?"

I nod silently.

"I like her, Stanton. I hope you don't plan on letting her get away."

"I have no intention of letting her get away—she just doesn't know that yet."

I look down into Jenny's baby blues, hold her in my arms—my dearest, sweetest friend.

"I'm glad you didn't let JD get away. You deserve to be looked at the way he looks at you."

She pushes my hair back from my forehead. "You deserve that too." She glances over my shoulder for a moment, and then her gaze is back to me. "Remember the other day by the river? When you said that Presley and I are your family?"

"Yeah."

Her eyes grow shiny with emotion. "We'll always be your family."

Warmth rises in my stomach—a comforting, tender sort of heat. Presley's voice catches both our ears and at the same time, we look over at our beautiful, laughing baby girl.

"We did good though, didn't we, Stanton? All things considered."

My voice is rough, choked with feeling. "Ah, Jenn—we did *great*. Just look at her."

And for a time, we do. Intimately joined by memories and the unending love for the same little person.

"If I could go back and do it all over again with you, I would," Jenny whispers. "I wouldn't change a thing."

I look into her eyes, and then I press my lips to her forehead gently. "Me too. Not a single thing."

And that's how Jenny and I say good-bye.

• • •

Later on, I sit on the wooden, two-seater swing beside Presley, watching the celebration continue. "And then, when school lets out, you'll come to DC for the summer."

"For the whole summer, right? You promise?"

"The whole summer," I say, nodding. "You have my word."

"Will Miss Sofia be there?"

"She will be, yes."

My daughter looks at me sideways, with round, knowing eyes. "Did you screw that up, Daddy?"

A little bit, yeah. But I'll make it right."

She bestows her approval with a quick nod of her head. "Good."

A blond boy in a button-down shirt and clip-on tie calls from a few feet away. "Hey, Presley! We're goin' down the river—you comin'?"

"I'll be right there," she shouts back.

My brow puckers. "That was Ethan Fortenbury, wasn't it?"

"Yep, that's him."

"I thought he was a horse's anus."

"Well," she sighs, "he said he was sorry for sayin' I had man hands. Tol' me he only did it 'cause his older brother dared him to."

This sounds uncomfortably familiar.

"Those big brothers can certainly be trouble."

Then she grins bashfully. "He thinks I'm pretty. And he likes how I throw a football."

Oh shit.

"He's got good eyesight, then."

"Yeah."

She stands up, smoothing her blue satin dress. Before she runs off, I implore, "Hey baby girl, can you promise me somethin'?"

"Sure."

"Just give me a few more years before you start turnin' my whiskers gray, okay?"

She laughs and kisses my cheek. "Alright, Daddy—I promise."

Then she skips off.

And I shake my head. "Ethan fucking Fortenbury. Sonofabitch."

23

Stanton

Brent and I make record time driving back to DC—I pushed my Porsche to the limit and she did not let me down. I refused to stop overnight, so one of us slept in the passenger seat while the other drove. For two men over six feet, sleeping in a Porsche is not conducive to happy fucking dreams, but Brent didn't complain. He knew it was killing me to be so far away and he put "Ride of the Valkyries" on repeat to help lighten the mood.

I park in front of his townhouse and jog down the block to Sofia's. As I get closer, I see boxes on her stoop and furniture stationed at her curb. My heart starts to hammer in my chest. Is she moving?

I knock hard on her front door, impatience pushing on my back. The door opens . . . and a giant looks back at me. Literally. Six-five, wide chest, arms like a professional wrestler, and a menacing scowl.

"What do you want?"

And I feel like a ten-year-old kid. "Is Sofia home?"

"Who wants to know?" From shoes to head, his eyes appraise me. *Hazel eyes*. Eyes I'm intimately familiar with.

I point my finger. "You're the brother—the one she said could kick my ass. The doctor." He doesn't nod, but he also doesn't say I'm wrong.

"I'm . . . your sister and I are . . ." I refuse to call her my friend, 'cause she's much more than that. So for the first time in my life, I stutter—like a goddamn idiot. "I'm her . . . we're . . . she told me all about you."

He crosses his arms, and they grow even larger. "She hasn't said a word about you."

Before I can respond, another guy comes to the door—this one more normal size, a little bit shorter than me. He has thick, short brown hair, a friendly smile, and teasing brown eyes—just like Sofia described him.

"Victor, come on, the couch isn't going to move itself," he says to Gigantor. Then he notices me. "Hey."

I hold my hand out, eager to introduce myself to Sofia's closest brother. "Stanton Shaw. You're Tomás?"

He shakes my hand and his smile broadens. "That's right. How are you doing, Stanton? Come on in, Sofia's told me about you."

Gigantor steps aside as I walk in. "Why didn't she tell *me* all about him?"

Tomás gives his brother a look that I've seen on my own brothers' faces. "'Cause you can't keep a secret—none of us tell you anything." Then he smacks me on the back and asks, "Have you come to grovel?"

I chuckle, maybe just a bit nervously. "Yeah. How'd you know?"

"I know my sister."

"What does he have to grovel for?" Gigantor asks.

"Doesn't matter," Tomás tells him. "As long as he's here."

Then we walk into the living room—stepping around boxes and furniture. Looks like the tornado hit here instead of Mississippi.

"Sofia felt the place needed a makeover," Tomás explains. "She gets like that when she's stressed. So she rallied the troops and here we are."

In the kitchen I see another dark-haired guy wearing round John Lennon glasses—Lucas, brother number two, I'm guessing. Near the couch is an older but still solidly built man with salt-and-pepper hair.

Sofia's father.

I walk up to him and hold out my hand. "Hello, Mr. Santos, I'm Stanton Shaw. It's an honor to meet you." I pause, trying to think of the right words. "I think your daughter's an amazing woman, sir."

He pins me with his stare for a few moments. Then he grins and shakes my hand. "It's good to meet you, Mr. Shaw."

All heads turn to the woman coming down the stairs. She's smaller than I'd imagined Sofia's mother to be, with shoulder-length dark hair and lovely, familiar features. Her eyes settle on me, filled with recognition—and animosity. And I know Tomás isn't the only member of her family Sofia poured her heart out to.

I approach her, holding out my hand. "It's nice to meet you, Mrs. Santos, I'm—"

She glances at my hand with disdain and cuts me off—in Portuguese. *"Você é um homem estúpido que machucou a minha filha. Se eu tivesse meu caminho, eles nunca iria encontrar o seu corpo."*

It would seem I'm a stupid man, and if she had her way they'd never find my body.

Nice.

I shake my head. *"Estou aqui para fazer isso direito. Sofia significa . . . tudo para mim."* I'm here to make it right. Because Sofia means everything to me.

At least, I hope that's what I said.

Her eyes flash with surprise.

"Sofia's been teaching me Portuguese," I explain with a shrug. "I'm a fast learner."

A reluctant smile tugs at Mrs. Santos's lips and her head tilts with begrudging approval. Then she steps aside. "She's upstairs, in the bedroom, painting."

I nod. "Thank you, ma'am."

• • •

I step softly through the open doorway. Her back is to me as she stares at fresh paint on the wall. I take the opportunity to soak her in, like a plant that hasn't seen the sun in a year. Her hair is pulled up, tiny wisps brushing the sweet-tasting skin below her ear. I take in her delicate shoulders under a red T-shirt, black yoga pants, the elegant curve of her spine that leads down to the luscious swell of her ass—also sweet tasting.

"What do you think, Mamãe?" she asks without turning, her head tilted. "I'm not sure about the yellow; it's duller than it looked on the swatch."

"I think it looks like dried dog piss, if you want the truth."

She whips around, eyes wide like she's seeing a ghost. "Stanton!" After a moment, she blinks, trying to rein in her surprise. To act casual. "When did you get home?"

But casual can kiss my ass.

"I haven't been home. I dropped Brent off and came straight here. To you." Now I eat up the view from the front—those lips, her amazing breasts that I want to rest my head on, the green speckles in her eyes, like precious gems.

I lift my chin toward the paint cans. "What's that about?"

She looks between me and the cans, nervously. "Redecorating—it felt like I needed a new start."

I move forward, needing to be closer. And I've held back about as much as I'm capable of. "Christ I've missed you, Soph. The last two days have felt like forever."

Her gaze drops to the floor. "I'm sorry I left like I did, but I needed to—"

"No." I stalk the rest of the way across the room. "You had your chance to talk. You rested your case—now it's my turn." I kick a folding chair toward her, and there's a definite warning in my voice. "So sit down and listen up."

Her eyes widen, and for a second I think she's going to argue. But then she does as she's told.

I stand in front of her. "It started at the softball game, with Amsterdam staring at your ass."

"Stanton, I told you—"

"Quiet," I snap, pressing a finger against her now-closed lips. "When I wanted to rip his eyeballs out for lookin' at your ass, that was the first time it felt like . . . more. It wasn't my place to tell him not to look at you—but I wanted it to be."

I push a hand through my hair, trying to explain so she'll understand. "That's the real reason why I asked you to come with me—even though I didn't see it at the time. Because I didn't want to be away from you—didn't want to risk losin' you to someone else. And when I saw you there, in my home—with the people who mean the most to me . . . it got more intense. Wantin' you, needin' you, feelin' so fuckin' grateful to have you. But it was all screwed up—mixed up with Jenny gettin' married, feelin' like I needed to do somethin' to keep from losin' her."

She's leaning forward, hanging on every word, her eyes breaking my heart—filled with hope and fear. "When I got it sorted out in my head, when I finally had the balls to admit to myself how much you meant to me . . . it was already too late. I didn't know if there was a chance you felt the same way. I didn't know how to tell you without it lookin' like you were just the rebound. And I never wanted you to feel that way—not for a minute.

"Jenny will always be my friend, the mother of the little girl who owns my heart, the first girl I loved." Then my voice goes scratchy, strangled with emotion. "But you, Sofia . . . I swear, if you let me . . . you will be the last."

There are tears in her beautiful eyes, rolling down her cheeks. I crouch down in front of her, running my hand over her shoulder, holding the back of her neck. "And I'm so fuckin' pissed off at you. I want to sit down on that bed, strip you down, and spank your ass till it's as red as that wall downstairs."

She hiccups. "P . . . pissed at me? Why?"

"Because you let me hurt you. You never said anythin'. When I think about how it must've been for you . . . like a thousand paper cuts."

I hold her face, brush her tears away with my thumb, because I can't not touch her a second longer.

She blinks up at me, swallowing a breath. "That was one hell of a closing argument, Stanton."

I gaze into her eyes. "It's what I do. So . . . what's the verdict?"

She runs her fingers through my hair, her expression tender and soft. "The verdict is . . . no."

I knew it. Never doubted my powers of persuasion for a second. I was sure if I just had the chance to explain, she'd . . . wait.

What?

I lean back. "What the hell do you mean, *no*? You can't say no!" Moisture breaks out on my brow and my heart protests in my chest.

She shrugs. "I just did."

My hands tighten reflexively around her jaw. "What the fuck, Soph? Two days ago, you told me you were in love with me! You don't fall out of love with someone in two goddamn days!"

"Exactly," she says in a small voice.

"I don't under—"

"I've watched you pine over another woman for the last week. For months, I've heard you talk about Jenny this and Jenny that. And now that she's unavailable, you suddenly realize I'm the one you love?"

"I haven't been in love with Jenny for a very long time, Soph. I just didn't know it until now." I swallow hard. "You don't . . . you don't believe me?"

She touches my face, tracing my jaw, watching her fingers' path with rapt attention. "I want to. I want to believe you so bad." Then she withdraws her touch. "But . . . I can't be your rebound. I won't. That would break me, Stanton. A week ago, I was okay with having any part of you I could—but I'm not okay with that anymore. I want *all* of you. For real. And forever."

I lean closer, looking into her eyes. "Darlin', you have me. By the heart, by the balls, and any other way you want."

A smile tugs at her lips as she gazes boldly back at me. "Prove it."

Teeth scrape my bottom lip as I consider all the glorious ways I can demonstrate what she means to me—over and over again. There's laughter in my voice when I ask, "Is that a challenge?"

Color rises in her cheeks and the air between us shifts. Growing more intense, more heated—not just with attraction, but with the promise of something deeper. A future. Together.

"Yes."

I pull her closer, and brush my lips against hers, a feather light touch. And I swear to her, "Okay. Then we'll start over, from the beginnin'. The way we should've started. No friends with benefits. I'm goin' to do it right—take you out to gorgeous places, keep you in for whole weekends. I want you to get dressed up for me so I can take my time undressing you. I want to memorize every inch of your body and hear every thought in your mind. And then you won't have any doubt that the only woman I want, the only woman I love—is you."

Sofia leans in, her cheek, her nose skimming my own. Her voice is slightly breathless as she wonders, "So . . . that was you asking me out, right?"

"Definitely."

And then her eyes are sparkling. "I'd like to make it clear that I'm totally open to sex on the first date."

I chuckle. "I was really, really, hopin' you'd say that."

Then I press my lips to hers. Her mouth opens, welcoming, her sweet tongue meeting me halfway. I feel her hands gripping my shirt, sliding over my shoulders, up my neck, cupping my jaw. I pull her flush against me, holding her, letting her know with every brush of my fingers, every whispered word that I never want to let go. And I feel the same in her—relief, joy with each sigh, every soft promise. Sofia and I have kissed hundreds of times—but not like this. It's different. Better.

It's fucking perfect.

• • •

Most stories finish at the end. But not this one.

This one finishes with a whole new beginning.

Epilogue

Stanton

September

We recline on a blanket on the grass at the Washington Mall, in a semisecluded little spot set back from the crowd. The sky is pitch black, but the lights from the city are too bright to make out a single star. Sofia leans back against my chest and my hands wander over her lazily, skimming up her sides, covered by a light pink minidress, and down her bare arms. The September air is warm, with a nice breeze. A contented sigh escapes her smiling lips, and I take a sip from the plastic cup of bourbon I've been nursing all night. I press a soft kiss against her temple as Elton John taps out the final piano notes of his latest song.

Events like this—a fall music festival—are free, first come, first serve. Even though Sofia was all quivery that Elton John would be playing, we didn't kill ourselves trying to get front-row spots. She was content to just sit back and relax after a hellishly long week at the office. To enjoy the music . . . and each other.

But as the familiar melody of "Your Song" pours out from the speakers, I place my mouth against her ear, my breath raising goose bumps along her supple skin.

"Dance with me," I whisper.

She arches her back to gaze at me, her eyes all soft and languid—the same way they are when I crawl up her body after bringing her to heaven with my mouth.

"Don't tell me you're actually starting to like dancing."

I kiss the tip of her nose. "No. I'll never be a fan." I rise, taking her with me, keeping her close within the circle of my arms. "But I'll always dance with you. Anytime, anywhere. Besides—this is your song."

It's a surprise I planned; a gift for her. I'm pretty sure it'll blow her mind, and I'm looking forward to her blowing other things in return when she's expressing her gratitude all night long.

Elton's perfectly timed announcement comes over the microphone. "We have a dedication, ladies and gentlemen. This is going out to Sofia, with love from Stanton." And then he starts to sing.

Her eyes go as round as quarters and she slumps against me just a bit from the shock. "Oh my God! I can't believe you did that—how did you do that?"

I shrug. "I know people, who know people, who know a few of Elton's people. I called in favors."

She lifts up on her toes and kisses me hard—making me think this was the best damn idea I've ever had. Against my lips, she tells me, "I love you."

As she rests her head against my chest I whisper, "I love you too."

"I have the best boyfriend ever."

My chest rumbles with a chuckle. "Yes, you do."

How wonderful life is, while you're in the world.

And then we dance.

. . .

November

"Push!"

"I *am* pushing. It's tight."

"Harder."

"If I do it any harder, I'm gonna fucking break something."

"Just shove it in."

"I'm trying," I grunt.

"Is anyone else getting turned on by this conversation?" Jake's detached voice floats over from the other side of the heavy-ass desk I'm currently jamming through the doorway.

With a shout, we get it through, then settle it gently in front of the window—like Sofia and I agreed. This way we can enjoy the natural sunlight while I'm fucking her on it.

"I'm too damn tired to get turned on," I gripe, wiping the sweat off my forehead.

Then Sofia walks into the room, and my eyes naturally fall to the magnificent way her snug black turtleneck highlights her tits. "Never mind—not too tired after all."

"This looks great in here!" she squeals with a smile. "This is the last of it."

Sofia asked me to move in with her last week. I'd practically been living here since midsummer anyway. But the idea that it'd be official—that'd we'd wake up together every morning and come home here together every night—is awesome. Her place is bigger than my apartment, and already furnished, so most of my furniture is staying behind with Jake. Except for Presley's bedroom set, which is now set up in the townhouse's third bedroom, the only item I insisted on bringing is my desk. So instead of a guest room, the second bedroom is now converted into a home office for both of us.

Sofia enjoys this oversized oak desk as much as I do. Especially for the extra space it allows while working at it, and like I said—for the fucking.

Brent walks in holding champagne glasses and Sofia pops the cork on the bottle in her hands. We fill the glasses, pass them around, and I propose a toast.

"My momma always used to say home is where the heart is. But I never really understood how right that was—until now." I gaze at Sofia. "You're my heart, so wherever you are, I'm home."

She plants a kiss on my lips.

"Okay, now I'm really turned on," Jake comments. Then to Brent he says, "You ready to head out? Hit the bars?"

"I was born ready," Brent retorts. Then he asks us, "Are you guys coming?"

With her arms around my waist, Sofia tells him, "I plan to shortly— and if history is any indication, more than once." Then she's kissing me again.

"Ewww," Brent says. "You guys are gross."

We walk them down to the front door. "But seriously," Brent asks, "you're not coming out?"

I smack his back. "Can't—I have a lot of work to do."

We say our thanks and good-byes, and I lock the door behind them.

Sofia looks up at me. "Do you still have work on the Penderson case?"

I chuckle. "No, Soph, I wasn't talking about that kind of work."

She smirks. "Then what kind of work *were* you speaking of?"

I scoop her up into my arms. "Christening every room in this house. It's gonna be a lot of hard, sweaty work."

• • •

February

It had been a bad fucking day. The bad started with a squirrelly client who was dicking me around about a prior out-of-state conviction for assault, then progressed into the notification of an appeal that didn't go my way. To top it off, an arctic blast had decided to descend upon DC, making it colder than a witch's tit outside—the kind of frigid that made it feel like needles are pricking your face every time the wind blew.

The only good part about the day was that it was almost over. And I was able to find a parking spot outside the courthouse, the steps of which I'm currently walking. After I pass through security, feeling starts to return to my fingertips as I slip into the courtroom and take a seat in the back. I take a deep breath—and watch her. Asking the final questions of her cross-examination, stalking back to the defense table, her black heels clicking on the floor. All eyes are on Sofia—not just because her ass looks phenomenal in the tight black pencil skirt—but because of her presence. Her posture, the tone of her voice —she commands the room and the attention of every person in it.

The frustration of the day ebbs away, replaced with a calm peace and swelling pride—because that amazing, fascinating, capable woman is mine.

After court is adjourned, I approach her from behind as she slides folders into her briefcase. I wrap an arm around her waist and place a brief kiss behind her ear. She tenses for a split second before relaxing into my embrace. Because without turning around, she knows it's me.

"Nice job."

She smiles over her shoulder at me. "Thanks. What are you doing here? I thought I was meeting you at home."

"It's cold outside—I didn't want you walking."

Then I pull the bouquet of roses out from behind my back. Her hazel eyes turn liquid and her perfect lips stretch into a wider smile. "What are these for?" She brings the flowers to her nose and inhales.

I kiss her forehead. "They're just because I can."

• • •

The lights glow softly through the windows, turning the townhouse into a beacon of warmth and comfort and home. Sherman vies for our attention as soon as we step through the door, his wagging tail and lapping tongue telling us he's been a good boy and Sofia's shoes have survived unmolested—at least for today. She pours me a bourbon and a glass of wine for herself, as I take the steaks that have been marinating in my special sauce out of the fridge. We talk about the events of the day, plans for tomorrow, and everything in between as I step out onto the balcony to fire up the charcoal. Because even though it's winter, even though it's not Sunday and not Mississippi—Sofia loves my grillin'.

Later, after the dishes are washed and dried, the news plays softly on the television as I step out of the bathroom freshly showered, a towel around my waist. Sofia reclines on the bed, one leg bent, her laptop resting on her stomach, clad only in a lacy pink tank top and matching panties. Her eyes rake over me, devouring every toned muscle—then she closes the laptop with a snap.

And I drop the towel.

I climb on the bed like a predator, my intentions as naked as my ass. She squeaks when I lean over her, cold droplets from my hair dripping on her collarbone.

"You're wet," she breathes in a husky whisper.

I lick my bottom lip and skim my hand across her soft skin, down between her legs, where she's already slick and wanting from watching me.

"So are you."

I take my time and make slow, easy love to her, that ever-present passion simmering just below the surface. Then, after, it's rough and loud—she'll have bruises on her hips tomorrow and I'll have scratches down my back. We fall asleep above the covers, our heated flesh more than enough to keep us warm.

The day may have been shitty . . . but the night was as fucking perfect as you can get.

• • •

May, Sunshine, Mississippi

Jenny's truck pulls up the drive of my parents' place, and as soon as the tires stop, Presley bursts out of the passenger side. "Hey, Daddy! Hey, Sofia!"

She hugs us both long and sweet.

"You look like you've grown three inches since I saw you last." That was over spring break, when she stayed with us in DC.

With her arm over my daughter's shoulders, Sofia looks down at her and asks, "You want to go horseback riding?"

Presley nods, and I just grin, teasing. "Someone thinks she's quite the equestrian."

Sofia twists her middle and pointer finger together and adorably insists, "Blackjack and I are like this. We have a whole mental thing going on—he understands me."

I'm still laughing as I jog to the truck to help Jenny out. "Hey." I kiss her cheek and give her a hug. Or, as close to a hug as I can, considering the size of her stomach. "Damn, Jenny, you're gigantic."

She frowns. "Why don't you go to hell and die, Stanton? What kinda thing is that to say to a pregnant woman?"

"A truthful kinda thing. I don't remember you bein' so big with Presley. You sure there's not two in there?"

She rubs her eight-months-pregnant belly. "No, just the one. One's enough—and I'm gettin' drugs this time."

I chuckle. "Not if Nurse Lynn's there, you're not."

Sofia hugs Jenny in greeting. "We would've come to your house to pick her up."

Jenny waves her hand. "Nah, it's good for me to get out. I've been nestin'—the floors are so slippery clean, JD said he's gonna put up hazard tape."

We catch up for a few minutes, then Jenny leaves and we head to the stable. Presley walks in front of us, and I hold Sofia's hand as she walks beside me.

"So . . . you ever think about that?"

"About what?"

I jerk my head in the direction Jenny just left.

"A baby?"

"A baby," I say.

"You and me?"

"Well . . . I'd be pretty pissed if it was you and someone else."

She laughs. "Stanton, I'm trying to make partner."

"I know."

"And you're trying to make partner."

"True." We walk silently. Then I lean closer to her, guessing, "So that's a yes, then?"

She grins. "Yes . . . I'll think about it."

I give her her favorite lopsided grin. "Good."

Sofia holds up a finger. "But not now."

"No."

"Make sure your sperm is aware of that. It has a history of going rogue."

I nod. "I'll send the sperm a memo and CC your ovaries."

She nods. "But soon."

"Soon is good."

I swing our joined hands. "We should probably get married first."

Sofia stops, staring at me. "Are you asking?"

I turn, cupping her jaw, tracing her beautiful lips. "Darlin', when I ask, you won't be wonderin' if I'm askin'." Then I kiss her sweetly. "But it'll be soon."

She smiles, big and blinding. "Soon is good."

Jake Becker loves his career as a hard, powerful defense attorney in D.C.

So there's no way a twenty-six-year-old raising her six nieces and

nephews would capture his heart

. . . right?

Don't miss the next installment in *New York Times* bestselling author

Emma Chase's Legal Briefs series

SUSTAINED

Coming Summer 2015 from Gallery Books!

Wednesday is a slow day. I lean back in my desk chair and look out the window at the sunny street below. A frustrated dog walker struggles with three four-legged clients as they tangle their leashes, fighting for the lead. A double-decker tourist bus rumbles past, leaving a cloud of black exhaust in its wake. A jogging father pushes an orange-colored running stroller, nearly taking out one of the yapping dogs, turning onto the grass at the last second.

Maybe it's the baby in the stroller, maybe it's the long-haired, rug-like dogs—maybe it's the fact that I haven't gotten any in two weeks—but the enticing image of Chelsea McQuaid slides into my mind.

Again.

It's the sole image I've conjured every single time I've jerked off, which has been pathetically often.

Those crystal blue eyes, her quick-smiling pink lips, her long, elegant neck that begged to be licked, her lithe limbs that I just bet are oh so flexible, and most important, her firm, perfectly sized tits. I mentally kick myself for not getting her number.

She's too old—and too hot—to be a virgin at twenty-six, but there was something about her that seemed . . . pure. Untouched. Undiscovered. And that's a particular course I sure as hell would love to chart.

I rub my eyes. I need to get laid. This "getting to know a woman first" shit is turning out to be a bigger hassle than I ever anticipated. Is the risk of contracting an STD really such a big deal?

And then I remember how it felt waiting for those test results. The sharp, cold terror of being saddled with a disease—possibly for life. Or, even scarier, with one that could cut my life short. Hell, yes—it's a big deal.

No fuck, no matter how spectacular, is worth dying for.

That should be the tag line in every high school safe-sex campaign.

My secretary, Mrs. Higgens—a great lady who looks like everybody's grandma—opens my office door. "Miss Chelsea McQuaid is here to see you, Jake. And she's got a whole brood of little ones with her."

My smile is wide and slow and completely gratified. I don't believe in signs—but if I did, this would be big, flashing neon.

I straighten my tie. "Show them in, Mrs. Higgens."

She nods, and a few moments later, Chelsea and her fidgeting, noisy gaggle of nieces and nephews come into my office. She's wearing casual "mommy-wear," but on that body, it screams Sexy. A dark green sweater that highlights the red in her auburn hair. Snug blue jeans tucked into high brown boots that accent those endless legs—and the tight swell of her ass. That's a pleasant surprise—I didn't notice her ass the first time we met, but it's fucking gorgeous.

She adjusts her grip on the baby carrier and her smile is strained. "Hello, Mr. Becker."

I stand up behind my desk. "Chelsea, it's good to see you again. What brings you . . ."

My eyes flick quickly to each of the faces that crowds my office, then to the empty doorway, as I realize someone is missing.

"Where's Rory?"

Chelsea sighs. Before she can speak, the grouchy girl—the fourteen-year-old, Riley—answers for her. "The idiot got arrested. He stole a car."

"A *car*?"

In a week, the little shit went from mugging to grand theft auto. That sure escalated quickly.

The small towheaded one, Rosaline, continues. "And then he crashed it."

The two-year-old supplies sound effects. "*Brooocshhh.*"

The smart one, Raymond, adds, "And not just any car—a Ferrari

458 Italia Limited Edition. The starting price is around nine hundred thousand dollars."

I look to Chelsea, who nods. "Yeah, that's pretty much the whole story. He's in juvenile detention—serious trouble this time."

This time implies there's been other times—my almost-robbery notwithstanding. *Jesus Christ, kid.*

Chelsea explains in a strained voice, "My brother has dozens of attorneys in his contact list, but none of them are defense attorneys. I had your card . . . and you seem like a good lawyer."

Out of curiosity, I ask, "What makes you think I'm good?"

She raises her chin and meets my eyes. "You look like a man who knows how to win a fight. That's what I need—what Rory needs."

I take a few moments to think—to plan.

Chelsea must interpret my silence as rejection, because her voice turns almost pleading. "I don't know what your typical retainer is, but I have money if—"

My lifted finger stops her. "I don't think that's going to be necessary. Wait here." Then I point to Raymond. "Come with me." And to the oldest girl. "You too, Smiley."

As they follow me out the door, the brooding teen corrects me. "My name is Riley."

"I know. But I'm going to call you Smiley."

"Why?" she asks, like it's the stupidest, most vile thing she's ever heard.

I smirk. "Because you're not."

Let the eye rolling commence.

I lead them into the office next door. Sofia Santos's dark head is bent over her desk, her perfectly manicured hands scribbling rapid notes on a document. She looks up as we enter.

"Hey, Sofia." I hook my thumb toward the sullen girl behind me. "This is Smiley McQuaid—her aunt is a new client and we have to head downtown for a few hours. Is it okay if she hangs with you?"

Stanton's daughter, Presley, is almost twelve. I figure if anyone is adept at dealing with a preteen female, it's Sofia.

"Sure. I'll be here all afternoon."

Riley moves to my side. "My name is *Riley*."

Sofia smiles. "Hi, Riley." Then she points to a chair in the corner, next to a wall outlet. "The phone charger's over there."

Riley almost cracks a grin. *Almost.* "Swag."

I turn to Sofia's office companion, who's staring at images on his laptop. And I hope to God it's not porn. "Brent, this is Raymond. Raymond, Brent. Can you keep him out of trouble for a few hours?"

Brent nods. Then, with the excitement of a boy allowed to watch his first R-rated horror movie, he asks Raymond, "You want to see pictures of blood splatter?"

The boy steps forward. "Is it as cool as it sounds?"

"Waaay cooler."

"Sure!"

And my work here is done.

I pop my head back in my office and crook my finger at Rosaline. She looks up at her aunt, who nods her permission, and Rosaline steps out to join me in front of Mrs. Higgens's desk.

"Mrs. Higgens, this is Rosaline. Can you mind her for a bit while her aunt and I head to the courthouse?"

Rosaline looks down shyly, and Mrs. Higgens pulls up a chair beside her. "Of course. I have a granddaughter about your age, Rosaline. I keep coloring books here for when she visits. Do you like to color?"

Rosaline nods eagerly, climbing into the chair.

"And what's your favorite color?"

She doesn't even think about it. "Rainbow."

Mrs. Higgens pulls out said coloring books and crayons. "Wonderful choice, dearie."

I stride back into my office, where Chelsea and the two youngest rug rats await. I point at them. "You both look like the real troublemak-ers in the group, so you're coming with us."

"Hi!" the two-year-old replies with a deceptively sweet smile.

I just shake my head. "Oh no, you're not roping me into that again."

I take the baby carrier from Chelsea's hands—and almost drop the thing. "Wow," I say, glancing down. "You're heavier than you look." He gurgles back with a drool.

I turn to Chelsea. "You grab Thing One. Let's go."

Her voice stops me. It's a whisper, quiet and inquisitive.

"Jake?"

It's the first time she's said my name. One small syllable that makes my gut tighten. That makes me want to hear her say it again—in a moan, a gasp. A pleasure-spiked scream.

"Can I ask you something before we go?"

I swallow, my mouth suddenly dry. "Sure."

"If it's not the money . . . why are you helping us?"

It's an interesting question. Noble isn't my style. I'm the more of an "every man for himself" kind of guy. So why the hell *am* I helping them?

Because I want in her pants, of course. Doing Chelsea a favor is the most direct route to doing her. Really not that complicated.

But I can't say that.

So I shrug. "I'm a sucker for a lost cause."

And because I just can't hold back any longer, I reach out and gen-tly stroke the ivory skin of her cheek. It's softer than I ever could've imagined.

"And for a pretty face."

WE WALK OUT to the parking garage, and as Chelsea buckles the kids into their seats, I check out her truck. Her gigantically large dark blue truck. She notices and remarks, "It's my brother's truck."

I lift an eyebrow. "Your brother—the environmental lobbyist—drove a gas-guzzling Yukon XL?"

She climbs up into the driver's seat. "He had six kids. A bicycle wasn't gonna cut it."

I give her directions to the Moultrie Courthouse, where she was notified by phone that Rory was taken after his arrest this morning. I don't have a lot of experience in family court, but I'm familiar enough with the process to fill her in.

"Rory will be assigned a probation officer who'll review the charges, his history, and make a recommendation to the OAG. The probation officer decides whether he's released to you today, or has to remain at the Youth Services Center until trial. They're also the ones I'll talk plea deal with."

The good news is, I know one of the officers at Moultrie intimately. We used to bang frequently—and thoroughly—right up until she got engaged. Our parting terms were friendly.

A soft V forms on Chelsea's forehead. "The OAG?"

"Office of Attorney General. That's who'll prosecute his case, but don't worry—it's not going that far."

Juvenile cases are different from adult ones. The system still has hope for delinquents—it's all about rehabilitation and redemption. Saving them before they've gone too far down that dark, wrong road to nowhere. In criminal courts, the main question is, *did* you do it? In family court, it's all about *why* you did it. An orphaned nine-year-old dealing with his parents' death by stealing a car will garner a shitload more leniency than an eighteen-year-old boosting a joy ride.

The Moultrie Courthouse is a concrete, intimidating building with a cavernous maze of hallways. After passing through security, we're ushered into a waiting room with a dozen nondescript tables and chairs scattered around and vending machines along one wall. A few other visitors occupy the room, heads huddled, speaking in hushed, confidential whispers.

Chelsea and I sit at an empty table. I put the infant carrier with its sleeping cargo on the table, and the blond, baby-haired Reggie squirms on her lap. A guard opens a door across the room and walks in beside Rory. He's still wearing his school uniform: tan slacks, white button-down, navy blazer.

His young lips are set in a hard frown, his dark blue eyes so full of resentment you can practically hear the "screw-you" thoughts. This is not the face of a sad, lost little soul who knows he messed up—it's the face of an angry cherub, desperately trying to look badass, who'd rather go down in flames than admit he was wrong.

For a second, I reconsider helping him—a few days in juvenile detention could be just what the doctor ordered.

But then Chelsea wraps her arm around him and kisses his forehead, murmuring professions of love, relief, and threats, all at the same time. "Thank God you're okay. Everything's going to be all right, Rory, don't be scared. What the *hell* were you thinking? A car? You're never leaving your room again. Ever!"

I lean back in my chair, just watching.

He brushes her off with a rough shrug. "Get off. I'm fine. It's not a big deal."

"Not a big deal?" She grimaces, and I see a flash of hurt feelings too. "You could've killed yourself—or someone else."

"Well I didn't, okay? So stop freaking out."

I've seen enough.

"Chelsea, go get Reggie a soda or juice." I pull a few bills from my wallet and hand them to her. She hesitates. I tilt my head toward Rory. "Give us a minute."

Still looking unsure, she sets the two-year-old on her feet and leads her away.

Once we're alone, Rory sits down. "What are you doing here?"

"Your aunt wanted a good lawyer. Lucky for you, I'm the best—and I happened to have the afternoon free."

"Whatever."

I pin him with an assessing stare. "You're in deep shit, kid."

So sure he knows everything, he scoffs, "I'm nine. What's the worst they can do to me?"

"Keep you here for the next nine years. At least," I tell him simply.

For the first time since he walked into the room, his confidence wavers. His cheeks bloom nervous pink and his voice rises half an octave as he says, "It's not so bad here."

It's a tiny crack in the facade—but still a crack.

I don't waste time telling him he's full of shit. I lean forward and explain. "Here's what's gonna happen. I'm going to call your aunt back over, and you're going to apologize for the way you spoke to her."

He wasn't expecting that. He squints. "Why?"

"Because she doesn't deserve it."

He lowers his eyes, almost ashamed. Maybe there's hope for the punk yet.

"Then you're going to sit there," I point at him, "and let her hug you and kiss you all she wants."

His chin rises, not yet ready to give up the fight. "And what if I don't?"

I look him right in the eyes. "Then I'll let you rot in here."

And I will.

He doesn't look happy; doesn't like being backed into a corner. He wants to come out swinging—to do the opposite of what I'm ordering, simply because it's an order.

I know what he's feeling. I know this kid through and through.

Once upon a time, I *was* this kid.

He needs an out—a way to give up the battle without feeling like he's lost the war. So I give him one.

"You don't need to show me how tough you are, Rory—I can see it. I was a lot like you when I was your age—a tough, pissed-off little asshole. The difference is, I was smart enough not to shit on the people who cared about me." I raise my eyebrows. "Are you?"

He watches me. Looks deep inside with that sixth sense that all children have, to see if I'm being straight with him or just fucking patronizing. After a moment, he gives the briefest of nods and says in a small voice, "Okay. I'll apologize to Aunt Chelsea. And I'll let her kiss and hug me if it makes her happy."

I smile. "Good. Smart and tough. I like you more already, kid."

I LEAVE CHELSEA with the kids and head upstairs to the probation offices. I knock on Lisa DiMaggio's door, even though it's open. She swivels around in her desk chair, her long blond hair fanning out behind her.

"Jake Becker," she says. She stands, giving me a perfect view of tan, toned legs beneath her black skirt, and hugs me. Parting on friendly terms most definitely has its benefits. "What are you doing in my neck of the woods?" she asks, stepping back with a smile. "Or is this a social call?"

"I'm here about a client."

"Since when do you play in family court?"

"Long story." I shrug. "And its name is Rory McQuaid."

"Ah." She retrieves a file from her desk. "My car thief. I did his intake this morning. Said he took the car because, and I quote, he 'wanted to see if driving was as easy as Mario Kart.'" She shakes her head. "Kids these days."

I lean back against the wall. "That's not why he took the car. There's extenuating circumstances."

"Enlighten me. I haven't had a chance to interview the parents yet."

"The parents are dead," I tell her. "Robert and Rachel McQuaid were killed in a horrific crash two months ago, leaving Rory and his *five* brothers and sisters in the care of their aunt—their only living relative."

She sits down in her chair. "Jesus."

"The kid's been dealt a shitty hand—he's not handling it well. But he doesn't belong in lockup. Talk to his social worker; I'll bet my left nut he was a saint until his parents died."

"That's really saying something—I know how precious your nuts are to you."

I nod.

"Unfortunately," Lisa sighs, "Rory picked the wrong person's car to steal." She rattles off the name of a cranky, influential former presidential hopeful. "And he wants the boy's ass in a sling."

"Fuck that," I growl.

I don't know if it's because I have a hard-on for his aunt or because he reminds me so much of myself, but if anyone wants a piece of that kid, they're going to have to come through me first.

"Besides, a public servant has no business owning a car like that."

"Okay," Lisa allows. "Then what are you offering?"

"Court-mandated therapy, once a week. Monthly progress reports."

"Twice a week," she counters. "And I want to pick the therapist. No feel-good quacks permitted."

"Done."

Lisa's gaze travels over me, head to crotch. "I'm surprised at you, Jake. I don't remember you being so . . . soft."

I move forward, bracing my hands on the arms of her chair, caging her in. "Soft isn't in my vocabulary—I'm still as hard as they come." I smirk. "And after."

Her eyes settle on my mouth. "Good to hear. Particularly since Ted and I broke up." She holds up her *ringless* left hand.

Lisa definitely falls under the "known" category, which means no awkward first-date dinner conversation, no twenty-goddamn-questions that I don't want to ask, let alone answer. Nope—it'll be straight to the fucking.

Excellent.

"It's a long story," she says. "Which I'm sure you have no interest in hearing."

Yes. Lisa knows me well.

"You still like tequila?" I ask.

"Absolutely. You still have my number?"

"I do."

Her smile is slow, and full of promise. "Good. Use it."

I stand up and walk toward the door. "I'll do that."

"And I'll get started on the paperwork."

A FEW HOURS later, after approval from child services and a quick compulsory appearance before an indifferent judge, Rory walks out of the courthouse with us. We head back to my office to gather his many siblings. They all seem happy to see him—if the affectionate "stupid idiot" and eager questions about his stay in "jail" are any indication. The sky is dark by the time I escort Chelsea and her charges back out to her car. I wait next to the driver's-side door as she gets them loaded and buckled in.

Then she comes around and stands in front of me, all warm eyes and soft gratitude. And I'm struck again by the smooth flawlessness of her skin beneath the glow of the streetlight.

Fucking gorgeous.

This close, I notice the adorable dusting of freckles across the bridge of that pert nose and wonder if she has them anywhere else. It'll take a slow, exhaustive search to find out. And I'm just the guy for the job.

She pushes her hair behind her ear. "Thank you, Jake, so much. I don't know what I would've—"

"Aunt Chelsea, I'm starving!"

"Can we get McDonald's?"

"Do you know what they put in McDonald's? Insects won't even eat it."

"Shut up, Raymond! Don't ruin fast food for me!"

"You shut up!"

"No, *you* shut up!"

"Aunt Chelsea!"

"Hiiiiiii!"

I can't help but laugh. And wonder if she owns earplugs.

Chelsea blows out a breath through her perfect, smiling lips. "I should go before they start eating each other."

"That may not be a bad thing. There's enough of them to spare."

She shakes her head and climbs into the truck, then rolls down the window. "Thank you again. I owe you, Jake."

I tap the side of the truck as she slowly pulls away. "Yes, you do."

And that is a debt I can't wait to collect.